Makarelle

Anthology ONE

Dear Kathryn and Roland
I hope you enjoy
Some of the stories and
poems in this anthology.
mine is on p. 311

love
H
xxx

DEDICATION

Our heartfelt thanks goes out to all contributing artists who have made our independent online literary and creative arts magazine **Makarelle** possible – and have agreed to have their work published in this beautiful book.

All profits from this anthology will be equally split between all contributing authors.

Thank you also to everyone who clicked on the PayPal button on our website www.Makarelle.com and donated their hard-earned cash to help us fund the running costs of Makarelle. Thank you in advance to those of you who will donate a pound or two in the future so we can keep going.

Finally, we thank Sarah Armstrong from www.fitzblocksberg.com for letting us use her lovely artwork 'Monsters' as our cover image.

Scan the QR code to find a short bio for each of our authors and visual artists:

CONTENTS

Makarelle Spring 2021: 'Coming Unravelled'

p2 Breath On The Glass: Toby Goodwin

p9 Rampjaar – Disaster Year: Gerry Stewart

p10 Lockdown – a Meditation: David Clancy

p17 The End Of The World As We Know It: Beth McDonough

p18 Intersection: Beth McDonough

p19 Unravelling: Caoimhe O'Flynn

p25 Watching From My Bedroom Window: Louise Wilford

p26 Lockdown Love Affair: R.E. Loten

p28 Sheffield, May 2020: Louise Wilford

p30 South Pacific: Jane Langan

p32 Coming Unravelled: Ben Lisle

p36 Blossom Thief: Alastair Simmons

p37 Beazley Faces His Bêtes-Noires: Ron Hardwick

p45 Those Who Can: Beck Collett

p46 Sometimes: Rosie Elwood

p47 Sorted: Jane Langan

p49 Consumed With Love: Dini Armstrong

p56 Here Now Nowhere: Clair Tierney

p57 Coming Unravelled: Sue Davnall

p62 Back To The Beginning: Helena Nwaokolo

p63 Who Parents The Parents: R.E. Loten

p66 Lockdown Wool: Lily Lawson

p69 Swarm: Suzanne Burn

p70 Between Two Worlds: D.H.L. Hewa

p77 Saved Marriage: GS

p80 Single Vision: Colin Johnson

Makarelle Summer 2021: 'Tattoo'

p86 The Bluebird: Sue Davnall

p93 Tattoo: Jeff Gallagher

p95 Symbolism: Mina Ma

p101 On Me: Yuu Ikeda

p102 The Brush And The Needle: Dovydas Jakstaitis

p108 My Ugliness: Yuu Ikeda

p109 The Drum Of Passchendaele: Henry Loten

p112 The Yellow Lily: L.C. Groves

p119 Trust: Suzanne L. Burn

p120 Strawberry: Sam Southam

p121 Phobia: Ken Smith

p122 The Tattie Tattoo Bird Of The Nile:
      Helena Nwaokolo

p125 Through All My Phases: Linda M. Crate

p126 Maybe Think of Me: Linda M. Crate

p127 Happy Birthday: Beck Collett

p129 The Edinburgh Tattoo: Elizabeth Eastwood

p134 The End Of Drought: Edward Alport

p135 A Demon Come Among Us: Edward Alport

p136 The Ballad Of Dove And Nate: Beck Collett

p141 Archie's Bolero: R.E. Loten & H.D.W. Loten

p148 Eternal Sunshine Of The Spotless Skin:
Dini Armstrong

p153 Stories: S.A. Pilkington

p154 The Butcher's Tattoo: Jane Langan

p161 Wilding: Jayant Kashyap

p162 Unique: Lily Lawson

p163 Mongoose (Fifteen Points): Toby Goodwin

p170 Tit For Tattoo: Amit Parmessur

p171 An Incriminating Tattoo: Ron Hardwick

p179 Invisible: Karen Honnor

p181 Lucky, Lucky Me: D.H.L. Hewa

p188 The Ballad Of Blackthorn: Jane Langan

p190 Tattoo: Louise Wilford

Makarelle Autumn 2021: 'Twisted Tales'

p205 Mimba's Hands: Ioney Smallhorne

p208 The Sting: S.A. Pilkington

p209 Mimicry: Ben Lisle

p211 Glimpse: Jane Langan

p212 'Tarosvan' or The Legend Of Logres: R.E. Loten

p218 The Linear Family: Ken Smith

p221 Don't Tell The Priest: Jonathan Willmer

p228 A Bumpy Ride To Heaven: Alain Li Wan Po

p235 The Art Lover: Maggie Small

p236 Violation: Suzanne L. Burn

p238 The Jungbots Of Frontier Scotland: Dini Armstrong

p245 Bile: John K. Ellington

p252 The Tale Of The Red Baron: Henry Loten

p254 Eagle One, Eagle Two: R.E. Loten

p261 The Strange Incident At Honeyman Cottage:
Ron Hardwick

p269 The Ghosts Of Fairfield: Jane Langan

p272 Crumbs Triptych: Laura Theis

p275 I Love This House: D.H.L. Hewa

p282 Georgie: Daniel David

p287 Pumpkin: Louise Wilford

p292 The Mirror At Midnight: Beck Collett

p293 Afternoon Tea: Diana Hayden

p294 A Special Occasion: John Bukowski

p302 The Inside Out Girl: Jane Langan

p307 Bridge Echoes: Lily Lawson

p309 Pitch Fork: Sharon Rockman

p311 The Worst Cyber Bully: Helen Rana

p313 Hard Bargain: Leila Martin

p315 Banshee: Louise Wilford

p316 Herculaneum: Edward Alport

p317 When She Comes Home: Cheryl Powell

p322 The Lady: Dave Sinclair

p324 The Visitor: Sue Davnall

Welcome, dear reader!

This time last year, we, Ruth, Jane and Dini, were nervously waiting for the results of our MA in Creative Writing. The Covid Pandemic was rife, and no vaccine was in sight. Everyone had spent the year in and out of lockdown and things were looking grim.

By the 2nd of December, a Covid vaccine was approved, and rollout had begun. Around the same time, we got our MA results and, exposed and vulnerable without the support of other writing students, decided to start a small writing group. We supported each other to follow Neil Gaiman's advice to 'write something, finish something and send it away' without succumbing to the temptation of the fridge, Netflix and TikTok thirst traps.

We wrote, we finished, we sent away, we stayed on track, we succumbed to the lure of Khaby Lame, we learned entirely new swearwords from each other - we even had some successes getting our work published. We did, however, notice how few webzines support emerging writers and artists. Well, you know the song …feeling like sisters already at this stage, we did it for ourselves. We introduced the Scottish word 'Makar = poet' to the French pronoun 'elle=she', the two fell in love and soon enough, we welcomed a brand-new literary and creative arts magazine to the world: Makarelle.

Having never met in person, we summoned the powers of video conferencing and dived in. Producing, designing, editing and promoting an online magazine is a huge undertaking. All three of us do this for the love of creativity. We don't get paid to do this (in fact, more often than not, we were paying for the webhosting, flipping book, Shutterstock images etc out of our own pockets).

Donations all go towards the upkeep of the magazine and website. Creating content for Pinterest, Facebook, TikTok, Twitter, LinkedIn and Instagram we slowly built a following.

Three issues in, having received submissions of brilliant writing and art from all over the world, the magazine is going strong. We have had over nineteen thousand visitors to our site www.Makarelle.com and counting. We publish quarterly online, in flipping book and pdf format. Our first issue was on the theme of 'Coming Unravelled, the other two on 'Tattoos' and 'Twisted Tales', all of which are represented in this book. While we have had overwhelmingly positive feedback from both contributors and readers, we had quite a few calls for a print version. And here we are. We were able to include most of the literary contributions. For the stunning visual art, alas, you still need to go browse our magazine issues – either by visiting **www.makarelle.com** or by scanning the QR codes at the beginning of each section.

Welcome to our first anthology, **Makarelle ONE** – hopefully the first of many.

Enjoy!

Jane, Ruth and Dini

Makarelle Spring 2021: 'Coming Unravelled'

If you would like to see the visual art of this magazine issue, you can access the flipping book for free by scanning this QR code:

BREATH ON THE GLASS
by Toby Goodwin

The window looks out on a quiet Glasgow street. Rows of postcards line the windowsill. Rows of tenements line the street. Cars punctuate it. It's a wide room, peeling floral wallpaper and wooden furniture. Hattie's nose almost touches the glass. She has rasping, unsteady breath and grey hair in a loose ponytail. She likes to keep the windows clean, but she cannae reach the outside bit. Too afraid of popping that hip out again. Well, she's not afraid for herself. She just knows what a hassle it would be for Graham. He's sitting in his armchair knitting. "Stupit hobby" she'd said, when she unwrapped the set their son Jimmy sent for her birthday. A sweet boy, but the brains ae a cabbage. Doesnae matter anyways; Graham was never one for waste, so he took it up.

"If they boys at the pub could see you now" she says, still looking out the window.

Graham snorts, "I may no live to see the inside ae anuthur pub, Hats."

She snorts, the glass fogs up. She wipes it with a woolly sleeve, nice blue cashmere. Another gift, from Sandra. Hattie thinks the family all feel guilty for not having seen them in so long, but she doesn't really mind. "Stiff upper lip an aw that, Grams."

"Pff, that's the English. Nothing stiff goin on here."

"Yer tellin me."

Graham laughs, "that's mean."

He knows she's never serious. Too old to be serious. They just had their gold two years ago, but the thing about being elderly is that nothing's about you anymore. Even your own anniversary. It's for the family, everything's for the bloody family. Christmas, Easter, whatever. Graham and Hattie would rather be watching

Noel Edmonds on the TV. They both think he's a wank, but they still watch him.

"Anhin gawn on oot there?" Graham says. He pulls a loop over the left needle and threads it through.

"There's that wee bouy with his dug, horrible hing. Big fat bastart."

On the other side of the road one of the local boys is taking the dog out for its evening shite. A big Labrador-something cross.

"It's no the dug's fault," Graham says. He's wearing that Old Spice aftershave. Always wears it, even though they've not had company in months.

"Aye, that's right. It's that Meryl. She lets that daft wee bouy take care ae it. He wouldn't know his arse from his elbow."

"Did I ever tell you about our Cathleen?" he teases out another loop.

"Who's that, fae the church?"

"Naw, growin up. My great-aunt Cathleen? She was always a bit mad, ken?"

"Oh aye. What was it she did?"

"She named her dug 'Piss'."

"Naw she never."

"Swear ae god, honestly. You'd see her running aboot Queen's Park screamin; 'Piss, PISS!'"

She smiles, still not turning from the window. Graham continues with the gentle clicking. The boy on the road is staring at his phone, tugged mercilessly by that Labrador. Hattie cannae hear it, but she's sure the dog's making a suffocating, panting noise. Stupit wean.

"Wan ae these days that dug's gonnae pull him into the road. He's always on that bloody phone," she says.

"Aye, but you'll be right there watchin to get the ambulance."

"Wheesht."

The dog tugs the boy round the corner. The skyline is sturdy, industrial. Gothic buildings and smokestacks. Hattie sees all the streetlamps begin to light up, as she does every night. Starting at the bottom of the road and working their way out into the skyline. The one on the corner flickers and then turns off. She doesn't look, but she knows Graham's little glasses are hanging low on his nose, and he's wearing that nice waistcoat he got in London. He always was a smart dresser though. One of the reasons she went for him in the first place.

She was working at a dry cleaner near the city centre, he was plumbing. A wee apprentice to this older guy. What was his name? John, Johnathan? She cannae mind, but Graham came in after one of the washers flooded. He was thin and tall, and he had an awkward gawkiness about him that she found endearing. The job took a couple of days and they got chatting. What was the line? He said something quite rude, naw it was her. He made some error and a pipe popped, spraying dirty runoff water all down his front. Hattie came over and went "I don't want to alarm you, but you've got a bittie something doon yer front there, pal."

He asked her out at the end of the job, and they went for a nice pub lunch down Candleriggs. He wore a sleek waistcoat.

Out on the street a bright light appears on the corner. A blue Ford comes in a little fast for Hattie's taste. It gets to the parking bit and stops. The car turns, but not quite enough. Forward, pause. Turn, pause.

"Graham, look at this. Got oorsels a twelve-point trick."

Graham heaves himself out of the chair, putting his knitting on the arm. The car tries it again, sticks, turns again.

"Shockin" he says, "isn't that they Polish?"

"There's nuhin wrang wi that, Graham."

"I never said there was anything wrang wi that."

"Sounded like you were slagging em aff."

The car stops. The headlights go out. Stalled. It shudders and starts again.

"I wasnae slagging em aff," he says.

"Wee, racist bam."

"Racist indeed, where'd you hear that wan?"

"Your nephew was tellin me aww aboot it. About time tae, they Polacks have had enough."

"I hink they're fine young folks. You're the racistic one here, callin them Polacks."

"Naw, I hink Polack's fine."

The car shunts forward again, turns slightly, and then finally gets into the space. Albeit at a bit of an angle. A couple get out of the car, clearly arguing about something. The man's taller with darker hair. He's waving his arms about dramatically.

"Mind when we used to argue lit that?" Hattie says.

"I mind when you used to argue lit that."

Graham and Hattie used to stay in a bigger place in Shawlands, but after the kids went away, they got a flat in Denniston. Cheaper, more practical. Less space to clean. Only problem's those stairs. It's just one floor up, but the pair of them are huffing and panting after a trip to the shops. "Character building" Graham always said.

The street's empty now. The sun almost down. But then, four or five boys round the corner, wearing tracksuits and hoodies. One's holding a bottle. Buckfast, she thinks. There's always a few cutting about. Wains wi naewhere to go, so they make a nuisance of themselves. It's all that pent-up teenage energy they've got. Makes them want to go out and fight, key cars and that. Hattie finds them intimidating, as well as feeling a twinge of pity for them. Poor wean's mothers probably dinnie give em the time of day.

"That's they ne'er do wells again," she says.

"Really?" Graham's wooden cane hangs off a hook on the wall. He grabs it and comes back to the window. "Where are they? Am sick ae those bouys. That Christopher was sayin he caught them all jumpin on his car the other day."

"Oh, sit doon Gram, whit you gonnae dae? Whack them wi yer cane?"

"I'll tell em aff. Boys lit that need an older man tellin them what to dae." Light appears in a doorway across the street. A woman comes out in her dressing gown.

"Oop," Hattie says, "there's big Julie."

"What's she sayin?"

"I cannae hear any better than you, can I?"

Julie has a shock of ginger hair flapping out the hood of an anorak, bright pink pyjamas on underneath. She launches herself towards the boys, they all jump out of their skin. One hides the bottle behind his back. Julie's quite wee, but she's very stocky. Hattie fancies she mouths the words, "I ken yer muther, Tony." The boys then seem to say something cheeky and Julie runs at them. They scatter, giggling. Disappearing into the semi-darkness.

"Mule ae a wumman" Graham says.

"Don't talk about wimmin like that."

"Not all wimman, just that een. Calm doon"

"Pff. I wish we coulda had that window open to hear what she said. I'm sure it was a belter."

"Aye. It'll never top Whiney-Johnson though, will it?"

Hattie throws her head back and laughs, "Whiney-Johnson."

"D'ya mind?"

Whiney Johnson was the name they'd given to this wee guy on a moped that they'd spotted a few weeks before. Chantelle's girl across the street was out having a sneaky smoke and this boy on a moped skidded over to her. It was like a scene from a romcom. The boy on the moped started giving this heartfelt speech, and his voice was so loud and whiney that they could hear it all the way up in the flat.

"I just know you're going to choose him over me, this always happens. I'm the stupid loser who gets dumped and it's always the big tough asshole who ends up with the girl. You know I'd treat you right, you just know it. And still I'm left, in DARKNESS."

The boy, with that final word then revved his wee moped and screeched off into the night without even letting the poor girl respond. The whole thing had Hattie and Graham in stitches, for hours. They took to calling the boy Whiney-Johnson.

"Am pure left in, lit, darknessssss" Graham says.

"I just pure ken you're gonnae leave me for him. This pure always happens tae me hahahahaha."

The door goes, sharp wooden tapping.

"Wis that the door?"

They walk over, Graham taking the lead. He looks through the peephole, sliding the metal cover off with a thumb. It's Arthur from downstairs. He's standing there in his own pyjamas, a nice tartan dressing gown and a cane. A grey, wispy beard.

"I can hear ye's through the door," he says "gonnae shut up likes."

"Arthur, is that you?"

"Aye, it's me."

"Arthur" Hattie says, "were auld, we canne be interact wi aebody. What do you want?"

"How fuckin convenient for ye's, I'm auld anaw. It's the middle of the night and yous are up giggling like weans."

"Oh, bugger off Arthur, it's only seven o'clock. This is why naebody likes you" Graham says, Hattie whacks him on the arm.

"Oh, is that how it's gonnae be, Graham? Come ahead then."

"Whit?"

"If there wasnae a virus, I'd be firein through this door wi a sledgehammer. I'll tell ye that much."

"You couldn't even lift a sledgehammer without putting your back oot," Hattie says.

"Aye, reel yer neck in Arty-boy. This isnae fuckin American ninja warrior. We're no kung-fu fighting you."

"Fuckin, cane-jitzu" Hattie says.

"Tai-Kwon don't"

"Bit ae Krav-Ma-Nahh."

"Just keep it doon, alright?" They hear the old boy moving away from the door.

The couple both go back to the living room. "What will we do the night, then?" Hattie says.

"Fuckin, same hing we do every night."

Hattie sighs, turning back to that window, "Try ae take over the world."

There's silence for a time, solid silence. Arthur's probably pleased. She picks a card up off the windowsill. "Sorry for your loss, call me any time. Pat X." That Pat's a good girl, thoughtful. Hattie looks over at Graham's seat.

Still empty.

Has it really been a month? Last time she saw him they had him belted to a gurney and they were taking him down those stairs. He couldn't even speak. Like drowning in your own lungs, they say. She was lucky, they said. You had very mild symptoms, they said. Very uncommon for someone your age, they said. No, you cannae visit the hospital, they said.

The room still smells like Old Spice. She sits in Graham's chair and picks up those needles. That half-finished sock.

"Cannae be that hard," she says.

RAMPJAAR – DISASTER YEAR
by Gerry Stewart
inspired by the life of Dutch artist Jan Victors

Those long stretches, flat and uncertain
as a Dutch flood plain, weeks, months
being attacked from all sides

Your small place in the world, ages to build up
a grain of sand, a paint dab at a time,
washed away by a carefully aimed volley of words.

Redeloos, radeloos, reddeloos,
senseless, desperate and without reprieve,
you'd cede anything for a moment's respite.

Contemplate closing up shop
and burying your artist's brush.
Running to the quietest corner you can find.

Someday you will be able to unpick
the tangled threads that knot you so tight,
sort the emotions from the enemies,

but in their midst you must follow
one silken path through morass and floods
in the hope it will lead you out to open sea.

LOCKDOWN – A MEDITATION
by David Clancy

The longer you stare at something, the more it frays. And unravels. And decays.

〇

I took up meditation in lockdown. I bought an app and sat comfortably in my chair and relaxed myself as best I could before listening to the monotone voice of a man I immediately identified as a person desperate to be thought of as smart. I felt a kind of affinity with this man. And a degree of loathing. Even if you can exchange the voice that appears in your head with someone else's, it seems you still can't change how you feel about it.

〇

The voice instructs you to keep your eyes open and stare into space, keeping your 'vision wide'. You sit, arms resting, body still, mind quietened. And you stare. Ahead of you is a pale blue wall. There are pictures on it but you deliberately focus on a blank area. One with nothing except a few lumps, an old nail hole and the pale, pale blue – shimmering cold in the sunlight.

〇

My science teacher had a monotonous voice too. He was a dour man who amazingly was called Mr. Meany. He said many things that have remained lodged firmly in my head. In first-year he told us that one of our class of 30 would be dead by the time we reached 25. He was right, and I thought of him as we attended a classmate's funeral 3 years later. Cancer.

Mr. Meany also told us that what we see, we don't really see. I see his face now though, I think, dispassionate and unchanging behind a well-tended beard and framed with mousy brown hair. He is telling me that most of our vision, what we think we see, is actually made up of memories that our brain 'fills in'. We really only see a small area in front of us with our eyes at one time. The rest is a simulation, presented as reality by the brain. A way to keep us calm and anchored in space rather than confronting a terrifying void at the edges of everything we peruse.

()

You keep your eyes open and stare at the wall. You breathe slowly, deliberately, your chest rising and falling, lungs filling and emptying. At the edges of your vision there is a cornice and the frame of a door. There is a couch below, a picture to the left. You are not looking at these things but they are there, incorporated but not focused in the pale blue widescreen of your brain.

()

'You're better off looking at it, than for it' my uncle Padraig says. Someone has just complimented him on his fine head of silver hair and he is smiling. I am 12, at my grandmother's house for a family gathering. His eyes are almost closed but a small twinkle is just visible, mirroring, I imagine, one from his silvery strands. The scary Sacred Heart picture is on the wall behind him, staring down at me with those wide blue eyes.

()

'This plughole is blocked' my wife says. 'Do you know anything about it?' No, I say, shaking my head. 'Well, it's clogged with hair' she says. This was the first hint I was losing my hair - that I would be looking for it, rather than at it. And after this I could only see further signs. Mundane things become profound in lockdown. I remembered my wife telling me a few weeks before that my hair was 'probably' my best feature. My mother-in-law complimenting me for passing such good hair genes to the kids. My son actually saying to me at the breakfast table. 'Imagine what it would be like to be bald, Dad?'

Each morning I dread putting hands to hair to wash my precious strands. I think of my other uncle,

Tony, balding from his late thirties, washing his hair in a tiny sink. He lived with my grandmother and they had no shower. When I stayed with them we would take it in turns to wash our hair at this sink in the drafty bathroom upstairs, its walls damp-cold to the touch, air fresh with 'alpine' scent. He rubs the shampoo onto his wet scalp so gently, as if washing a baby. His hands, gnarled from years working outdoors as a postman, move in small shallow circles, lightly touching, taking care to barely disturb the remaining hairs. This morning in the shower, I notice myself doing the same.

I try to avoid looking at my hands after I have rubbed them through my hair. But I always do in the end, eyes flitting down to count the number today. How many have I lost? How much closer am I to baldness? To death?

◊

Another lockdown video call but now I have turned my camera off, preferring the reassuring, stopped-in-time image of me that appears, to the sunken-eyed, wispy-haired live version staring back. I think I may have looked at my own face more in the last few months than ever before. The longer you stare at something, the more it frays.

◊

It was around this time I first heard of the No-hair Theorem. A voice on the radio explains new developments in Quantum Physics which may have resolved the Black Hole Information Paradox. This paradox arose from work by Stephen Hawking and Jacob Bekenstein, whose findings on radiation appeared to suggest that information could be permanently lost inside black-holes. This violated a core principle of modern physics, namely that information cannot be destroyed, it must be preserved somehow. Tangled up in this is the No-hair theorem which says that all information about a black hole apart from mass, electric charge and momentum disappears behind the event horizon. A black hole has no hair. I wonder why the universe chose this moment for me to learn of this.

◊

I stare at my 10 month old son. He is making 'oooh' shapes with his mouth, while he slowly, carefully picks up a small piece of cheese with his fine fingers. He is becoming a little boy, emerging from the baby world. He was born a few weeks before lockdown began and serves as a reminder that time still moves forward and life still goes on. That growth is possible, inevitable even, despite the nagging feeling that the world has stopped these past months. I see his growing features before me, his eyes widening, his movements becoming more natural. His golden hair grows thickly, especially at the back. I wonder if there is a law governing the preservation of hair. If I must lose so he can gain.

◊

The news about black holes potentially meant something even more profound. A recent paper suggested that the paradox could be resolved using error correction codes from the completely separate field of Quantum Computing. To a certain type of mind this seems to suggest a link between human-made, but extremely complex algorithms, and the very fabric of space-time. In other words something, possibly similar to a human mind, but more advanced, had created space and time. And perhaps reality itself.

◊

Nick Bostrom had a paper published in the Philosophical Journal in 2003. In it, he argued that at least one of the following 3 options must be true. Either the human race is likely to go extinct before it reaches a post-human stage (that is a stage where humans are capable of creating complex computer simulations which resemble our existence); that any such post-human civilization is unlikely to create such simulations; or that we are almost certainly living in one of those computer simulations. Bostrom concludes 'In the dark forest of our current ignorance, it seems sensible to apportion one's credence roughly evenly between [options] 1, 2, and 3'. That is, there is a 33% chance that we are living in a computer simulation.

◊

Apophenia is a potentially disordered tendency to perceive meaningful connections between seemingly unrelated things. The more you look at things, the more they seem to be connected. During lockdown it seems to have become easier to see patterns between things. And then believe in these patterns.

◊

A study from the University of Glasgow in 2012 revealed that faced with a monotonous voice, the human brain will talk over it and make the speech more vivid and interesting in order to better remember it. Is it possible that faced with the monotony and fear of lockdown our brains work overtime to give us more vivid and interesting versions of reality?

◊

During lockdown I do things that remind me of faraway places. Other worlds. I watch films in the same way that I seek out food from restaurants that seem to 'take me away'. We watch movies with the kids, like Disney's 'The Frog and the Princess' or 'Spirited Away' from Studio Ghibli.

New Orleans. Japan.
Southern gentlemen. Eastern magic.
Ghosts. Spirits.
Voodoo.

◊

The other day my six-year-old son called the time before lockdown 'the olden days'. I have no idea why. But the phrase fits so perfectly, I have started to use it too.

◊

Fragmentation is a structural device used in writing. The writer creates a series of images or thoughts in sections, sometimes separated by asterisks or other symbols. The sections are linked, perhaps like a hidden network, but there is no explicit bridge between them or straight narrative threading them all together. The reader is encouraged to make their own connections. To become involved. One rationale for using such an approach is that some subjects cannot be tackled linearly or head on. That the full gaze of examination on a topic will yield nothing of substance. Staring too much will cause it to atomize and disappear. In these cases a meditation on floating images or fragments can bear greater fruit.

◊

A year ago, just before lockdown began, I was reading 'The Year of Magical Thinking' by Joan Didion. 'Jesus', my wife said, 'you need to read something more uplifting.' The news had already started to darken by then. The black shadow of the virus was moving inevitably towards us, east to west. I still took the bus to work in the last of these olden, normal days. The route had been changed due to road works so I needed to walk down an unfamiliar street and initially put the strangeness of these bus journeys down to this. But while reading Didion's descent into grief and disorientation, I noticed something else. Silence. Deathly silence.

On these days no one dared open their mouth it seemed for fear they would cough, or splutter, or somehow give themselves away as a carrier, as part of the problem we all were beginning to fear.

◊

Wikipedia tells me that magical thinking is '…the belief that unrelated events are causally connected despite the absence of any plausible causal link between them… ' A year of magical thinking. How can you not see patterns everywhere?

()

The man's voice is back, willing you to the pale blue wall and the meditation. You stare and slowly the colours start to change. They buzz and glow and fade. Whites seem to illuminate, burn bright and then dim. Shadows lengthen and multiply before receding. Still you stare at the pale blue patch. It is a locus of stability, a core, but outside everything is changing, in flux. Like a reverse black hole, there is substance at the centre but around it all is void.

You blink. Once. Twice. But the view, this silhouetted image remains. Now it begins to vibrate, to shake at the edges, become less solid. Your sense of control, of reality, shakes too. It could all disappear, be revealed to be an illusion.

'Look for the one who is looking' the voice in your head says. But you see nothing.

The longer you stare at something, the more it frays. And unravels. And decays.

THE END OF THE WORLD AS WE KNOW IT
by Beth McDonough

Whenever we guessed, we sensed
how Armageddon must arrive
in sweating flanks, in muscled necks,
with percussive hooves,
thunder splats,
in ripped retinas of lightening.
Not like this

under bowed awnings,
by drippy cafes, stripped
of prettiness, stopped off
with sticky of incident tape.
With coffee served in take-out cups,
which offer themselves to compost,
without the gift of segregated bins.
Sandwiches stuffed in styrofoam,
fruit boxes turned lobbed barriers,
defensive lines across shop floors.
Ineffectual visors. Masks worn as beards on chins.

No Durer. Dante absent. No Revelations to St John,
just soggy sheep depressions,
the sink into whatever bores you most,
while a suspect taste of wormwood
runs through orange burns.

INTERSECTION
by Beth McDonough

That man I will not meet today
has crossed and gouged my path,
scratched out his thin diagonals.
On this stamp-packed mud,
I fret across these scores of scores
he's knifed, under autumn-weighty trees.
I met him once in rain. He sheltered, gathered in
his blade and spade, put aside
a compass and detecting kit. His distance
kept us safe. In tripping ivy darkness
on the day I met this man
he did not find one 1850s French coin.
Below the beech, by cut-down trunks,
I taste air thick with wicked blooms,
pinked up in usurper balsam, and a deeper accent.
The man I cannot meet today, without a sou,
has molehilled earth, already marked his time.
In jigsawed works of light, he's incised tiny lines.

Here beside the Sweet Burn, on a different day,
he found that coin. Today I will not meet that man.
But he is is plotting all this messy puddled wood.

UNRAVELLING
by Caoimhe O'Flynn

A smack in the face. Forceful. Red, raw cheeks. Intense. Blood flowing from the nostril to the elbow. Then, a laugh. Forceful, red, raw. Cheeky, intense.

My god, why won't you shut up for five fucking minutes?! It stays lingering, crawling. It needs to find space to inhabit. To take up space. To bear the four corners with its thoughts and speculations. All Intense, all forceful.

It thinks of every past mistake. God why did I say that when I was sixteen? Should I call him? Maybe he misses me too.

Photos. Plenty of photos. Friendship. Family. Oh, would they ever just fuck off-

Language! I know, I know. What can I say?

Language itself is a hard one to fathom. Sometimes the tongue will roll to mimic certain phonics.

A-fraid.

Be-wil-dered.

Con-fused.

Dazed.

En-vi-ous.

Oh, and now a hard one. Fri-vo-lous-ly.

Good job, you haven't lost all your knowledge in your little box.

It continues. It's now high pitched. Afraid. Bewildered. Confused. Dazed. Evious.

And then I said-

Oh stop, that is hilarious! I'm going to piss myself. Keep going.

Wait, why is it still here? I don't know. I guess it just wanted to be. I don't make the rules.

You do make the rules. You can change it.

Can I? They told me I couldn't. Besides, I don't think I have the strength. There is an anchor tied to my neck.

They are the anchor. I am the ship sailing into the void. To an island where the waves will erase my footing.

Footsteps. Close and yet so far. Pounding and then tip-toeing. A rasp on the door.

Knock, knock, knock.

Who's there?

It's me, your friend from the dark. Can I come in?

No. I don't want you.

Why?

You know exactly why.

Ah now, I didn't mean what I said last time.

You meant every single snarling word. Don't you dare try and gaslight me. I have had enough of it. All the petty bullshit. The lies. The grit on my eyes. The sour tongue, the sifting lungs.

A wheeze. A cough. A choke.

You don't mean that. You can't say that.

Yes, I can. I have power over you. You can't control me.

Their friend comes along.

What's happening now?

They're at it again.

No, I'm not. If you would just listen to me-

Oh, that's a shame. Were they after a glass or two?

They now judge the empty bottle by the sink. The crisp ooze of spring permeates. The bottle conceals echo springs of hidden truth. Even I cannot escape each drip. Sip, sip, sip. There I go again, fading.

Hey, I am entitled to have a glass if I want. That is not the point. I think we need to talk about everything.

Oh, here we go-

Don't you dare roll your eyes at me. You don't know what it's like.

Oh yes, we do.

Yes, we know everything.

No, you don't. Stop it.

Well from what I can see, you leave your paint brushes in that same cup hoping for a miracle.

You also never pick up your underwear thinking it's invisible.

You also tend to listen to your music a little too loudly.

Your feet dance offbeat.

You turn off your phone notifications proudly. It ebbs the hunger you know is sweet. Taste it, let it become meat. Foul rotting refuge you take as a treat.

Speaking of hunger, we know why you won't touch chips. Did you read that book on dieting in discreet?

Oh yes, that is a good point. Perhaps it's from that one time when you started pinching your -

Stop it. Don't bring that up now.

No, let us speak.

It becomes gradual. Honey pours from their lips into yours, each drip suckling on your naked truth.

We know what it's like the past few days. These months on end have eroded your brain.

You see us in rhymes, in singsong and grace. But you don't get that what we're saying is grave.

Come along, let us see. Let's get the scalpel and cut open your bleeds.

Let it pour, let it rain. Let the maggots invade.

This pain of yours will always enslave.

This is ridiculous. Why are you rhyming? I don't get it. It's ridiculous. Stop it, right now. I need to clear my head. I didn't sleep too great.

But don't you see, that is the mystery of your misery.

You not sleeping is our bookkeeping. You are crushed over hushed sobs, wailing into the waters.

Waters…waters…what rhymes with waters? Daughters, slaughter, trotters? Why word describes best the hunger you crave in this very age?

When I think of waters, I think of drowning. Drowning them out might be the cure. Yet they do not leave me. They continue to infest.

At best, there are a warm toilet seat. No toilet paper.

Yellow wee. Cold tea. A half-eaten apple.

A chair screech, a slam.

Loud burp. A fart. Constant passing remarks

Some would think of it like the blight of the Famine, leaving nothing to digest. Eroding from the inside till there is nothing to be kept.

I think back on history and memory and longing to being, and all I can think about is how awkward it is to be seen.

I call out, I cry. I want someone to be there at night. Yet the only comfort comes from the howls of my mind. They heckle and taunt, leaving nothing. I have become gaunt.

Looking in the mirror, there is paleness. There is shrewd. Withering of the consumed. Revealed ribs. Wide hips. Fat on the calves. Nothing in the head.

I could whack myself. I could grab a hammer and bash it out.

Be gone wild thoughts. Let me be.

Yet the suffering is contagious, perhaps even fleeting.

"This doesn't read well." They would say.

Who are they? What do they want? You have us.

Do I? I do not know. Do I have anyone at this stage?

A parting glass. A triumph. A roaring cheer.

We made it at last!

Made it where?

I don't know. Success maybe. Or defeat. Acceptance. This is it. I can't stop it. No one can.

Well, that's a bit sad.

But is it? Is it really?

Acceptance has always been defined as something scattered, whimsical, offbeat. You can accept many things in life. The passing of a friendship. No food in the fridge. Death.

Is this the acceptance I want?

I would like to thank my mother, my father, my old English teacher, my grandparents, my mind, my body, my aches, my pains, my glory-

Or do I wish for a gentle sign? An outstretched hand to tell me that it's alright.

I do not know. I don't think I ever will.

How do you feel now?

Okay, I guess. A little confused even. I know I'm avoiding things.

Staleness evaporates. I can see faintly. I think I should tie my hair up. It helps with the concentration.

Sunlight creeps in. It is ten to twelve. My bed is not made. I am shaken. Fingers shaking, heart racing. Thump, thump, thump. Unacquainted rage. It is ten to twelve.

I brush my teeth. I fix myself. A deep breath in and out.

I want to let out a cry. It is lost. Word empty, void.

I grew up with silence. Speak up they said. Don't let it get to you.

A board game of scrabble.

Five points. I win.

A competition. A game.

Oh, you think you have it bad? Well, I –

-No, I have it worse than you. You wouldn't get it. Bless you. Achoo!

A canvas that does not speak. Bleeding paint with no meaning. Of crimson red and bright greenery. Are these the colours of my thoughts that others can see?

Expulsion of the lungs. Frail limbs, exposed skin. Dear breath, let me speak.

I cannot find the words. I don't know if I ever will. There is not enough time. There is not enough space on the canvas of life. This jigsaw is fragmented. I cannot find the pieces. I cannot find the image. It is bleak, dishevelled, nothing.

It is all nothing. Yet is it something?

To come out of the dark. To stretch out our limbs. To hear another beating heart.

To dance in the kitchen, to hum to a tune. To let our lips part. The rise and fall of the sweetest perfume.

To tell another you love them. To find new flavours in food.

It can all be done, and I cannot wait. This heaviness I carry is something that is bound to break.

It will become torn up and crinkled, digested into small miracles. It will be what our ancestors will speak of. Speak. Let the tongue rest. Let the mind believe.

Belief. A siren rings. Traffic spins. They all carry on to their destinations.

There is comfort in the noise. For noise means something. Doesn't it? I don't know.

Perhaps I will never know. That is something I will take for granted. My footsteps will softly trail over passages that have not been constructed, like waves erasing the sand.

Carry me. Hold me. Let me be.

I have had enough. I want it to end. I want hope. I want it all in this moment. An entirety. An infinity. All everlasting.

So, where do we go from here?

For that, I do not know.

WATCHING FROM MY BEDROOM WINDOW
by Louise Wilford

How intimate the washing on the line;
How colourful its lace and silk, how fine;
As if the life these things adorn is mine.

It's hanging on the nylon cord next door.
I spy it from my window, wanting more –
a sneeze, a sigh, a mutter or a snore,

a hint of other life beyond my fence.
But all is silent. All is quiet and tense,
as if observed from far off through a lens.

No children in the garden, just a grey
cat, statue-still, beneath the gold heat of the day.
The edges of the flimsy garments play

a little, stirring in the hesitating breeze.
A bird half-sings somewhere up in the trees,
as if afraid of summoning disease.

I cannot catch my breath, as if entombed.
My chest hurts like the whisper of a wound.
Is this the way it ends, without a sound?

LOCKDOWN LOVE AFFAIR
by R.E. Loten

Angie took a last look at the list of people who were working a shift that day and stretched out in her chair, her whole body tingling with anticipation. She stroked the name at the bottom of the column, imagining it was his naked chest she was touching. She glanced at the clock on her desk. Not long now. Her phone rang and the smile slipped from her face. Ian.

'Hello love, how's it going?'

'It's hard with so few staff in, but we're getting there. What have you been up to?' She forced herself to sound interested.

'Oh you know us furloughed-types, we just sit around watching TV and laughing at the rest of you still going to work.' Angie could hear the laughter in his voice and couldn't help a slight smile emerging despite her irritation.

'What have you really been doing?'

'Prepped all the veg for dinner and cleared out the shed this morning. You got a good team today?'

'The best.'

She paused a moment and loyalty won out over truth. 'Ian... I'm sorry I had to furlough you, you know that, don't you?'

'Course I do love. Don't be daft. I'll get my turn at work in a few weeks.'

She glanced at the clock again. Almost lunchtime. 'I've got to go. We've got a shipment due in any minute. I'll see you this evening.'

Putting the phone down, she checked her face quickly in the mirror and strode out of the office onto the warehouse floor. She'd timed it perfectly. The workers below were all filing out of the door heading to the canteen for lunch. All except one. Jack was leaning against one of the shelves watching her as she descended the stairs.

'Not hungry?' she asked, nodding towards the door as it banged shut behind the last worker to leave.

'Plenty hungry,' he said, 'But they don't serve what I want in the canteen.'

It was a terrible line, but she smiled anyway, knowing exactly why he was there.

'Did you find somewhere?'

Angie smiled and crooked her finger. He followed her through the warehouse to the deserted loading bay and pulled her into his arms as soon as they were concealed by the half-loaded lorry. One kiss later, he had her pressed against the wall, skirt hitched up, his fingers fumbling with his zip. Then he froze.

'What about the cameras?'

She tugged his zip down impatiently.

'Out of action,' she muttered against his mouth. 'System's down.'

'You're a genius,' he panted, finally freeing himself from his trousers. 'Only you could furlough your husband and keep your lover at work.'

Angie didn't reply. She didn't want to think about Ian. Not now.

On the other side of the building, the security guard waved goodbye to the electrician as he got back in his van.

On the wall in the loading bay a red light blinked and a faint whirring sound could just be heard over the noises floating up from below.

SHEFFIELD, MAY 2020
by Louise Wilford

A wind has scoured the streets,
shuttering the shops, bolting tight the doors
that used to lead to dingy staircased rooms.
No more taxi-cabs. There are whispers weeds
have flowered between the rain-washed paving slabs.

Sow thistles lift their heads
to sneer at grating ragwort threads, while scores
of oxeye daisies idly stare. Pink spikes of
rosebay willowherb stab up between the bench's slats,
and form a blushing mist between the asphalt and the
kerb.

A badger on the station;
roe deer in Hunter's Bar. Between the floors
of office blocks, the lifts have stopped; trams dead
in their tracks. All's still around the snoozing city hall;
Boots, napping; John Lewis shivering in the evening chill.

The Showroom dreams of old
Dirk Bogarde films. Under glass, the Wintergarden
snores.
The catnapping cathedral chimes,
a row of sleepy groans, bouncing soft as lead
against the tricksy old-town cobblestones.

A fox stands on a crossing,
wondering where the world has gone. A grey rat gnaws
a chicken bone beside the bins. Wrung clean, air hums
round chimney stacks, whistles along gutters, rests
in cashpoint crevices, blows dust down pavement cracks.
□

A street cleaning machine
lumbers along, alone, past rows of lifeless stores,
a tired diplodocus sneezing in the dust. Pigeons watch
litter fall and lift, observe the empty, pointless alleyways
and lanes through which the muted noises dip and drift.

Tumbleweed memory of traffic.
The city's bones laid bare to expose its flaws.
A lone police car stalks the streets, a cigarette end
idly flicked, its driver wondering how the caffs
on London Road could look so quickly derelict.

SOUTH PACIFIC
by Jane Langan

Life repeats. Wake up, breakfast, kids to school, work, boring meetings, working lunches, pick up kids, make dinner, watch tv, sleep, repeat.

How do people do this for their whole lives? What is their point in being, what makes them get out of bed every day? Why bother?

I heard a story about a man who stopped, jumped off the rat race and instead decided that he could just stay home, he didn't need to go out or go to work or do anything. He just stayed in bed. To begin with, this was fine. He would order food online, he would take in the delivery, his cupboards were full and so was his stomach. Then, as time went on, his money started to run out. He looked at his finances and decided on the things he didn't need. He made a list:

Soap
Shaving Foam
Deodorant
Detergent (Clothes and the Dishwasher)
Cleaning products for the home

He reasoned that as he wasn't going anywhere or seeing anyone (except the food delivery person) these were useless items. He also stopped paying the electricity bill. He had plenty of books, he could read, he could sleep, he could stay warm under his duvet. His dirty duvet.

As time went on, his house became cold, damp, dirty and dark. Everything, including him, began to smell. He started to get bed sores. Occasionally, the sores would burst. They exploded pus all over the already filthy bacteria covered covers. His money completely ran out after six months. He remained determined that it was still fine, there was plenty of canned goods in the cupboards.

The fridge didn't work so there was no point having fresh food. He didn't empty the bins.

One day, a small pregnant mouse climbed through a damp rotted sill of a window. Daintily she avoided the sharp shards of peeling paint. She set up home amongst the discarded baked bean cans and cereal boxes. It was a perfect home for a small mouse family. They thrived and bred and thrived some more.

Meanwhile, the man in the bed of pus and scabs and skin and grease and all sorts of unmentionable bodily fluids got sick. One of his many bedsores became infected, then another and another. The mice visited him on the bed. He could have sworn they spoke to him as he lay dying in his own filth.

Hallucinating from Sepsis he smiled at his mouse friends. They wore little hats and tap shoes and had canes in their small paws. Tip tapping across his chest, they produced an excellent version of South Pacific. He thought it was delightful. He was completely unaware of them nibbling away at their newly found protein source. Yum.

Obviously, the man died. It was months before anyone found him. By then he was little more than a skeleton. The mice family had grown exponentially and flooded out of the house when the police broke in. It was like a tiny brown furry mouse tsunami, brother upon sister upon father upon mother. On the plus side, the only smell was that funky smell from mouse droppings and ammonia from all the gallons of mouse piss, instead of the stench of a rotten dead human. There is always a bright side, after all.

COMING UNRAVELLED
by Ben Lisle

Life had always been too busy to notice the loose threads. The commute to the office with audiobook in your ears, chats with co-workers, lunch, too much work, the bus home again, dinner, a film, bed, sleep. Do it all again the next day. Out at the weekend, a hike, games, fleeting romance, drinks, and loud music. A rush, an escape from the world, from the cycle of the week, exciting enough to carry you through until the moment the alarm signals the start of another commute. Too busy to notice anything.

Then the world stopped.

It won't be for long, people say it's just a small thing, over in a few weeks. Maybe longer, if you listen to the doomsayers. Wash your hands, be careful, and everything will be fine. Few places close, but really, it's just a flu. You can still meet up, and the office carries on with a few more bottles of hand sanitiser around. A few plans are cancelled, but it's just a bit of a bump. A change might be good for you, more time to yourself.

Now people are a bit more worried. It doesn't look like things will be over as quickly as hoped, but it's not too bad. The office has some people very seriously holding new thermometers, but you know that it's just a precaution. No one is really at risk, but it might be best to put off that party to next month, just to be sure. You've learned about Zoom, and had your first virtual hangout. It's not the same, but the drinks ease you through, and soon you're laughing like you always have. It's even cheaper, no expensive cover charge or overpriced cocktail. You giggle as you finish off the bottle, toasting your friends, and making half plans to have a big get-together soon.

Now the office has shut, and you're home again on furlough. Some time off work, and the company has it sorted. Slight dip in pay, but you're saving so much on travel and god knows you enjoy the extra time in bed. A bit lonely at times, but your friends are never more than a few swipes and taps away. A few of them work in healthcare, and are working more than ever. So brave, and you tell them just what an amazing job they're doing, and cheer for them in the street. You hear that one of your colleagues lost a grandparent, but you don't really know them very well, and it might be weird to push into their private life like that. You'll give your condolences in person, soon enough you're sure. Your job is covered by the government, so even if things are tough, you'll be fine. The Zoom parties aren't really happening so much now but you've kept drinking, binging through some TV series you've always meant to see with glass in hand, delivery boxes starting to stack up.

Your job sends out an email to say that due to the current situation, they would unfortunately not be able to keep everyone on right now. Your job will be there once things pick back up and they're very sorry that things have come to this, but right now they will regrettably no longer be able to keep you on furlough. You can't really read much more of the message through the tears, and open another can. Why not? You can't go out, can't see anyone, can't touch anyone. It's been too long since you washed your clothes, and your hair is a state. Doesn't matter, you can smile through it all, wipe your face off and be brave. Your uncle works in a hospital, he's got it much worse than you, you just need to stay home for a bit. The landlord is understanding, and you say that you won't let the rent get behind. You re-watch things you've already seen, sinking into the familiarity, trying to lose yourself in the past. You wake up to the crash of broken glass after the bottle slips from your fingers.

Your uncle died. He wasn't even old, did all the right things. Sure, he was around sick people, but he had all the right gear on, should have been safe. It's not fair. You haven't left the flat now in weeks, get food delivered, struggle to get out of bed. The spirits keep you going, make the world less awful somehow. Your friend is sick and isn't getting better. You text them that you're sure everything will be fine, unable to admit to yourself that you're terrified it won't be. The landlord has been getting more unreasonable, starting to demand the rent. You've tried to get a job, but who's hiring? A delivery driver? No way, you don't want to have to go near strangers, not after what happened to your uncle. You sell a few things online, manage to scrape things together, dip into your small savings. You can start thinking again in the future about a house deposit when this is over. You can't even pretend you know when that will be.

It was your mother, she never told you she had it. Didn't want to mention she'd had a cough. It was Christmas after all, and it had been so long since you'd seen anyone, be a shame to spoil it all. You'd been drunk for most of the visit, but everyone drinks in the festive season! There had been a big fight about politics, about how bad things were, about how the world had failed, about how this was just hysteria. Your uncle's name had been shouted, and then it had got quiet. You'd stolen the last of the wine and disappeared to your guest bedroom, not able to deal with the bleakness of the world without a friend to comfort you. The drink was all you could rely on to take that pain away, to make you forget how desperately lonely you were.

You can't get another credit card. You'd never been bad with money but now you're drowning in a sea of red, finding any way to make your rent. You had an interview with a local takeaway, even gone in for a shift. One drink, just to help face the world, just on the way out the door, maybe two. They'd smelled it through the masks and sent you home again, offer withdrawn. They didn't hire drunks. You'd been angry, screamed at them that you weren't like that, and that you needed the job, even started crying in the middle of the shop. They'd threatened to call the police if you didn't leave. You'd slammed your door hard, hit the wall, snatched up the dregs of something and finished it. Then curled up into a corner sobbing and wanted to die, for everything just to stop. No more, please. Just... stop.

You'd woken up in the same corner, cold and hungry. Needing someone, anyone to listen. Your phone battery had been low, but it was enough to let you find a number and call.

"Please, I... I just need someone to talk to."

"Take all the time you need."

BLOSSOM THIEF
by Alastair Simmons

You stole the blossom before the April wind
Plundered the fruit for your feasts
Cut down the trees to stoke your fires
Dug the soil for your own gardens
Quarried the rock to build your houses
What is left?
Now
Let us begin

BEAZLEY FACES HIS BÊTES-NOIRES
by Ron Hardwick

'Stand over there, please. Make sure you're the mandatory two metres apart from that chap with the trilby.'

'I'm sorry,' said Jack Beazley, 'I didn't bring my tape measure with me. Could I stand approximately two metres away from the chap in the trilby? I mean, who said you have to stand precisely two metres away? Does this blasted virus always travel exactly two metres? What happens if there's a strong wind, or if the perpetrator is under five feet tall?'

The staff nurse didn't favour Jack with a reply. She turned her attention to a confused-looking woman in a pink scarf.

Jack reluctantly stood where the staff nurse indicated. He was outside the hospital waiting for his Covid-19 jag.

'Why Covid-19?,' he had said to his long-suffering wife, Enid. 'Why not Co-vid twenty-six or even Uni-vid four and a half?'

'Calm down, dear,' replied Enid. 'You're getting yourself worked up over nothing, as usual.'

'How long are we going to have to stand here in the freezing cold?' Jack asked the staff nurse.

'As long as it takes.'

The queue shuffled forward. Another nurse stopped Jack as he was about to enter the hospital.

'Put your mask on,' she said.

'For pity's sake, I'm fed up looking like the Lone Ranger,' said Jack.

'Put your mask on.'

No sense of humour, these nurses.

Jack fumbled in his pocket for the cotton mask Enid had made for him. She fashioned it from his grandson's vest and it sported tiny images of Paddington Bear in purple on a yellow background. Jack was of the view that Enid did this on purpose to make him look an absolute fool. If so, she had succeeded beyond her wildest dreams.

'Which arm?' asked the doctor, a young man who was already going bald.

'What do you mean, which arm?'

'Which arm do you want the injection in?' said the doctor.

'Oh, my left.'

'You were supposed to wear a short-sleeved shirt so that I could more easily make the injection,' said the doctor.

'Have you seen the weather outside?' retorted Jack. 'Snow up to your oxters. Coming here was like Captain Scott crossing the Antarctic. I would have frozen to death in a short-sleeved shirt. I'm not twenty, you know.'

'I can see that,' said the doctor, drily. 'Take off your woolly and roll your sleeve up as far as you can.'

Jack obeyed.

'There, that didn't hurt, did it?' said the doctor.

Jack had to agree.

'Now, if you'll go out into the corridor, you'll find a number of booths,' said the doctor. 'A volunteer will direct you to a vacant one. You will need to remain seated for fifteen minutes before you can leave.'

'Why?'

'In case you have a reaction to the vaccine.'

'What, you think I'll keel over just because I've had a little prick in my arm?' asked Jack.

'A little prick, indeed,' said the doctor, who hustled Jack out the door and ushered in the next patient.

'Over there, sir,' said the volunteer, a tall girl with a pony-tail. 'I'll tell you when your fifteen minutes are up.'

Jack sat down. In the next booth was the woman from number five. Across the way, was the chap from number eighteen.

'Bloody Hell,' Jack said to himself. 'A street reunion.'

'Time's up. You can go now,' said the volunteer.

'Thank God,' said Jack.

'Betty's not well,' said Enid, as they sat on easy chairs in the lounge that afternoon.

'Who's Betty?'

'Betty Smith, from Warburton Avenue.'

'Never heard of her.'

'Yes, you have. She came to the tennis social last Christmas.'

'She the woman with the flared nostrils – looks like a horse?' asked Jack.

'She doesn't look anything like a horse. She's quite an attractive woman, reminds me of Penelope Keith, in a way. Tall.'

'Tall in the saddle,' remarked Jack.

'She's got the flu.'

'Perhaps it's the dreaded lurgy,' said Jack.

'It isn't. Her temperature's normal and she hasn't lost her appetite.'

'If I recall, she ate like a horse. Half a dozen vol-au-vents in twenty minutes.'

'Jack, why are you so nasty?' asked Enid.

'I'm not nasty. I'm witty. Ironic.'

'Nasty.'

'Well, if you must know, it's this blasted lockdown and this rotten weather.'

'It's the same for everyone.'

'No, it isn't. My tennis is stopped. My badminton's stopped. There are only two shops open in the town. Fancy having to tell people the highlight of your day is a trip to Tesco for another supply of bog-rolls.'

'You've got little Hamilton.'

'He's two. What sort of conversation can you have with a two-year-old?'

'He can say 'dinosaur.'

'Can he say 'Quetzlcoatlus?' asked Jack.

'I'm not sure even I could say that.'

'Well, then. And what sort of name is Hamilton, anyway?'

'I think it's a nice name. Sort of distinguished,' said Enid.

'You know what he'll be called when he grows up, don't you?'

'Hamilton?'

'Don't be daft. He'll be Ham, or Hammy.'

'I hadn't thought about that,' said Enid.

'Neither did your son or his idiot girlfriend.'

'Partner.'

'I refuse to use that word. A partner is someone in business, like a group of lawyers.'

'You know, Jack, you're a peculiar man. We've been married all these years and you've still got an aptitude for being really silly.'

Two days later, Bob West, one his tennis chums, rang Jack up.

'Hey Jack, fancy a ramble?'

'A ramble?'

'Just thirteen ks or so. No need to overdo it.'

Jack was so desperate to avoid the tedium of his lockdown life that he agreed. Even a bloke like West, who was so boring that Jack would rather try and read the Dead Sea Scrolls than listen to him, was preferable to watching 'Can't Pay, Take it Away,' on daytime television.

'When?'

'Claire's got a dental appointment tomorrow and I'm at a loose end. Will tomorrow do?'

'Suppose so.'

'Don't forget to bring a picnic.'

'Jugged hare and Veal knuckle in aspic sandwiches,' said Jack.

The earnest West wasn't great at sarcasm.

'I'll just be bringing cheese and pickle.'

They met at the old school. There were six inches of snow lying on the ground.

'I know some splendid tracks you won't have even seen,' said West.

'Oh, goody.'

They walked through a new housing estate full of nondescript houses and onto an abandoned railway track.

'We go left here' said West, and they struck off across a farmer's field full of virgin snow, much of which lodged in Jack's socks.

'Look, a hare,' said West.

'Where?'

'Tracks. Can only be a hare. Paws close together and almost in a straight line.'

Jack rolled his eyes.

After an hour of tramping through hedges and trees, slithering and sliding as if they were on a slalom, they arrived back at the railway track.

'We'll stop at Cockburn Sidings for our picnic,' said West. 'I've two bin bags in my pack that will keep our trousers dry.'

He would.

They ate their sandwiches in silence.

'A bullfinch,' said West.

'How do you know?'

'Pink breast, black cap, white rump. He's a handsome fellow.'

A bloody ornithologist as well as an accountant.

'Did you know Heather and Eddie are splitting up?' said West.

Who the hell are Heather and Eddie?

'I had no idea.'

'Oh, I thought I'd told you. It's amicable. They each have the children three days a week.'

The penny drops. Heather is one of the two West daughters.

'Do they abandon them on a Sunday, then?' asked Jack.

'Certainly not. Eddie's mother takes them. Gives them some breathing space.'

'They blame the lockdown, of course,' said West, 'each getting on the other's nerves due to their close proximity to each other and them having to work from home.'

'I know just how they feel,' replied Jack.

Oh, God, give me strength. I cannot stand to listen to any more of this drivel.

They started off again, walking in a wide semi-circle until they reached Elfingside, a tiny hamlet not far from the main road and the beginnings of civilisation.

'Bryony's had her second novel published,' said West. 'She's arranging a five-book deal.'

Bryony is West's other daughter.

'You'll have read Stars Fell On Dockray, of course?' asked West.

'It's on my reading list after the complete works of Dickens, the collected poems of Rudyard Kipling and twenty volumes of the Encyclopaedia Brittanica,' replied Jack.

'Ah, good. As long as you intend to read it.'

They walked on until they reached the main road.

'Now, if you're willing, we'll just do another five ks. That track takes us down to Bigbie,' said West.

'Bob. Nothing would induce me to walk another yard. My feet are soaking and aching, and I'm going to catch the bus home.'

West shrugged his shoulders and walked on. Jack flagged down the town bus.

'Put your mask on,' said the driver.

'I haven't got a mask.'

'You can't get on, then.'

The driver closed the doors and drove off.

'You Marxist swine,' yelled Jack. 'Come the revolution and you'll be the first up against the wall.'

He dragged one foot after another for a long walk home.

'Enjoy your stroll, dear?' asked Enid, up to her elbows in self-raising flour.

'Enjoy it? Of course not. Having to listen to that buffoon West for two hours whilst he drones on about his precious offspring, his rotting windows, his solar panels, his addiction to oatcakes and bitter marmalade, his tai-chi, his ballroom dancing and that ferocious topspin serve of his is enough to drive anyone into an early grave. And then, a recidivist bus driver wouldn't let me on his bus because I didn't have a mask. I had to leg it all the way home, even though I've got blisters on my bloody blisters.'

'Oh, how awful it is to be you, dear,' remarked Enid.

The next day was wickedly cold, with an unforgiving wind blowing straight in from the Urals. Jack went out to his car after breakfast. He needed fuel. He sat in the driver's seat, switched on the ignition, and went to close the door. It wouldn't close. He tried several times, banging the door more firmly on each occasion.

'You swine,' he yelled. 'You bloody obstructive swine.'

He examined the door lock assembly. The catch was frozen into a position where it couldn't engage with the latch on the pillar.

'How can you freeze, ay? You've never frozen in all the time I've had you and now you choose a morning when I've only got the sniff of a petrol rag in the tank.'

Jack stomped off to the garage and returned with a can of WD40. He pointed the nozzle at the frozen catch and pressed. Nothing happened. Jack shook the can. There was plenty of penetrating oil in there, he could hear it sloshing about. He shook the can violently and pressed the button again. Still nothing.

'You sod. You useless, dismal, rotten little sod. I'll teach you.'

With that, he hurled the can to the ground, where he had painstakingly cleared away the snow, and jumped up and down on it until it was as flat as a lemon sole. He picked it up again, pressed the button and fluid issued forth in some quantity.

'How the hell is that, you evil swine? I didn't borrow you from West, did I?'

'Good Morning, Mr Beazley.' It was Matt Dobson, his next-door neighbour.

'Good? What's good about it? Day after day of doing the same thing in this bloody lockdown, bored witless, stuck indoors with a woman with a brain like a colander, friends so tedious you wish you were Romanian, a grandson whose greatest joy is throwing plastic bricks at your face and now a tin of spray that only works when you've smashed it to smithereens. As I say, what the hell's good about it?'

'You haven't contracted Co-vid 19, for a start.'

Jack was silent. There was no answer to that.

THOSE WHO CAN
by Beck Collett

'But I know what it means, and the answer's "a."'

'Yes, I know you know what it means, but I don't, and I need to know, see? I can't help you if I don't know myself, can I?'

'But I already know it, I'm going to press enter. No, don't google it – that's cheating! What if I tell Mr. Evans?'

'Don't tell Mr. Bloody Evans! We haven't had training for this, have we? We don't know how to bloody well teach! And I can't even remember learning this when I was your age. I can't even remember being you age, let alone identifying which one's the f*****g quadrilational—'

'It's quadrilateral, not—'

'Right, ENOUGH! Google says it's "a" so—'

'Just what I said, why don't you ever listen to—'

*Sound of failed attempt to slam doors, and muffled effing and jeffing *

Later that day…

'Yes, Mr. Evans, she is very good at maths, isn't she! Yes, everything's going great. OK, will do. Bye!'

'What did he say, Mum?'

'He said how well you were doing, and how well I must be doing, too.'

'And?'

'Not until Easter.'

'Oh, for the love of—'

SOMETIMES
by Rosie Elwood

Sometimes sadness pulls its string
and I can't help but unravel

line by line
stitch and purl
until I fall

unsightly, limp upon the floor

pause

my feet move me forward

inch by inch
then mile by mile
pulling my yarn

purl and stitch, line by line
until formed once more

SORTED
by Jane Langan

She is surrounded by socks. Which ones to keep? That one can't stay. It's the wrong colour and the wrong size. It won't fit in the drawer. They need to be rolled then colour matched and then arranged into perfect lines within the draw. Nothing else will do. 'I'm NOT joking.' She closes her eyes. She knows nothing else will do. The offensive socks are abhorrent, ghastly, patterned, nasty coloured, too thick, too thin, unnecessary. Into the bin.

When she is finished, she knots the black plastic bin bag tight, no one needs to see inside. Terrible. How did she let that happen? She takes the bag out, first checking if there is anyone around who might see her put it into the large refuse bin. No. No one. She runs out, drops it in and returns.

And relax. She opens the cupboard in her kitchen and stares at all her mugs, the handles matching, pointing towards her. She takes one and puts it on the surface in front of her. Then she returns to the cupboard and adjusts the mugs, so they are all equidistant apart. She gets a ruler, just to double-check. OK. Good. She puts the ruler away. She takes a measuring jug and puts 270mls of water in the jug for her cup of tea. She gazes at the mug on the counter as the kettle boils, she moves it several times until she is happy that it's central. She considers getting the ruler again. A voice in her head screams. 'STOP BEING RIDICULOUS!!!' so she doesn't. Another voice says, 'Gosh, that was a bit noisy.' 'FUCK OFF!' shouts voice one. She shakes her head gently from side to side and puts her hands neatly over her ears, making sure they a) don't mess up her hair, and b) are in the same place on both sides. The kettle switches off. She pours all the water into the cup then she puts in a teabag. She pushes the bag down with a spoon and leaves it there.

'Alexa, alarm twenty seconds.' Alexa replies, 'Alarm set for twenty seconds.' She goes to the fridge and takes out a bottle of milk and places it three centimetres away from the cup. She looks at the tea as it slowly seeps into the hot water. The alarm goes off. 'Alexa, stop.' She removes the teabag with a squeeze to the inside of the cup and puts the bag in the bin. She adds a splash of milk. A splash is measured by tipping the bottle then immediately lifting the bottle to vertical again. That is a splash. She puts the lid back on the milk and puts it back in the fridge. As she closes the fridge door, she sees a thumbprint. Her hands clench into fists. She stares at it for a moment. Voice one says, 'YOU DISGUSTING DIRTY WHORE, LICK IT CLEAN – YOU FILTH!!!!'

At the sink she washes her hands with bleach, they are raw.

CONSUMED WITH LOVE
by Dini Armstrong

The phone starts ringing the second she pushes a cream egg into her mouth. Half-chewing, half-choking, she grabs the TV remote with her left and freezes a naked Bill Nighy mid song, guitar strategically placed over his privates. Simultaneously, her right hand digs out the headset from under a sofa cushion. Her tiny frame disappears under a yellow Pikachu onesie.

She presses connect. Her voice as gentle and professional as she can manage, she says:

"Rognum Mental Health support line, my name is Tanya, how can I help?"

No one speaks, but the line is not silent. Tanya can make out a sloshing sound, wind is blowing against the mouthpiece of the caller. Her display spells out number withheld. A small green LED dot confirms that a live connection is in progress.

With her silkiest voice she coos:

"Take your time. That's ok"

After a further two seconds of silence a male voice, Scottish, mature and pleasantly hoarse, asks:

"You still there, hen?"

Tanya carefully pushes the tip of her tongue into the corner of her mouth to clear away a stray trickle of sugary goo.

"I am here, Sir. I'm not going anywhere. How can I help?"

Another pause.

"I ... ,I ... ," the voice stammers at first, but then the words come, each syllable working its way out of quicksand

"... I am eating my wife."

I am eating my wife? Shuddering, she feels naked in her onesie. No colleagues around that she can alert. No one who can sit beside her, plug into the call, and notify the emergency services. She has given him her real name!

In slow motion she reaches across to the sofa and manages to get hold of her personal mobile. Who is the senior on call clinician? On auto pilot she double-clicks on a file marked Easter rota on her laptop, while asking as gently as possible, and without even a hint of being patronising (psychopaths don't appreciate being patronised)

"Sir, did you say you are eating your wife?"

The excel spreadsheet on her screen reveals that Nicola is the SOCC. Reaching for her mobile, she scrolls for Nicki's number, then fires off a text

Red flag. Potential homicide in progress.

"Sir, it's ok. This helpline is confidential."

This is technically a lie. In case of mortal danger, emergency services can be involved without the caller's consent. The telephone counsellors have been told on day one of their training that it is better for a client to hate them than to end up dead. No mention in the red flag protocol of how to handle callers who are eating someone though.

"I feel such a failure. I'm letting her down." The caller is sobbing now. Not quite the composure of a Hannibal Lecter.

"You sound exhausted."

"I am," he sniffles, "I am puggled, hen. The water's jeelit, and even the wet suit isn't helping anymore."

Wait, what?

"Sir, are you near water just now?" She sends off another silent text to Nicki.

Callr mihgt b eoutside.

Typing with two thumbs is hard, and she is in a rush.

"Of course, I am near water," he bellows. "It's the only way I can get her back!"

Yep, clearly nuts. She regrets that thought as soon as it flashes into her judgmental brain. Come on, girl, empathy and unconditional regard! This guy might be raving bonkers, but he is in distress and outside somewhere. Find him.

"You mentioned a wetsuit. Sounds like you are on a boat? Maybe in Scotland? Loch Ness maybe? I am a bit worried that you are not safe. Maybe cold?" She exaggerates her Queen's English and hopes the ignorance of an English woman might provoke a slip up.

"It's Loch Torridon. T-h-o-i-r-b-h-e-a-r-t-a-n." He spells out the name with the shortened patience of someone who has to do this a lot. "And obviously I am not on a boat just now." Tanya breathes a sigh of relief, when he adds: "It's a kayak, one of thae sit on tops."

Why is Nicki not answering her texts! How long had the wife been dead? Did he have her with a nice Chianti and some Fava beans? Bollocks, her supervisor has warned her not to use humour as a shield.

"That's a relief, Sir. I am glad you're warm. And what's your name? I think I already told you mine, it's Tanya." Maybe an appeal to his good manners might work.

"Oh, so sorry," he apologised, "it's Rory. R-u-a-r-a-i-d-h. McGregor." His voice sounds calmer now, almost business-like. Gotcha.

"Hi, Ruaraidh. Do you go out on the kayak a lot?"

"She bought two of them within weeks of moving here. We have a jetty at the bottom of our garden."

Remember your training. Deep breath in, deep breath out.

"Help me to understand," she pleads. "What happened?"

She texts Ruaraidh McGregor, lives on Loch Torridon, jetty in garden

"She was sick," he murmurs, suddenly so quiet, she has to adjust the volume on her headset. "She was always going to die, we knew that. You should have seen her when she told me. Gutsiest woman I ever met."

So maybe it was euthanasia? A mercy killing?

"She had made me mince and tatties. My favourite. She used to put her own spin on it, too, added some herbs. I was never able to make it taste the same. She was wearing that dress I loved, the blue one, really short. She didnae need it, like. A pretty face suits the dish-cloot. She had great legs, even at her age, you know, but she was always a wee bitty conscious about that small scar on her knee. Used to nick it when she shaved her legs.

"'Pass me the ketchup,' she said, 'and by the way, the cancer is back, and this time there's nothing they can do about it, so no use crying over spilled milk. You're just going to have to figure it out without me, Chainey.' She called me Chainey because of my red hair. It's Gaelic. T-e-i-n-e."

"She sounds like quite a woman."

"Oh, she was, hen, she was, you've no idea. She used to say she was the cheese and onion to my salt and vinegar. We were so different, Beauty and the Heffalump, but when we snuggled up on the sofa, sharing a bag of crisps, we just never had any leftovers. Her breath would be honking but I kissed her anyway. Even in the end, when she was nothing but a bag of bones, bleeding gums and mouth wash. She hated me looking after her, but to be honest...," he took a sip of something, "it made me feel like a wee hero for a change. They don't talk about that in the stories, the knight in shining armour, scoopin' up his loved one, takin' her to the cludgie. Wipin' up efter her when she cannae quite make it anymair. She'd given that cancer a right rammy, but in the end, ... , in the end ..."

"She was lucky to have you."

He hesitates.

"She said that, too. Not in those words, mind. Left me a note. Included the instructions for the washing machine and the dish washer. And the phone number for the local Chinese. Cheeky mare. She never did like my cooking. And that's just it. I tried, but I can't make it work!"

Her mobile vibrates briefly. Finally, Nicki is responding. She picks it up. A text from her mum. Happy holidays, sweet pea, sorry we couldn't see you again this year. Ibiza is amazing. Wish you were here. Dad says hi.

"What's not working, Ruaraidh?"

"The recipes are all wrong. It's all wrong. She tried to teach me to cook, but I never had a knack for it. Give me a lawn mower to fix any day. I guess I'm a bit old school."

Time to get him back on track. "Ruaraidh, what happened?"

He pauses, and she can hear him sipping.

"She was a wee fighter, lasted three months longer than they gave her credit for. One night, her breathin' got weird, she lay on the sofa, starin' upwards, mouth wide open, gaspin' for air. Sun came up, I woke up, she didnae, and that was that.

"Of course, she had already planned it all down to the nth degree. Dead classy, like. You know that Monty Python song, Always Look on the Bright Side of Life, that one? She wanted that on full volume while her coffin disappeared behind the curtain. People didnae know whether to cry or whistle along. Hard to do both.

"It was so fast, so fast, before I knew it, I was driving home, with her ashes in a little scattering tube, eco-friendly, floral design. She'd bought it for twenty-four quid online."

They are silent for a while. Eventually, Tanya asks "What was her name?"

"Shonagh," he declares, pride in his voice, "it was Shonagh. I tried, ye ken, I really did. I kayaked out on the Loch, just as she telt me. I opened the tube and scattered the stuff, it was like icing sugar, just grey. It floated there for a bit, then it started to sink, just down, like, into the deep black, where I couldnae see her anymair. And so I plunged the stupid tube into the water again and again to try and scoop as much of it back up as I could manage, but the damn thing started to fall apart and ...". He sobs. "But I had to get her back, I had to."

He tells her how he started to go fishing every day, three times on some days. He would catch Mackerel by the dozens, smoke them, boil them, grill them, find new and elaborate recipes. Every time he felt he was unable to do her justice. He would eat as much of the flesh as he could, but there were always bones. Sometimes he would grind them up and mix them into smoothies. He couldn't waste a single gram of her.

"I think I understand," she lies.

"No, you don't," he snaps back, "you don't have a scooby. When I eat too much of her, I get sick and then I throw up. That way all I've achieved is turn my wife into vomit. If I manage to keep her down long enough, she comes out the other end as ... well, ... I can't hang on to it, I can't flush it down the toilet. So I keep it in the garden, in a plastic barrel.

"It was ok in the winter, but now it's spring, I hardly catch anything anym..." He stops dead. Then he exclaims: "Oh, yer fuck!" Tanya hears splashing sounds.

"Ruaraidh? Ruaraidh? What's going on?"

"It's a seal," he shouts, "one of thae wee ones, just waiting, staring straight at me, the little shit, it's mocking me, the wee fuck, I nearly went in after her." Tanya jumps in her seat when she hears him screaming:

"Gie's it back, gie's it back!" His voice has cracked, then he lets out a growl, more beast than man. She hears thumping noises, water splashing, then nothing.

She stares at her display. *Caller disconnected.*

Tanya has to take a sip of water to wash down a lump in her throat before she picks up her mobile.

"You said 'her', Ruaraidh," she murmurs, "You nearly went in after her."

HERE NOW NOWHERE
by Clair Tierney

A winter forest
waiting for a blade
soft talon of spring
pushing up from
sealed ground.

Children climb trees
making each bend
a new room in the arms.
They pull carpets of moss
off the old and big stones
and lay over branches,
fashioning a nest.

Outdoors takes on a potency
a poetry
the here, now, nowhere
day-white technicolour
technisound,
their sound of playing
pulling me out
from sealed ground.

COMING UNRAVELLED
by Sue Davnall

Unravelling. Losing the plot. Coming apart at the seams. Some of the words my friends have used to describe their experiences of lockdown this year. My pal Julie, for example.

'You've no idea what it's like, Mia. I could maybe just about cope with working from home, crouched over that crappy kitchen table cos Matt's too stingy to buy me a proper desk. But it's doing my head in trying to fit in the kids' schooling on top of everything else, never mind stopping them tearing up the house when I'm on a work call. You're so lucky you don't have kids.'

I thought Matt and Julie would have enjoyed spending more time with their children. They were always complaining pre-covid about how little quality time they had together as a family when they had to commute for work. But it appears that the grass isn't greener after all. Mind you, more than thirty minutes in the company of young Chloe and Benjy would have me throwing a pot plant through the window too. Yes, that really happened, according to Matt anyway. Luckily, the window was open at the time.

Then there's Beth. Super-disciplined, figure-of-a-goddess Beth. Up at 5am for a six-mile run before her commute up to the City, an hour-long session at the gym every lunchtime and triathlons just about every weekend. And now? Two stone heavier with a serious alcohol problem and an addiction to home baking. Lives on her own and has to eat everything herself before it goes stale. Or so she says. Of course I'm not gloating. Not at all. She's a very dear friend.

George and Lizzie Brown next door are Zoom refuseniks, and I admire them for it. For most of us, the steady cycle of work meetings, coffee mornings and heavily lubricated Friday night quizzes has taken its toll on our eyesight, our posture and our livers. The Browns drew a line in the sand early on in a bid to keep their health and sanity. Sadly, their enforced dependence on each other for company means that they're both now ready to commit murder in the most ingeniously horrible ways. I know that because Lizzie told me so the other day: her chosen weapon is George's golf club and she's not going to hit him with it.

You're probably wondering about me by now. Well, I haven't got kids, I was never a fitness fiend, I have no problem with Zooming and I don't have to deal with the annoying habits of a dearly beloved. So while I listen diplomatically to my pals as they offload on WhatsApp (or, in the case of Lizzie, over the garden fence), I feel blissfully free of the trials of a lockdown existence. In fact, I've positively enjoyed the experience.

I should explain that I'm a writer. Spending time alone is the norm for me. I lose myself for weeks in the world I'm creating for my current project. That is, I do when time allows. I'm still trying to find the right publisher for my epic saga Warlords of Wisbech – I know I'll get there in the end, J K Rowling was turned down seventeen times before she hit the jackpot – and in the meantime I keep a roof over my head with a tedious little office admin job. Lockdown has been a gift: apart from the odd online meeting I've been able to devote myself entirely to my writing. Yes, an unravelling, but a welcome one, a freeing from the bonds of my previous existence which in turn has released the full force of my creative powers.

Shall I tell you a little of my latest work? It's fairly under-developed as yet but I can give you a flavour. You might even be able to advise me on a couple of the plot twists.

In short, I have been turning over ideas for some time on how to commit the perfect murder. Hardly original, you're thinking, and you're right. But the reading public has an insatiable appetite for the dark and gruesome. I was taken with the idea of something contemporary, in a lockdown setting in fact. You'd think that committing a crime in such circumstances would be harder, with everyone at home most of the time and getting more involved in each other's lives. But that in itself offers new opportunities.

The first thing I noticed was that folk living in the same street who had hardly exchanged a word in decades started calling round to check up on each other, deliver groceries, exchange misdirected Amazon parcels. More interaction means more possibilities for fallings out, the bringing out into the open of long-nurtured resentments. I was in the garden the other day when I overheard the following conversation.

'Oi! You! Chappie in the blue jumper. What have you done to my forsythia?'

'Trimmed it back. The bits overhanging my garden. Like I always do, every year.'

'You lunatic! You've killed it!'

'You've never complained before.'

'That's not the point! I've never caught you red-handed before. I've always been at work.'

'Well tough. It's dropping leaves all over my hot tub.'

'I couldn't give a toss about your hot tub. If that forsythia dies I'll…I'll…'

'You'll what?'

'I'll come round and I'll sort you out.'

'Oh yeah? You and whose army, grandpa?'

I didn't hear the outcome but there's a murder waiting to happen, don't you think?

The other useful development, from a potential killer's point of view, is the springing up of a host of unregulated services. So many people baking in their kitchens and selling their wares on local social media sites, so many purveyors of home-made beauty products! How difficult could it be to intercept the supply chain, the deliveries left unattended on customers' doorsteps, and introduce an appropriately lethal substance?

Tell me, dear reader, what would you find more convincing? A murderous baker or a sinister delivery driver? At what stage of the proceedings should I introduce the fatal dose? Or doses: perhaps I should go all out for a serial killer.

Now, I have to confess that I have already carried out a small amount of practical research: it goes without saying that a good author should always test the plausibility of his or her plot line. I borrowed a couple of recipes from Beth and tried my hand at a Victoria sponge and some fairy cakes. They turned out rather better than I expected, and when I posted some pictures online I received a most gratifying response.

Next, I looked into the lethal properties of various common household substances. I didn't want to make life difficult for my murderer by requiring him to obtain, say, a Novichok agent. I eventually settled on rat poison; a bit of a cliché, I know, but easy to obtain and to administer. I experimented with a small amount in a crumbled-up fairy cake on the bird table and was rewarded with two dead pigeons and a parakeet. I felt quite sad about the parakeet: such a pretty bird, I love to see them in the garden.

Then I needed to find out how much might be needed for a larger creature. George and Lizzie own a decrepit old tabby that pees on my lawn and dumps dying mice on the step outside my kitchen door: I knew I would be doing them a favour by helping it along its way to the Great Cat Litter in the Sky. Unfortunately, I underestimated the amount and found the mangy creature vomiting copiously behind the shed: a loose stone in the rockery resolved the problem and also gave me an idea of where to dispose of the body. I was more successful with the vicar's mutt – I lobbed a well-laced sausage over the hedge when he was lolloping round his garden. The dog, obviously, not the vicar. (Almost) instant success!

I confess that I am now terribly excited at the prospect of completing the final stage of my research. The book that follows will be my best ever: so vivid, so true to life. The bonds of my imagination have been unravelled: I have been set free.

BACK TO THE BEGINNING
by Helena Nwaokolo

In searching for the end
The beginning was found

Before its unravelling
Her life was tightly bound

Around itself
In random layers of tracks

Not chosen or planned
With misplaced hope just travelling

But loose paths fell away
Safe routes were obscured

Steps faltered at
Faces grinning through the layers.

Decades on
Reflections in life's foliage

Showed a face of someone strong
Who could travel

Not to an end
But back to a beginning.

WHO PARENTS THE PARENTS
by R.E. Loten

'My turn CH-O-P, chop. Your turn.'

    'CH-O-P, chop.'

    'My turn, SH-I-P, ship. Your turn.'

    'SH-I-P, ship.'

    'My turn F-U-CK, fuck. O-FF, off.'

This last was inside Nina's head rather than on the home-learning video her five-year-old daughter was watching. She wondered if the teachers were ever tempted to say this as they had their clothes tugged by sticky hands and listened to the incessant whining of the children in their class. She didn't know how they did it. She could barely cope with one five-year-old, let alone thirty of the little darlings.

Her husband ambled past on his way to the fridge.

'You're doing so well darling. Very good,' he said.

'Patronising bastard,' Nina thought, before realising he was probably talking to their daughter rather than her.

'Could you do this with her for a little bit so I can get a shower?' she called through the open kitchen door.

'Sorry darling,' he said, 'I've got another meeting in twenty minutes.'

'That's okay,' Nina said. 'I can be quick.'

'But I wanted to make a cup of tea to have in the meeting.'

Nina gritted her teeth.

'You still can. I won't be long.'

She pushed her chair away from the table and pointed at the laptop screen.

'Her work's all there on the website.'

Inside the bathroom Nina turned the shower on then took a deep breath and leaned her head against the door for a moment, fighting against the threatening tears. Why is it always me that has to give? Why is my work less important than his? She knew why: money. It still wasn't fair though. Lucy was a good kid, but she needed constant supervision to get through the work. If they didn't do it, the school would be on to them, checking everything was ok. They'd done that the first week.

'Everything's fine,' Nina lied when Mrs Edwards rang. 'Lucy's had such fun, I just forgot to upload the pictures, that's all.

The reality of that first week was Lucy sobbing because she couldn't see her friends and her teacher, while Nina tried to be a caring parent at the same time as having a Zoom meeting with her boss, while her silenced mobile buzzed with angry texts from Steven hiding upstairs in the study. Can you get her to stop that infernal wailing. I'm trying to write a report and I can't concentrate. What the fuck did he think she was trying to do? She'd noticed she swore a lot more nowadays but reassured herself it was only in her head until yesterday when Lucy had knocked her drink over and shouted, 'Shit' at full volume while Steven was on the phone to a client.

There was a knock on the bathroom door.

'Nina? I can't work out what she's meant to do and my meeting starts soon.'

Nina looked in the mirror. A blurry smudge peered back at her through the mist. She felt more like her reflection than a real person: slightly out of focus, smeared around the edges and somehow not quite there. She'd been completely consumed by Home-Schooling Mum. Nina the person no longer existed. Nina wondered if she ever really had. Was there more to her than mum, wife, cook, cleaner? She thought there might have been once. She touched the face in the mirror and a single droplet slid down the glass from the corner of its eye.

Steven knocked on the door again.

'Nina, seriously! I've got a meeting. Hurry up!'

The shower would have to wait. She could feel herself unravelling, patience and sense of self unspooling in tandem. Time was running out for the person she used to be and there was nowhere to run. She sank to the floor, hands over her ears while Steven pounded on the other side of the door.

'Nina. Nina? Nina!'

LOCKDOWN WOOL
by Lily Lawson

I entered lockdown after emerging from a fog of grief following my Mam's death. After the reality of the situation sunk in, I went into panic mode. I felt sure that this Covid beast would take away everyone I cared about.

My main concern was for my Dad. He was determined to carry on as normal. I tried to reason that he was being careful.

My anxiety would not let me relax if anyone I cared about displayed any deviation from normal communication levels until they got in touch or posted on social media. In some cases, I manage to get an agreement from people that they would communicate in a regular pattern and what steps I could take to check on them if they broke the pattern.

It was only for a few weeks; the risk would diminish or treatment would be found so it wasn't fatal. These were my naïve thoughts. I saw it as a pneumonia strain. I knew lockdown would last longer than the original broadcast stated. I figured as it takes 21 days to form a habit that time frame had been chosen to lead with and after 21 days, we would be told how long it would be. I never imagined this!

My life wasn't affected too much beyond my concern for my friends and family. It was weird to feel that they were in danger just by venturing out the door. Unlike War it was unclear who the enemy was and where an attack might come from. It took me a long time to relax and realise that if everyone was careful, the odds were, they would be ok.

I got to grips with Zoom, caught up with my uni work and even managed to record some of my poems and songs to share privately. My writing did suffer from a lack of attention at times but thankfully it didn't desert me completely.

My insecurity had other ideas and would not leave me alone. I lost some people completely and some wisely put distance between us.

My Dad had a mini stroke. The hardest part was not being able to see him. He recovered well. I never doubted he would make it; my concern was whether it would take away his independence.

One of my closest writing friends got the virus. She was her amazing, inspirational self. It is unclear how it will affect her in the long term but she survived that's the important thing.

My time in lockdown has given me experiences I would never have had otherwise. I saw people in a different light. I did a fair bit of unravelling.

Unravelling sounds messy, the image I have is a ball of wool rolling across the floor. You roll the ball back up again, trying to secure it so it doesn't happen again.

In life when we unravel it starts slowly, we may not even notice it at first, or we may recognise it and deny it even to ourselves. We think by ignoring it, we can pretend it never happened.

I have unravelled several times in the past. I examined what I thought were the causes and promised myself I would not let it happen again. It did, just differently.

A bit like clearing a garden of weeds unless you dig them out by the roots they will just come back. It takes longer to do that. You may have to turn the garden over to make sure you have removed any old roots that were missed in previous weeding sessions.

I tided up my unravelled wool in a somewhat careless fashion, thinking one day I will get back to it and do it properly if it really needed that. The balls got messed up in the box and got tangled with each other. It got completely out of hand.

Over the last few years, I have been trying to unravel it all properly to really see what wool was worth keeping and what belonged in the bin. I didn't always do this alone. In some cases, the 'help' created another mess but even that helped me see what the wool was worth. I was fortunate to have the assistance of some professionals and some very caring amateurs who had learnt through their own experiences. Their suggestions and patience in trying to teach me have made the process easier than it might have been.

Unravelling can be a positive experience. It has led me back in the direction of who I was before the initial unravelling took place.

As we unravel our lives and examine them, we see the repeated patterns. We have to be brave and unravel all the wool before we can see what we can make with the good bits. We may need to buy more wool, this time carefully chosen. There is no guarantee we won't make a mess again. If we do, we know what steps to take to sort it out. It is easier one ball at a time.

SWARM
by Suzanne L. Burn

In my brain, the deafening drone
from high in the baobab tree.
Cells crammed full with seething black
bodies on transparent wings,
So dense, blighting an African sun
fight or flight, nowhere to run,
survival relies on reflexes
falling to the ground, curling tightly
like an unborn child
cocooned in the womb.
The swarm surges down, pulsing
threatening, like a throbbing mass of fury
undulating just inches above -
barely any room to breathe, I play dead
as day turns to night, only my dreams
will set me free.

Note from the author:
I've taken inspiration
for this poem from Sylvia Plath's bee poems, and my childhood in
Africa.
Swarm is a metaphor for my anxiety which can be crippling at
times, and this is when I start
to unravel. I frequently need to block out my fears which are so often
unfounded, yet so real.

BETWEEN TWO WORLDS
by D.H.L. Hewa

How could I not be scared?

There's a stealthy silent enemy moving amongst us. Hiding within friends, and family. A single hug, the touch of a hand, any human contact having the potential to kill or maim us. It's three months after the man behind the lectern gives his permission, but I still feel like I'm facing a pack of hungry lions in a colosseum. We've already cancelled two holidays this year.

The leaves on the trees are changing to red, yellow, orange, and brown, as our last booked break of the year approaches. Should we leave the safety of our home? Venture out to accommodation vacated by the previous occupants only hours before? Should we trust our health to the vigilance of the cleaning crew? My father-in-law used to say that if you live your life being scared, you may as well lock your front door and throw away the key. Remembering this, we make our decision.

It's the day after our arrival in Devon.

Juddered awake by the flickering blue lights of the television, and my husband's lap top, I pull the duvet over my head. It's six thirty in the morning. Breakfast is served in bed, but no, it's not to give me a lie-in, but to get me up and ready. Ready to make the most of the weather which is forecast dry for the morning. Ready to make use of the fact that there's no live firing today. Ready for my first ever, in fact our first ever sojourn into the depths of Dartmoor.

'We need to leave by eight or eight-thirty.'

My husband, aka the holiday planner and activities manager has got the ten day itinerary.

'Can't we leave later?' I ask, sitting up, and pulling the covers up to my chin.

'Not if we want to be back by lunchtime. Before the showers…' he says.

For goodness sake. We haven't even unpacked properly yet, and he wants to be off out. It's already quarter past seven! Puffing out a loud, long deep breath, I pull back the covers fiercely, stomping out of bed. Rushing through my morning routine, I push up the suitcase lids, letting them go with a bang as I throw on my walking clothes, whilst hubby gets our snacks ready. Rushing out, we stumble across a family of blue-green peacocks, the only other early morning risers. Strutting slowly, oblivious to social distancing and sanitising, they wander the highly landscaped grounds. Quietly, quietly, we move around them. Getting into our Mazda, we stir it to life. Negotiating farmers on tractors and quads, and cars doing morning school runs, we finally arrive at our destination.

Only one other car there.

Empty of occupants.

'That's our destination,' husband says, pointing at a hill in the distance.

It looks innocuous. Nowhere near the height or steepness of Scottish mountains. A gentle amble is in store.

Stepping out of the car, I raise my head, letting the wan October rays caress my face.

So quiet.

So tranquil.

Togging up, I pick up my trekking pole, bought for a mere ten pounds. Bargain. Hubby gathers his camera and map.

'Putting your waterproofs on already?' he asks.

'Thought you said it would be soggy,' I reply.

Shrugging, he stares at the map in his hand. He knows the real me. Hating to put on leggings whilst underway.

'Come on then,' I call, striding off, grinning.

The route initially along a path, is dry. Waterproof bottoms probably a bit overkill. Entering a field, we squelch through the water running down it. Wish I'd brought wellingtons.

Aha. A stream. Test my new stick. Have to find a way across. Hubby's already on the other side,

'Be careful, just got a boot full of water,' he says.

'Cheers,' I reply.

'Might be better to extend your stick to full length,' he advises.

I pull the bottom part. It comes off. Quickly pressing it back in, I twist the catch, tightening it. Choosing where I want to cross—I move from tussock to tussock—but as I lean my weight into the pole—it slides straight down.

'Bloody hell, stupid cheap piece of shit,' I say.

'What's happened?' hubby asks.

'It's not tightening properly and gone back down.'

I wave my stick in the air.

Stretching out his hand, hubby steadies my skip on to sturdier ground.

'Let me see,' he says, taking my pole off me.

'Trouble is, you never test your equipment before you set off,' he grumbles.

Oh, so it's all my fault that something doesn't do what it's supposed to. Biting my lip, I give him my best glare which hits a stone wall, as he fiddles with the damn thing.

'You've broken it,' he says.

'I haven't!'

'There. It's done,' he says, passing it to me.

'Thanks,' I reply.

Winding our way around the mire, we trudge, tutting at each change of course. Reaching the bottom of the summit, we go up, up, up. One highland cattle, miles away from home, watches us through its lock down fringe. A herd of black cows stare askance as we advance. Scrunching grass and gravel, we reach the top. Ravens glide and soar, jet black shapes above us.

'Look, a flagpole, they put a red flag on there when there's live firing,' hubby says, pointing at the empty contraption.

He always keeps me well informed.

Standing together next to the grey flagpole, we catch our breath, taking in the expansive views.

'Choice of routes now. Through that boulder field, or down the back of the slope,' hubby says.

'Down the back,' I say, looking at the vast expanse of unremitting grey stone.

Edging our way slowly down the steep back of the hill, we finally make it to level ground.

Squelching, we move on, watched by bored black cattle. Best keep my head down. Been chased by calves on a walk along The Ridgeway path before now. Concentrating hard, I lose sight of hubby. Getting splashed, clambering over small rivulets, balancing precariously on top of mossy stones and knitting needle tussocks, sinking, slipping on slushy mud. It's only when I stop—find myself all alone in the middle of a vast expanse of moor—listening to a fast flowing stream—seeing rolling hills and a few skeleton bramble bushes in the distance that Sherlock Holmes and the hound come to mind. Shivering, I pull up the collar of my fleece. Then walk, walk, walk. Oh. Thank God. There's hubby, waving his arms, pointing at the best way to get to him.

'The path has disappeared,' he says, as I catch up.

'It's not me then,' I grin back.

'Let's go down towards the stream. We can follow that back,'

Clambering down, now every step is a tussock. I go back up. More tussocks. My teeth grind. My knees groan. Stopping every three steps to pull my knee guards back up from around my ankles, I stem the scream rising in my throat. Seeing a sheep track, I battle my way back down. Stepping gingerly along the grassy clusters of the quaggy trail—I meander—falling further and further behind. Looking up, I see hubby waiting for me on the slope ahead. Rushing forwards, I head straight toward a monumental bog.

No way.

Straight through?

Go to the right on to steep-sided tussocks?

Go to the left and slip into a raging river?

What choice?

Inching forwards, I pick which lumps in the bog will appreciate my weight.

'Nooooooo!'

My left foot slides off a moving clump, entering the mud. Ugh. Water bubbles into my boot. Pressing my right foot into a tussock, I jerk my left foot.

Splash.

The walking stick slips off into the peat, followed closely by my right foot.

'Oh no!!!!!'

I pull my left hand out of the water. Grabbing the nearest bit of solid earth, I push down, and rise up. Heaving back a sob, dripping, I squish up to hubby. Sky blue eyes wide, he stands prickling by my side.

'It's horrible. Thought it was going to be an easy walk,' I whimper.

'Right. I'll go on my own next time,' hubby shouts, hotfooting it off.

Pursing my lips, I trudge behind, eyes stinging wet, until I see hubby contemplating the river.

'It looks easier on the other side, but there's no way across,' he says.

We search upstream, then down. The deafening torrential roar taunts us. Just have to carry on as we are. Scrambling down a rocky fern strewn path, at long, long last, we reach the valley bottom.

'Right. Better change your clothes before you get cold,' hubby says.

I now see a muddy purple fleece, dripping brown hands. Pulling off my now brown pack, I dump it on the nearest cement coloured rock. Fleece, jumper, long sleeve top, is nothing sacred to that bog? My teeny pink t-shirt is the only top that's dry.

'Got a towel? Spare clothes?' hubby asks.

'No,' I whisper.

'Brought an *empty* pack?'

'Have a few thing…' I mumble.

Yes I do, Scarf, gloves, waterproof top, two packets of wet wipes, bottle of water, wallet, purse, mobile phone, sun cream, sun hat. All very useful, other than if one falls in a bog.

Removing my clothes on the now chilly hillside, I use the dry edges of my dripping clothes to wipe myself down. Opening the wet wipes, I scrub at the stubborn mud and grit on my hands and lower arms.

'You'd be better washing in the river,' hubby pronounces.

'What? Balance on those stones and fall in?' I squeak.

Honestly!!!

'You'll be cold. Take my fleece,' hubby says, getting ready to take it off.

'No. One of us needs to stay warm. My waterproof top will keep the wind off.'

Grateful that there were no other walkers about, I change my attire. Munching banana, and chocolate, we look at what's ahead. A boulder field, stretching far into the distance. Great. We climb up one side, and down the other—step into and out of root holes—up again, down again. Using both hands to grab at trees, bushes, edge of boulders, my now not so great bargain of a stick helps just enough. Sliding on my bottom off slippery large boulders—I totter and stumble. There's not so much as a smooth straight path in sight.

'You're right about your walking stick. I've just seen the bottom half of another one, in a bog,' hubby chuckles.

'See, told you,' I smirk.

Chortling together we continue our journey. The rising wind whips our faces, as the sky turns brooding, darkening the landscape. The rain makes an early entrance, pelting our cheeks. I pull my hood up tight around my face.

'I'd better put my waterproofs on. Can you hold the map and camera?' hubby says, chucking his pack down on a flattish rock next to the river bed.

Putting one booted foot into his trousers, he teeters on the other.

'Sit on the rock, and pull them on,' I instruct.

'I'll get my walking trousers wet,' he retorts.

'You're wet now anyway.'

I take a deep, deep breath, and hold it.

Losing his balance, hubby knocks off his glasses, sending them somersaulting into the rumbling river. Bending into the coursing water, he grabs, stemming their journey downstream.

Hey, they're cleaner than they went in,' he says.

'Well done. Never seen you move that fast,' I cackle.

'At least I didn't go down like a wobbly, shaky skittle in slow motion,' hubby chuckles.

'Anyway, we've found one way of forgetting the pandemic,' I say, my mind on a hot shower in the safety of our holiday lodge.

SAVED MARRIAGE
by G.S.

I looked cautiously at the stranger sitting at the other side of the table, quietly eating his food. I felt his quick, curious eyes on me as I looked down. None of us dared to stare too long for fear of rejection. We had both been equally guilty of rejecting each other for a long time now. Years of being stuck in a cycle of shift work, stress, anxiety and tiredness. Sex was practically nonexistent. We moved on each other like robots, with no feelings, because we both felt we had to 'fit it in' to our schedules.

Six years since that first passionate kiss, four years since our beautiful wedding. We were so passionately in love. I had never had time to think about just how much things had changed, until now. Did we even know each other anymore? Did we even like each other? Did I love this man in front of me?

Lockdown came rushing into our lives like some sort of therapist and we had both been told to work from home. For the first couple of days, we had been busy setting up equipment, so our workplaces were ready. Now it was the weekend. Usually, we would be out in a restaurant with our friends, letting their chat drown out and distract us from each other. Instead, we were alone, our doors closed to the outside world.

I was immediately nervous, first date nervous! I quickly downed my red wine. I felt I needed courage. His sparkling brown eyes were smoldering as he gained the courage to fix them on me, and I quite suddenly remembered why I was so attracted to him. My face felt like it was burning red. My heart thudded wildly because I remembered what he was capable of doing to me. I wanted him to do it. I took a calm, shaky breath and smiled.

"Is something the matter?" he said, looking concerned.

"No," I said, shaking my head.

He bit his bottom lip and beckoned me over with his index finger. I sat frozen to the chair. I did not know what was wrong with me. He looked a bit dejected.

"I'm just a bit nervous," I said, thinking it best to be honest.

"Why? It's just me," he said, raising his shoulders and laughing.

"It hasn't been 'just us' for so long. I'm scared you won't like me anymore," I said, sheepishly.

"We will see about that," he said, raising one eyebrow and disappearing under the table.

"Chris, Christopher, what are you doing?" I laughed nervously, but at the same time wanted him so badly.

I felt his hands slowly run up the sides of my hips and under my dress. He tugged the sides of my underwear down. He pulled my hips forward unexpectedly, my back resting now against the back of the chair. I felt his warm hands on my knees as he steadily parted my thighs. His warm lips began kissing and teasing my intimate part. His tongue moving on me, in me, causing an intense feeling I had forgotten I could feel. I arched my back and moved my hand under the tablecloth and into his thick blonde curls. I groaned and thrusted trying to push myself further into his mouth. I felt his fingers join in as he guided them inside me. My body couldn't take the excitement anymore and I came helplessly into him.

I caught my breath as he pushed my chair slowly backwards and stood looking seductively down at me. I wanted to give him what he had just given me. I unzipped him and tugged everything down, taking him inside my mouth. He groaned, wrapping his hand around my hair as I picked up speed, but he didn't let me finish. He wasn't ready to finish like this. He lifted me under the arms and turned me backwards so that my buttock rested against the table edge. Leaning over my shoulder, he began to move the plates, letting them crash to the ground. I leaned back eagerly helping him, feeling liberated.

He lifted me up onto the table, I took in his manly, musky scent, sending my desire for him wild. I unbuttoned his shirt impatiently, throwing it to the side then pulled his shoulders down on top of me as I lay back on my forearm. He moved his hand up my body, reaching and pulling down the front of my dress, releasing my beasts. He cupped and massaged them as he pushed himself inside me. Moving faster and faster. I wanted him, all of him. I screamed with the mounting orgasm; my body hadn't felt so alive. He came into me, as I did to him, both slowing. He leaned over and kissed my neck as he reached around me, pulling me up slowly to sit as we caught our breaths.

"Where have you been?" I said, stroking his face and bottom lip.

"I know... Lockdown is going to be fun," he said, with a wry grin.

We both looked around us at the broken glass and china and laughed.

He picked me up under my thighs, I clasped my hands around his neck and cradled myself into him.

We continued to love each other over and over and we quickly got to know each other again. Re finding, not only what we had physically together, but learning about each other and enjoying each other's company again.

Lockdown had unraveled us from our busy lives. A life that had slowly and sneakily pushed us apart.

SINGLE VISION
by Colin Johnson

Nice of you to come, mate. Thanks.

It started when we was on holiday – Malaga – nice place, plenty of sunshine, even in October.

Yeah, we got back just before this new lockdown. Started while we was there. I could see okay most of the time – the hotel pool, people in the bar, the bar staff. I could still read the labels on the bottles lined up at the back. So at first, I just rubbed me eyes a bit, and had another beer. Don't worry, I said to myself. Relax. Unwind.

Hard to unwind though, if you can't take it all in – the people swimming, the girls in their bikinis. The women laughing together underneath a sunshade.

Don't get me wrong, I was still enjoying sitting by the pool. It was just the people – well, it was odd. Not a lot of staff in the hotel. Couldn't figure it out, the room was done each morning, nice as you like, but I never saw a cleaner. Same in the restaurant, hardly anybody working. The waiter on our table every night was fine, though – cheerful, always a little joke and a smile. Left him a decent tip.

Coming home, it was worse. When we checked in at the airport, I was all ready with the passports, put them down on the desk. Thought the girl must've gone to get something. It seemed like there was no one there, then she asked me to put a bag on the belt. That threw me, I can tell you. I felt a real wally, waiting to be asked to do that, then looking round to see who had spoken, before I picked up the bag. My face went all hot, then, and it wasn't the sunburn.

Well, I didn't tell Barbara, did I?. No need to worry her, not then. But I could tell it was gettin' worse. Even she was getting' a bit fuzzy.

On the way home, I couldn't hardly see the cabin crew. There was just a grey blur where their faces and shoulders should've been. Makes you wonder, something like that, what's going on.

Couldn't ask for nothing on the plane, didn't have nothing to eat, not even a drink. I just couldn't work out how you talk to a voice, when you cant see where it's coming from.

A couple of days after we got home, we were sitting watching the news, that's when I told Barbara. Had to didn't I? She made some comment about that Emily woman that reads the headlines, you know, before the specialists come on and explain what's really happened. Barbara said her neckline was a bit low for the BBC, wasn't it?

She always gets huffy, if I say someone on TV has a short skirt or a good figure, like I'm not supposed to notice stuff like that. But it's okay for Barbara to find fault with their necklines.

'I can't see nothing wrong with it, love,' I said. 'In fact, I can't see her at all.'

Well, the shit hit the fan then, didn't it?

– How long's it been going on?
– Why haven't you told me?
– Could I see her – Barbara?

To tell the truth, mate, her face was all blurred out, but her outline was clear, so I blagged it a bit. Told her I could see her okay, but I'd still go down to the optician next day.

Well, they put me straight. Loss of sight, that's an emergency.

Barbara was out, of course. Coffee with friends, as usual, every Tuesday morning. God knows what they find to talk about, week after week. Thought I'd better not drive, not with eye problems, so I walked round to the doctor's and explained to the receptionist – or to the grey cloud floating there, where I knew she was sitting. Then I waited for an emergency appointment with the GP registrar. Nice chap, sharp dresser, none of that stubbly beard some of them have these days. Seemed to know what's what.

'Eyes,' he said, looking right at me, 'need specialist care. 'Get to the Eye Hospital quick as you can, he said.

He sounded like a school teacher talking to a slow learner. 'You need to go to the Eye Hospital now. I'll call you a taxi.'

Well I've been called some funny things in my life, but I wasn't gonna to tell him that. I was holding onto that chair so hard, my knuckles cracked. I could feel the plastic cover, cold and swaety in my hands.

'You really need to get there now,' the doc said again.

At the hospital, everything happened real fast. Lights in the eyes. Up to the ward. Scan. Fancier scan. All this Corona virus going on, and they were giving me the red carpet treatment.

When they'd done all the tests, the consultant herself come to see me. The nurse had just brought a plate of macaroni cheese for my tea. Smelt good, too, but now it was going cold. The grey cloud was telling me what they'd found. My eyes were okay, the problem was in my brain. Some fancy name, she gave it. Agynopsia, I think she said.

There's me, shit-scared I'm going blind, and she's giving me some medical bullshit, and saying it's all in my head. If I could've seen her face, I might have had a better chance of working out what was going on.

Calm voice, she had, though. Firm.

She told me how your brain has like a screen on each side, at the back of your head. Pictures from both eyes go to both screens. Then some fancy wiring matches them up – so you can see 3-D. Complicated, ain't it? Well in my brain, they'd found this "abnormal activity" next to my right ear. She reckoned it was sending out signals that spoiled the pictures.

By now I was in a right state, I can tell you. The old ticker took off like Usain Bolt on speed. I started with the heavy breathing. Then I was smacking the side of my head, hard, with my hand.

'Please don't do that,' she said, 'it won't help.' And she took a hold of my wrist. I saw her hand before it went blurry – I hadn't realised 'til then, she was Indian or something. Sounded English, see?

So, like she explained, the only treatment is surgery. On my brain. They can't cut out the place where the interference starts. Too big, too deep inside.

The way she put it, I've got a choice. I gotta decide. I can wait, see if things get better. Or I can let them try and fix it.

What's that, mate? Yeah, they can try, she said. No guarantees.

They can cut the wiring that crosses over, left to right and right to left. That way, she says, one eye, one screen. The other eye, the other screen.

Or I can wait and see, maybe try some tablets. It might get better. She didn't sound hopeful, I reckon they're as much in the dark as me.

Sounds simple, don't it? But it ain't.

Yeah, I can see you've got that. Makes you think, though, don't it? The world'd be a funny old place without any women. If you'd asked me a month ago, how'd I feel if I never saw Barbara again, well, I might have laughed, and taken a shot at that, y'know. But not now. Now I seen her turn into a grey cloud – well, it ain't right.

Oh, thanks love. Gasping for a cuppa. You got one for matey here? Lovely stuff, thanks.

Which one was that mate? All I seen was the cup appears on top of the locker, and heard the footsteps. Couldn't tell you if it were the cleaner or the ward sister.

I'd like to know what that doc was thinking, you know, when she told me – but I couldn't see her face could I? It's a fifty-fifty chance, she says. Depends which screen my brain decides to look at. It'll make a quick choice, then it'll stick to that side, always.

One side normal. The other side all these grey blanks.

'Think about it,' she said. 'I'll come back tomorrow.'

I tried to talk it over with Barbara. She sounded like she had tears in her eyes. I couldn't see. Dunno if she was hopeful or afraid. She squeezed my hand, but the rest of her was a blur.

Well, thanks for coming, mate. It's been good to talk to you. No, don't say no more. It's up to me. I gotta decide. I can wait and see, it might get better. If I go for it, it's fifty-fifty. Cure or permanent.

Makarelle Summer 2021: 'Tattoo'

If you would like to see the visual art of this magazine issue, you can access the flipping book for free by scanning this QR code:

THE BLUEBIRD
by Sue Davnall

They fished her out of the Thames just east of Blackfriars Bridge. She was wedged against the southernmost arch of the old London, Chatham and Dover Railway, barely alive. They took her straight to Guys, her lungs half-full of water, a deep but bloodless wound on her right temple.

In the ICU they hooked her up to a saline drip and oxygen. The clipboard at the end of the bed said simply 'Patient N'. Three days passed. She did not wake. DNA samples were taken, and photographs. A media appeal was made. No-one came forward to claim her, no name was found. In due course they moved her to a general ward. Around her the occupants of the other beds chatted and moaned and cried out in the night. She remained mute, immobile, eyes closed, like a stone angel on an elaborate tomb.

A week after her transfer, a nurse giving her a bed-bath found on the nape of her neck, just on the hairline, a small and stubborn stain. On closer examination, it proved to be a miniscule tattoo.

'Doesn't look that old. The colour's still nice and strong.' Dave the ward orderly had been called in to advise, being something of an expert on the subject of tattoos. If he had an area of skin that was still its natural shade, it was well hidden.

'What do you reckon, Dave? Is it some sort of bird, do you think?'

'Maybe. It's so small it's hard to tell. A bluebird maybe? Symbol of happiness, seems an odd thing to hide under your hair. Pretty common design, though. Don't think it'll tell you much about the lass's identity.'

The nurse sighed. She felt sorry for the girl, lying there with no-one to talk to her, no one to light the spark and get the synapses firing again. Every day she tried to make time to sit with her for a few minutes but as often as not she was called away before she could get settled.

***

At Southwark police station DS Carol Jacob was cross. Since she'd re-united an amnesiac pensioner with his anxious relatives a few months ago the guv regarded her as the go-to person for every other misper case that came in. Not that this was a misper, of course, quite the opposite. They had the person; they just didn't know who she was or where she was from.

She stared gloomily at the screen in front of her. No useful info at all: no ID on the girl, no record of her fingerprints or dental treatment. It was hopeless. At least with a corpse you had a post-mortem to go on. The docs couldn't even tell Carol whether the blow on the head was accidental or deliberate. At least they said they couldn't: she'd got the distinct impression at the hospital that she was under everyone's feet and they wanted her to go away and leave them to their insane schedule.

Biker Dave had pointed her in the direction of his favourite tattoo artist, who he said would be able to tell Carol pretty well anything she needed to know about the possible origins and meaning of the tattoo. It had turned out to be a dead end.

Stig, the aforementioned artist, had confirmed that it was a bluebird, and expertly executed.

'Looks like she must have had an undercut at some point,' he opined when shown the close-up photos.

'Undercut?'

'Long hair on top, shaved underneath. You wouldn't be able to get that level of precision unless the hair was completely cut away.'

'Why would anyone have a tattoo there?' Stig shrugged.

'Reactionary boss? Parental disapproval? She looks young enough.'

Carol pointed out that people in comas commonly look a lot younger than their years because of the relaxation of the facial muscles, a lifetime of stresses and cares washed away by the waters of oblivion.

'Are there any criminal associations that you know of with this kind of symbol?' 'Criminal?' Stig snorted, 'A bluebird? No self-respecting bank robber or trafficker is going to have a tattoo of a bluebird.'

'OK, OK; I had to ask. What else can you tell me about it? Who would get a tattoo like this?'

'Hard to say. It's not native to Europe, you know. Forget Vera Lynn...' Carol did a double-take at the thought that Stig even knew who Vera Lynn was. '... very much North American is the bluebird. But it's revered in many cultures as a symbol of happiness, transformation, growth, good things to come.'

'Perhaps the girl had it done as sort of talisman then. Maybe she thought it would bring her luck.'

'Could be.'

'This may be a daft question, but is there any way of telling from the design or the ink used where it might have been done?'

'Probably not on a living person. There's been some research on dead bodies to see what happens to the tattoo ink, where it travels, after it's been injected. Don't see how you could do that with your girl, though – not at the moment, anyway. You might get a clue about the type of carrier used, depending on how deeply the ink's sunk into the skin.'

'Carrier?'

'Tattoo ink isn't just ink – it needs to be mixed with a carrier fluid – might be distilled water but could also be alcohol-based. Acts as an antiseptic and opens up the pores, allows the ink to go deeper into the skin.'

'That wouldn't help with narrowing down who did it though. Would it?'

'No, sorry. The ink composition is about as individual as the artist.'

Carol gave up. She thanked Stig, declined his offer of an introductory tattoo 'on the house' and headed back to the hospital. She wanted to sit by the girl's bed for a while. Maybe one of the nurses had spotted something that would give Carol another line of enquiry.

***

What is it like, being in a coma? According to those who have been lucky enough to come out the other side, Nothing. With a capital N. No awareness, no sensation, zilch. The body's involuntary reaction to stimuli, increased brain activity, doesn't mean that the patient is picking up the signals in any meaningful way. All those desperate hours of sitting by the bedside reading favourite books and poems, playing music, chatting about what the family's been up to "while you've been away" probably isn't making a lot of difference.

The girl lay unmoving day after day, then week after week, then month after month. Periodically the doctors ran tests to see whether she was still in there, capable one day of rejoining the rest of humankind. She certainly wasn't dead but neither was she showing any signs of swimming back up to the surface. The nurses cut her hair, trimmed her nails, kept her neat; the wound on her head closed up until there was just a faint silver line running across her temple. She became known to all of the ward staff as 'Bluebird', in the absence of a more definitive way of identifying her.

After a year, the hospital moved her to a care home in Bromley. It wasn't the ideal destination, being a home for senior citizens and not geared up for rehabilitation. But there was a vacancy there, and no known relatives to raise objections. So off went 'Bluebird' to Sunny Park Court. The nurses who had cared for her at the hospital shed a tear for her then knuckled back down to work. No time to dwell on her once she had moved on.

***

Carol had a shedload of other cases to pursue. A change of guv had given her a new lease of life and she had set her eyes on the inspector's exams. She became a specialist in human trafficking and modern slavery. From time to time she checked the woebegone women whom she rescued from private houses, nail bars and brothels across South-East London but she found no-one with a bluebird tattoo on the nape of their neck. That comforted her a little; her suspicion that the girl in the Thames had been another victim of this most heinous of enterprises appeared to be unfounded.

She never forgot 'Bluebird' entirely but over time she went weeks without thinking about her. Once a year she headed down to Bromley to sit with her a while. The girl was very well cared for and looked peaceful as she lay for all the world like Sleeping Beauty in the middle of the large bed with its crisp white sheets. Carol was usually there in the summer and the window stood wide open to let in the soft breeze and the alluring scent of the roses below. There were worse places to be.

***

On the tenth anniversary of the girl's arrival at Guys, Carol persuaded her boss to let her put out another media appeal. It backfired spectacularly: several thousand people phoned or e-mailed to say that they knew who the girl was, or knew someone who thought they knew someone who had disappeared ten years ago. Many more offered to interpret the symbolism of the bluebird tattoo, while others believed that they could identify the girl through the intervention of the spirit world, the exercise of water divining or the passing of crystals over her body. Carol spent several weeks trawling through each and every one of the contacts in the rapidly dissipating hope that there would be a genuine nugget in the middle of the fool's gold. Her boss looked more thin-lipped every time she saw him in the corridor, and eventually he banned her from following up any more calls. The file went into the 'cold cases' cabinet and that was that.

***

Kieran heaved the holdall onto his shoulder as he walked away from the carousel. He felt disorientated by the crowds swarming towards the Customs controls. The babble of his native language around him sounded harsh and hostile after so many years away. Passing straight through into the arrivals area he realised that he didn't know where to go. Ever since he'd got out he'd been trying to call Cara but she'd never picked up the phone.

Twelve years in a Thai prison for alleged drug smuggling. His lawyer told him he was lucky not to get the death penalty. He'd declared himself innocent throughout the trial and ever since: a complete lie, of course, but he was a convincing liar. It was one of the reasons Cara had broken with him in the first place; she'd had enough of his repeated failures to live up to his promises.

'Mum would have been heartbroken,' was her usual mantra.

Emotional blackmail, which he'd resented in the past. Now, he'd had plenty of time to examine his life and to realise that if he didn't take a different tack the prognosis wasn't good. He'd been wanting for a long time to tell his sister that he was ready to listen to her, but she clearly wasn't yet ready to hear that.

He wondered what her life had been like while he'd been 'away'. They'd been everything to each other for a long time after Mum had died, he couldn't imagine Cara coping on her own. A beautiful soul but fragile. As he stood by the Costa wondering what to do next he rubbed the back of his neck. It was still there, he knew, the tattoo that he and Cara had got together when they were still speaking to each other. In memory of their mother who had loved the Wings song 'Bluebird'. His sister wasn't keen on the idea but was persuaded when he promised that it would be discreet, somewhere that only the two of them would know about.

***

Thirty-five miles away, Bluebird's eyes flickered open.

TATTOO
by Jeff Gallagher

Identity fashioned through punctured skin
and your true nature defaced by
the replication of another's design
are now preserved like cartouches
in your drooping senescent carcass.

You were driven to this precise scrawling
of crop circles across your skeleton
by the need to etch sgraffito
and reveal some truth or reality
in your other imagined self.

For this is no longer you, this facile
doodling endured to excite imagined
admiration in the fellows of your tribe
or to thrust your personal brand
into the world's shop window.

The colouring in of your blank life
and the desire to look different
cannot hide the moko hastily scrawled
and set for life in this stick
of rock that carries your name.

Our genes are who we are, determining
which side of the brain will dominate,
whether the shape of our jaw or the slant
of our eyes is appealing, whether
we are good or bad at games.

To tattoo is to bang a drum, demand
attention from a world that has already
made up its mind; or to gather in groups,

hoping to assume the identity of the strong
through some feeble attachment.

Paint, sculpt, fashion yourself as you will:
adding a layer to your overworked canvas
will never prevent posterity from uncovering
the real work of art, the original beneath
this artifice of temporal decoration.

SYMBOLISM
by Mina Ma

Gerry is cute, like a pixie. His face is round, and his ears stick out. Long shiny black hair, tied back. Petite, as many Southeast Asian men are. He's shorter than me. Younger. He holds out his hand, and we shake. His touch is gentle, his fingers long and thin, suitable for the artist that he is. When he laughs, I can see small, white teeth.

I like him right away. I trust him. I choose him.

I connected with Gerry on Instagram. It sounds like a dating cliché, but it isn't like that; there's no romance in this story. I saw a recommendation on a website, so sought him out. I looked at photos of his artwork. It resonated with me. Delicate, intricate details. A spiritual theme: blossoming lotus flowers, rising suns, crescent moons. Mandala – a meditative geometric circle. Unalome – a line that begins straight, then spirals out, like a person's path through life. black lines, dot work, shading. I wanted to purchase a piece. We exchanged messages, I told him what I wanted, and we arranged to meet.

I flew all the way from China. Well, that's not the whole truth. I was done with China. I'd been living in China for too long. I left. I will never return.

It was a Friday. I headed to Shenzhen airport just before midnight, and tried to stay awake until the 3am departure. None of the shops or cafés were open. Outside was black. The high glass ceiling drew up the other passengers' voices. A little bird fluttered about, trapped and confused. We started boarding just in time, and I was asleep before we were in the air. An unceremonious departure, like I was walking out on the country after a twelve-year relationship with it, without even saying goodbye.

I arrive in Kuala Lumpur, Malaysia. I disembark, wander, board another plane. I arrive in Denpasar, Indonesia. This is Bali, the island of the gods.

I'm used to humidity, so it doesn't affect me the way it might the other new arrivals, but it's sunnier here than it was in Shenzhen. My final three weeks there were marred by rain and thunderstorms, so fierce it felt like the world was ending. My driver is waiting with my name on a sign, and we head to Ubud, home of ancient Hindu temples, lush rice terraces, a sacred monkey forest, and Gerry.

But I'm not meeting him right away. I have some time.

There's a Starbucks backing onto a temple honouring Saraswati, the Goddess of Knowledge. One of her roles is to impart wisdom. I buy lemon hibiscus iced tea, and take it to the covered seating area beside the temple's lotus pond. As the ice melts in my cup, marking the table with a dark wet ring of condensation, I watch tourists posing in front of the flowers and temple buildings, local children trying to catch fish in the murky pond water, and hawkers peddling their wooden elephants, metal necklaces, and rattan bags. There's a kind of peace in observing the chaos of others.

I return to the pond the next morning, and capture a photo of a single pink lotus surrounded by green lily pads and browning, curling leaves. 'Did you know that the lotus flower takes the skanky, muddy water from the bottom of the pond, and turns it into something beautiful?' I ask my Instagram followers.

Today is the day. I arrive at the studio early, and have to wait beyond my appointment time because his previous appointment is overrunning. It's fine; I don't mind waiting. I'm nervous. It's taken a lot of courage to walk through that door.

In Bali, there are lots of doorways leading to hidden wonders. I pass by an unassuming open doorway near my hotel, glance through it, and see a beautiful stone

Goddess adorned with offerings of flowers, food, and burning sticks of incense. Later, I visit Lempuyang Temple, and look through the Gates of Heaven – a doorway through which, on a good day, you can see the distant and perfect cone of Mount Abang, a volcano; but the day I'm there there's too much cloud to see anything. There's a secret doorway near the swimming pool at my hotel, 'A shortcut,' according to the man on reception; I don't know why, but I feel scared to walk through it.

When I leave Bali, I'll be starting a new life, somewhere else.

In the studio, I sip water and look at the art on the walls.

There's a painting of Kali, the Goddess of Death. She's blue, with gold jewellery on her wrists, neck, and head; her pink tongue sticks out, contrasting with her blazing orange background. 'She's new,' the staff tell me. 'She was created last night.' Kali is a misunderstood deity; fearsome, she brings death and destruction, but only in order to create new life.

I make temporary friends with a blonde American woman whose dog just died. She's the only other customer. I can hear in her voice how much she loved that dog. I drink more water. I pee a few times. I'm scared of needles.

Gerry comes out to meet me. He uses an iPad to draw out my design. His dark eyes turn to me when I speak, so I know he's listening to what I'm saying. He keeps asking my opinion, giving me options, making amendments; he wants to get it right. This calms me.

When it's ready he prints it onto transfer paper in three different sizes. He puts on surgical gloves, and holds the paper – the flash – against my skin to check its placement. I'm naked from the waist up, except for a thin white cotton shirt that's unbuttoned and taped over my breasts. The studio is also a café; there's a glass partition between the tattoo room and the seating area where people can enjoy cappuccinos and smoothie bowls. Fortunately, the café is empty today.

We choose the smaller size. My skin is wiped with an antiseptic solution, and the design is transferred onto me, onto my sternum, in blueish-purple ink. He makes me stand and look in the mirror. He inspects me. He's not happy; it's not straight. He removes it with his cleaning solution, leaving bluish-purple stains on my skin. He reapplies the flash, and nods his approval.

The American is getting a paw print on her bicep, its design modelled on a photo of her dead dog's paw. She checks the placement of my flash, and nods too.

'I'm glad you're here,' I say to her.

'Your guy knows what he's doing; it's perfectly straight,' she says with a reassuring smile.

That wasn't what I meant. I meant that, although I don't usually take my clothes off in front of strangers, I'm glad of the company, and I'm glad someone is going through something similar to me, but I don't clarify, because she doesn't need to know.

I lie back on the plastic-wrapped bench. Gerry gets another pillow for me. He lays out his implements on a steel table beside us – a pot of black ink, vegan, imported from the States, and the tattooing device, which is a thick needle attached to a purple gemstone handle.

I'm getting a hand-poked tattoo. This means the ink is tapped into the skin with a single needle controlled by the artist's hand, rather than by a machine that uses multiple small needles all at once. Hand-poked tattoos are comprised of multiple dots created by this single needle; if the dots are close enough, or dense enough, they create smooth lines, or shading, so any image can be produced. My first and only tattoo, which I got fourteen years ago, was hand-poked. If I get another tattoo in the future, it will be hand-poked. For me, hand-poked tattoos feel more in keeping with the tradition of tattooing; more tribal. They're also supposed to hurt less than a machine tattoo, but I have no frame of reference.

Gerry tells me, 'If it hurts, breathe deeply; breathe through the pain.'

He positions the needle over my skin – I can't really see, because I'm lying down – but I do what he said, I breathe, and he begins.

This isn't something I've rushed into.

It came to me one evening, as I lay on my bed in Shenzhen, the curtains closed against the heat and noise and pollution, the air conditioning struggling to cool me, my escape so close yet so far; I wanted a tattoo. Something meaningful. That's when I started looking, and found Gerry.

I decided what it would be, and where it would go.

Many times, I stood naked in front of the bathroom mirror, staring at the place where the ink would be embedded under my skin. I traced its likely position with my fingers. It's hard to imagine the permanence of a tattoo before getting it. Some things that are meant to be permanent and forever simply don't last; but this is real permanence, real forever.

Gerry asks where I'm from, and I ask him back. He's from a small city on Java, one of the many islands that make up Indonesia. He says it's beautiful there. He encourages me to visit.

Because he's from a different place, I ask him about language, and if he understands Balinese. He shakes his head. I ask if his colleagues speak to each other in Balinese, and how he feels about it. 'Yes, they do,' he laughs. 'But it's okay. I'm used to it'. I know how that feels. I speak Mandarin, but there are lots of dialects in China, and at one point I had four languages or dialects in my life at once. Feeling lost was sometimes fun, and sometimes not, and, in the end, no fun at all.

Although hand-poked tattooing sounds brutal, it isn't. For the majority of the tattoo, I can't feel a thing. It was the same with my other tattoo. Towards the end, the pokes become uncomfortable, but not excruciating; like I have sunburn and someone's repeatedly pushing their fingernail into it. I ask which part of the design he's doing – it's the top part – he's reached my chest, where the nerve endings are more sensitive.

'Breathe deeply,' he reminds me.

It takes over an hour, about twice the time of a machine tattoo, then it's finished.

I rest in a chair, admiring my new art. One of the other artists, an Australian, comes to have a look. Gerry tattooed her, too. 'He's so gentle, isn't he?' she asks.

My favourite Hindu god is Ganesh, the elephant god. On my way home from the studio, I see a statue of him outside a hair salon. He's the God of Beginnings; patron of arts, letters, and writing; believed able to overcome any obstacle in his path. His large head represents knowledge. His trunk, adaptability. His single tusk, retaining the good and rejecting the bad. His trunk and palm are tattooed with golden symbols. Orange garlands have been placed around his neck. He looks serene. I take a photo for Instagram.

Back at the hotel, I can't stop studying it in the mirror.

But I won't be sharing it on Instagram, and because of where it is on my body, it's like a secret; unless I want them to, no one will ever see it, so no one will ask me, 'What is it? Why did you get it? What does it mean?'

If I ever do decide to show someone, though, and if they do ask me, I will say something like, 'There is no easy explanation'; 'How I see the world is different to how you see it'; or, 'Much like when reading a story, you need to engage your inference and deduction skills, fire up your imagination, and interpret the symbolism for yourself'.

ON ME
by Yuu Ikeda

Tattoos that you carved on me
are the oath,
and also atonement
to love

I feel them,
by pain of tattoos

Wings of a dragon
and lips of a flower
prove that
you love me
and I love you

THE BRUSH AND THE NEEDLE
by Dovydas Jakstaitis

Beauty is pain. That was one of the first great lessons I learned upon becoming an adult. Children, as a rule, are vain, convinced of their own importance, and so it is only natural that they should be unbeautiful. For if beauty is pain, it only follows that pain is beauty, and the recklessness of children's self-love serves as proof of their incompatibility with pain. But everyone learns of their shortcomings eventually. When the time came for me to make this discovery, I was surprised more than anything else. Dreams of grandeur and importance crumbled away with nothing but shards left to commemorate their departure. I thought that if I was wrong about this, I must have been wrong about other things, too. So, presented with the ultimatum of a lengthy cross-examination that would span every assumption I had ever made in my life, I decided to take a path of lesser resistance.

For a while, I imposed a Spartan regime upon myself. I rose early each day to go on a run through the empty morning streets. When my legs threatened to melt under me, I would go to the gym and lift weights. By the time I was done, it would be around 10am, so I would spend some time reading through recent fashion magazines over a light breakfast and an espresso at a local coffee shop. For the first time since I was seven, I started learning the piano again, and playing chess, and watching classic movies. After a few months of this, though, I realised that I had still not managed to become truly beautiful. Clearly, I had been too optimistic. I thought back and realised that pain was the only thing that would help me amend my unkind fate. And what articulated the delicate link between pain and beauty more than the underappreciated art of the tattoo?

My tattoo was a small, slender rose with symmetrical leaves that curled inward at their edges. The flower circled around my forearm like a hawser rope around a rowboat, and the colours were muted, aged somewhat, as if their vitality had haemorrhaged out of the severed stem. As I rode the bus back home from the tattoo parlour, I couldn't stop looking at my arm. The dull burn of the ink numbed my skin like dry ice. As I expected, the whole process had been painful, thoroughly so. I realise now that the pain involved in such a small tattoo was, relatively speaking, a trivial matter, but it provided sufficient impetus for its image to bloom within my mind. That brief pain represented the rose's birth, its decay. Each movement of each needle buried a separate, parasitic seed into my bloodstream, until my blood was rendered into little more than a solution of plant nutrients. The rose would accompany me to my deathbed, distorted only by my own thinning, wrinkled skin. I had not become beautiful in myself, but was rather the canvas for a beautiful thing, which gains its beauty by harming its host. I lost more to this new, immortal part of myself than I realised, and I quickly set myself to work recovering whatever I could.

A few months after I started as a tattoo artist, a man called George started coming to the shop I worked at. A well-fitted suit defined his slim, tidy silhouette, which was rounded up at the top by a close-cropped head of hair. Not once did I see his expression budge. It was as if his facial muscles had ceased working after being pasted on by a lazy, would-be Frankenstein. He probably wasn't the type of person most would take for a tattoo enthusiast, but by that point it wasn't much of a surprise. All types of people walked through those doors. The surprising thing was the tattoo itself, a curious-faced monkey, roughly the size of a hand, around the area of his left shoulder blade. It wasn't his first either. His back was interspersed with an ecosystem of rodents, birds, insects, and lizards, all in different styles. A dainty, blue hummingbird decorated the right side of his spine. Smooth, pencil-like lines portrayed its slightly upturned back, which seemed ready to burst out of my client with the momentum of the wings rising dramatically at its sides. A clumsy, angular spider climbed up his back. A cartoon-like bumble bee stared out at me as I wielded the tattoo gun. I stole a glance at my client's blank face, then at the lonely rose that I'd made a habit of hiding behind my sleeve.

He came back once every three months or so. He always requested me, I supposed that the monkey must have been to his satisfaction. On one appointment, I drew a curvy gecko on his shoulder in the shape of an S. On the next, a square platypus. In the months between each appointment, I felt myself improving rapidly, so that it was no longer as necessary for me to work around the barriers of my inexperience. The fewer restrictions there were on my art, the more I saw my tattoos as portraits of myself. I stared at myself from within the critters decorating George's back. I was only truly in my element when I was working on him. The act of creating a tattoo itself became a sort of exhibitionism with him, our shared secret. Looking back at my own work became a cause for shame, yet beauty seemed closer within my reach than ever before. The carnivorous thorns draining my body lost their grip, until they were almost forgotten. My only regret was that my ambition would make a sacrifice of my most prized canvas. I pumped poison into his veins with my tattoo gun.

During the December of my third year working at the tattoo parlour, I had my only proper conversation with him. I had gone to shake his hand as he walked through the door, and carelessly failed to notice the flash of red peeking out from under my sleeve. He pounced on the discovery.

"Oh…" he said. "I didn't realise you had a tattoo of your own. Probably should have guessed." His eyes tried to burn through my sleeve. I pulled my sleeve over to the base of my thumb clumsily.

"Ah, this isn't anything much. Just a small piece I got done a few years ago. Only really bring it out on special occasions these days." To my frustration, he continued to pursue the matter with a surprising persistence.

"I didn't see much of it, but I could tell that it's very well-made. Where did you get it done?" he asked as I motioned him towards a seat.

"Here, actually, before I started. The guy who did it got out before I got here, though. Guess he was trying to flee the crime scene." I forced a laugh and quickly changed topic. We spent a while discussing the specifics of his next tattoo. He decided on a snake that would run through the few sections of his back there were that remained tattoo-free. I went meditatively through my preparations as I imagine the artists of old may have done before dedicating their art to God. Only, I was not so cowardly as to aim for imperfection. His naked back struck the light like a kidnapped painting, honouring whatever nameless warehouse it had found itself in. The more you looked at that menagerie of mismatched animals, separated vaguely by patterned bumps of muscle, the more you felt that they belonged together. Not even I had lost ownership of my body so fully.

I wiped down his back with a cloth, dried it off, and began. I worked the oscillating blades of the tattoo gun, purring like a lion cub, slowly along his spine, wiping little bits of excess ink away with my spare hand. I didn't notice George's meek voice until he'd spoken my name for the third time. "Yes?" I asked.

"Do you have any other tattoos?"

"… No. One was enough. I'm not great with needles, I'm afraid."

"That's a shame… As soon as I got my first one, I couldn't stop." He hesitated guiltily between words, as if he saw me as some harsh schoolmaster who would cane him for speaking out of term. I remained silent to let him speak. It was the least I could do. "It was that hummingbird. A bonus at work came in so I kind of…"

"Any particular reason why you chose a hummingbird?"

"No. I don't know. I watched this documentary a few days before I got my appointment… Once I got it though, I couldn't imagine life without it. I don't like speaking, really. Or I'm not very good at it, anyway. I don't know. But, having some sign of my personality on my body, even if it wasn't a place that most people would see… it was quite reassuring. I felt like a different person. The more work I got done the more I felt like myself, I suppose." His skin grew warmer under my hands, and I felt my own cheeks heat up as I heard him speak. "…You do good work."

"I'm happy to hear that. We can never have too much business over here." The edges of my lips curled upwards against my will. I strongly felt that the snake I was in the process of outlining commemorated some sort of graduation for the both of us. Even his prior tattoos, his prized hummingbird included, were now images of me. He was my perfect tragic hero, but his moment of realisation would never come. My perfect, happy fool.

When I was done, we arranged another appointment so that I could finish the inking, and I walked him over to the door. Out of sheer joy, I footed his whole bill. I thought it was only right that he receive some compensation. He shook my hand with a firm familiarity and his skin, turned brittle by the inactivity of his facial muscles, gathered unevenly in a facsimile of a smile. His image as he left was like that of a man who willingly went to the hanging block after smiling at his executioner. I sat down and cracked open a soda to celebrate. Glancing at the mirror on my desk, I could have sworn that for a moment I saw that wide-eyed monkey staring back at me.

MY UGLINESS
by Yuu Ikeda

Beautiful butterflies
hide my ugliness
On my waist,
they are whirling
and weeping
On my buttocks,
they are trembling
and laughing
Wounds that I made
are parts of butterflies
I can gaze at my body
because they are
fluttering and gleaming
on my body

THE DRUM OF PASSCHENDAELE
by Henry Loten

Most think Hell is a huge fire
a boiling inferno of blood
But here we know, hell is a brown wasteland;
a machine gun that echoes through the night;
mortars firing across scarred fields
that once wore green,
now scorched beneath trench and wire.

And they march their feet to the beat.

Filth is the norm,
Slurry and sludge drip off everything
and pile onto rising decay.
Roads and farms: all are gone
Is there glory to be won?

And they heave to the high hat.

Know, many will suffer.
Know, many mutilated
Know, many will die
How many shall they take?
And the dusk falls,
And the raids begin
And the killing carries on.

And they scream to the snare.

Clocks crawl in the light of day
The night covers the sky like a cloth
Time picks up, it moves in a blur
and the dreams of home flutter
Like blossom from trees as they tumble to the ground,
a gentle breeze that fills an empty heart.
A fire, long extinguished, relights.
Flowers of yellow, red, white and blue
all billowing like smoke in the wind,

And they stumble to the cymbal.

Know, many have suffered.
Know, many are maimed.
Know, many have died.
No glory will ever be won.
And the dawn breaks,
And the battles begin
And the killing carries on.

And they slog on to the toms.

A forlorn Tommy pushes on,
waist-high in mud.
Stuck in the trenches.
Stuck in the slush.
And the men crawl
And the brass hats plan
Will the killing carry on?

And they march their feet to the beat
And they heave to the hi-hat
And they scream to the snare
And they stumble to the cymbal
And they toil on to the toms

And they die
to the Drum
Of Passchendaele

THE YELLOW LILY
by L.C. Groves

Linda took one last look around reception. Light bounced off the chrome and glass, lifting the smart grey interior and lending it an extra air of elegance. She smiled, satisfied. Her employees in their deep purple uniforms stood at the doors to their individual suites, ready to welcome Conquiesco's first customers of the day. Behind the closed doors, tattoo guns, aromatherapy oils, gel polishes and beautifully scented shampoos lay waiting to be called into service.

A slight frown twitched at the corner of Linda's eye and she forced down her rising anger. Josie's face was too heavily made up again. It was happening more and more often and something needed to be done about it. Maybe she could speak to Steve. Josie was one of their own after all. She was sure he'd be happy to have a word in the right ear.

Pushing that problem aside for a later time, she clicked across the tiled floor and unlocked the doors. Swiftly and with minimal fuss, she checked each client in and directed them to the correct person. Murmured greetings soon disappeared behind closed doors and silence once again descended over her domain. Only then did she allow her thoughts to return to the problem of Josie. She was a good girl and a hard worker – her nail designs were the most highly sought after in the city – but there were standards to be maintained. 'Conquiesco' had to come above all other considerations. She'd sacrificed too much to allow the business to fail. She tapped a 'Rouge Rite' coated fingernail on the desk. The familiar technique worked and she felt the usual sense of calm rise up through her body. Yes, something definitely had to be done about Josie.

The girl herself appeared to farewell her client and Linda beckoned her over. She waited until the woman had tapped her credit card on the machine and made another appointment before she acknowledged her anxious employee.

'We've been a little heavy with the foundation again this morning, Josie dear, haven't we? What is our make-up mantra?'

'Keep it neat and be discreet.' Josie's head hung low. 'I'm sorry, Miss Linda, I –'

'Head up dear, we talk to faces not shoes.'

Josie raised her head but twisted her face away. Linda stretched out a hand and gently turned the chin towards her. Her jaw tightened and the fingers of her free hand clenched into a fist.

'What was it this time? Caught it on the cupboard door, did we?'

'Yes. No. I mean…' Josie's miserable expression made Linda's breath catch in her throat. 'I opened the cupboard and a tin fell on me.' The words came out in a rush and she exhaled sharply.

'I see.'

'Please, Miss Linda… I know you've had to warn me before, but… I can't lose this job…'

Linda patted her hand.

'Now, now,' she said briskly. 'There's no danger of that.'

The outer door swung open and Linda waved Josie back to her suite, then turned to greet the new arrival.

'Good morning, Madam. How can I help you?'

'I'd like a tattoo.'

Linda's eyebrows rose. The woman in front of her was the most exquisitely turned-out creature she'd ever seen. Firmly middle aged and definitely part of the twinset and pearls brigade that haunted the rotary club dinners, she certainly fitted the description of

Conquiesco's usual clientele. However, Linda would have expected to find her at the manicure table not under the tattoo gun. Steve, her supervisor, kept all his eyes firmly fixed on the people who worked in the building (the third eye, which was tattooed in the middle of his forehead always slightly disconcerted Linda) and Linda knew he'd be intrigued by this new client. Steve was an excellent tattooist in his own right – he was responsible for the beautiful blueberry that lay beneath the strap of Linda's Cartier watch. However, his main role was to deal with the other side of Conquiesco's business. The side that stayed hidden beneath the refined and elegant facade. He had a separate client list and his suite had a separate entrance to the rest of the business. It turned over a good profit but most of the time Linda liked to pretend she didn't know it existed.

'Lovely. Did you have something particular in mind, Mrs... Miss...?'

'Armstrong-Jones. Mrs Armstrong-Jones.' Mrs Armstrong-Jones shook her head. 'No idea at all, I'm afraid.' She looked around and lowered her voice. 'I don't even particularly like tattoos. I'm only getting one as revenge.'

Linda remained quiet. Experience had taught her that interrupting the confession often ended it. It had also taught her that an opening of this nature often led to the client being referred to Steve for a further consultation.

'It's my husband, you see. He hates them with a passion. When our daughter got one last year he threatened to throw her out of the house. I found out he's been having an affair, so I'd like a tattoo of something that means 'I know'. That way, when he asks what on earth I think I'm playing at, I can just tell him what it means and watch his face as he realises I know all about the little slut he's keeping in a flat in St. James' Square.'

Linda nodded sympathetically, ignoring the slip in both language and accent. Mrs Armstrong-Jones had clearly not been born to the life she was leading and was desperate to cling onto it. Linda admired her tactics though. 'Don't be sad, be smart' was another of her little mantras. That one had seen her through her own husband's infidelity.

Reginald had been one of those men who always had to have his own way in everything. When they'd met, Linda had been a beautician, but he'd insisted that she give up work when they got married. She'd been happy to turn her back on her old life. Her family was… complicated. Too well-known in the city. With her surname she hadn't a chance. She'd tried to distance herself from them even before meeting Reginald and he'd seemed the perfect solution. He had money, he had status and he loved her. Or so she thought.

He kept her at home and wheeled her out now and again for work purposes. She always had to be immaculately turned out in case he unexpectedly brought colleagues home for drinks. He got so cross if she wasn't prepared for them. At first, it had been a relief when he spent more and more time away from home. He'd told her he was going to the gym after work. The doctor had warned him there was a problem with his heart and he needed to lose some weight before he could have surgery. She'd encouraged him to go, pleased he was taking care of himself. Then she realised why. In Reginald's case, the flat had been on the Royal Crescent. He laughed when she confronted him over dinner. He was still laughing when she served him the blueberry pavlova she'd made specially for him. He stopped laughing when the deadly nightshade berries did their magic.

Of course, his widow had been thoroughly bewildered by the flat he was paying for. Did she wish to continue paying the rent on it? No, she didn't think so. Whatever he'd been using it for, it was surplus to requirements now. The money from his life insurance had paid for her to do various courses, including one in fine art. Then she'd bought Conquiesco and paid others to carry out the work needed to bring her visions to life. She only employed the very best of each profession and took pride in the knowledge there were people queuing both to be clients and employees of her establishment. It became common knowledge in the local community that the people who worked for Linda were treated like family. Her rules were strict and enforced, but any problems and they knew she could be relied upon to help.

Similarly, with the business, Linda quickly established a reputation for excellence. Nothing happened in Conquiesco without her approval: she designed each tattoo personally, she advised on new hairstyles, she was an expert in matching clients to colours which suited them. Nothing was beneath her notice. The best in the business did nothing more than carry out her instructions and she revelled in it. Where Conquiesco led, the rest of Bath soon followed.

'Where were you thinking of having the tattoo?' She asked.

Mrs Armstrong-Jones considered for a moment. She tapped the inside of her thigh. 'He likes to… you know…' she whispered. 'It will be the perfect time for him to see it.'

'In that case, how about an iris?' Linda said. 'They symbolise knowledge. They're quite tall flowers, so it would work well, I think.'

She sketched out the delicate violet petals and slid the paper across the desk. Mrs Armstrong-Jones nodded.

'Very well,' Linda said. She clicked the mouse and brought up the grid of appointments. 'We could book you in with Angelica at 10am on Thursday if that would be convenient?'

It was. Mrs Armstrong-Jones left, clutching an appointment card and with a much lighter air than she had arrived with. Linda watched her go then returned her attention to the drawing she'd just created.

'I wonder…'

She hesitated for a moment. Should she just speak to Steve? No. In this case, better to bypass him and go straight to the top. Reaching into her handbag, she extracted the mobile she never used. It only had one number stored on it and she pressed the button to dial it.

'Hello Charlie. Yes, it's me. Yes, I know it's been a while. Listen, I need your help. The same kind of help as before. No no, I'm fine. It's not for me this time. It's one of my girls.'

After a few minutes of conversation she ended the call. Extracting the SIM card, she broke it in half. She must remember to get rid of it on the way home and buy a new one.

A few weeks later, Josie phoned in sick. When she eventually came back to work, Linda held her customary 'return from sick leave' meeting.

'Is everything okay, dear?'

Josie bit her lip but nodded.

'I'm alright,' she said. 'It's Mark. He's dead.'

Linda arranged her face into a suitable expression.

'Oh my goodness, what happened?'

'He'd been on a night out with his mates and he fell into the river on his way home. The police said he must have been really drunk.'

A tear ran down her cheek and she dashed it away.

'You poor thing,' Linda said, patting her hand. 'How awful for you. Are you sure you should be here?'

Josie nodded. 'I'm fine, really.' She rubbed a hand over her face. 'I know I should feel sad, but I can't help it. All I feel is relief.' She looked at Linda. 'You knew, didn't you? You knew I was lying about the tin.'

Linda nodded.

'If he'd come home that night, it would have happened again. He just got so angry when he'd been drinking. When he didn't come home, I thought he'd decided to stay at a mate's and I was just so relieved I didn't have to worry about what he'd do. Does that make me an awful person?'

Linda patted her hand again.

'It makes you human.' She tilted her head. 'I know what will make you feel better. How about a little tattoo?'

Josie gave her a watery smile. 'I had been thinking of getting another one,' she said.

Linda passed her a piece of paper. 'A yellow lily, perhaps?'

Josie frowned.

'It symbolises gratitude. You are grateful he's gone, aren't you?'

Josie nodded slowly. 'But how did you...' Her voice trailed off as Linda raised a hand. 'I know. Never ask, just do the task.'

Her employer smiled 'Good girl. Book yourself in for the tattoo whenever you're ready. It's on the house.'

Josie stood up unsteadily and left the room. Linda sat back in her chair and smiled. Good old Charlie. Family was family after all.

TRUST
by Suzanne L. Burn

You and me, we share inked skin.
Yours, a stylised blend of crosses and angels
a quasi interpretation of death,
mine, a number allocated to me amid the horrors
of the camps at Auschwitz.

Your tattoos are too visible to your patient
in her vulnerable state.
Why would you choose to blight your skin?
I don't trust you in your paramedic green.
How can you call yourself a professional?

I hide my number like a disgrace.
I don't want to see it every day,
yet in my darkest hours, the faces
of those I loved, they parade before me
regimented lines of families waiting for the chambers.

Three hours since I've fallen on the stairs
and you are here in my time of need
speaking gently, tending my wounds without delay
you lift my wrist to insert a drip,
there is deep compassion in your eyes.

My mind begins to clear, I see
the numbers on the crosses on your arm.
You tell me they are the service numbers
of fallen comrades in Afghanistan.
You and me, we share inked skin

STRAWBERRY
by Sam Southam

They tried their best not to let it slip, but they had forgotten about the tattoo of a strawberry on her hip. It stood there proud, small, and pink. The details of the seeds exquisite against her skin.

Still sore, a faint red ring around the striking image.

Trying to catch the attention of the young man standing a foot away from her, his black hair falling into intense green eyes. A nervous smile on his handsome face, scuffing his shoes on the kerb. Did he smile, or was it her imagination? As if he had known her for his whole life, he took her hand. They walked and breathed, not saying a word. The moonlight making his appearance change, but she wasn't afraid. She just moved, one foot at a time, like she had been told by her mother.

He was the reason she had the tattoo.

He held her hand as the needle shot blissful electricity through her body. The pain was only bearable because of his presence, standing by her side, smoking a cigarette. When it was over, she felt proud as a peacock, and she hitched down her jeans so the strawberry was visible to everyone that mattered.

The night was a blur, she danced, she spun, she forgot about the pain of the tattoo, the pain of the loss she had cherished for so long. She gave herself away.

When they found her the next day, there was only one thing that stuck in the youngest officer's mind, and it refused to leave him alone. The pinkness, the tiny seeds, the soreness. The tattoo of a strawberry on her hip.

PHOBIA
by Ken Smith

It was her skin.

Smooth and soothed and warmed by sunshine. It was alive, with the knowledge of blood moving beneath the taut and tender surface. It caught the eye and the breath, in those first, small areas allowed for public view.

It was skin to be inhaled. Touched and lingered over. Pressed into. It was skin to be tasted; to be bitten hungrily, tenderly. It was the essence of temptation, skin to make you understand the lust of vampires. It whispered the desire to consume and be consumed. Seeing it suggested that oppositions could be merged: the need for union. And within a second of seeing, it ignited speculation.

And then later, in a private place, after conversational manoeuvrings, after an infinite moment of anticipation, as fabrics were unclipped and fell away, there it was, her skin.

Oh, but the transgression – the crime. Emerging from dark spaces that wanted to be filled, tendrils sprang in floriated rage, as if reaching out for prey. It was skin desecrated with ink, pictorial screams from an anxious biography, a storm of skulls and brambles and occult signs and imprecations. Skin pulsing amid a tangle of boldness, horror and private causes.

Those public fragments of soft, inhalable, immaculate surface that had triggered appetite and intimated perfection; they had given no warning of this. That when seen complete, it was skin wretchedly compromised and violated, its texture broken. The full revelation of it was egregious. Desire choked in the agonised foliage. There was a shrinking back, a falling away. A need to escape. A simple, overwhelming fear.

It was her skin.

THE TATTIE TATTOO BIRD OF THE NILE
by Helena Nwaokolo

In the tall grasses on the fertile and lonely banks of the River Nile as it nudges past the ancient kingdom, now named Uganda, there lives the rarely spotted Tattie Tattoo bird. It is rarely spotted due to its dullness of colour which easily merges with the dung coloured stems of the reeds and by its disheveled body which is camouflaged within the feathery heads of the same fauna. Its near neighbours are the hippopotamuses, crocodiles, baboons and the bathing elephant family all finding comfort around or beneath the cooling waters in the heat of the day.

A little way down river, where the water widens, a modern fish farm has been built. It is secure within the river with strong steel fences rising from the deep. It is serviced by a gang of patrolling boatmen who keep watch each twenty four hours so the fish within are never lonely. Tattie Tattoo birds visit the fish farm daily. While the boatmen are distracted by the many other birds, the scruffy little fellows swoop across the water to steal the smallest, baby fish. They carry them in bulk, Puffin-like, in their ridiculously big beaks to the safety of their riverbank homes.

The other birds who are so distracting are a vibrant mixture of colour, shape and size. A five-year old's imagination, a new box of paints and the instruction to design birds who might live in a magic land, could produce close to the variety and flamboyance of Ugandan bird life. The birds that find the fish farm irresistible mostly balance on spindly, fishing line legs or swoop on rainbow wings. They have long elegant beaks that spear their prey or short stumpy ones to store their catch. Some wear crowns or ruffles, some legs are rusty red, others sunshine yellow.

The Tattie Tattoo birds living so close to the water, see their own drab feathers and stumpy beaks reflected back to them, continually. The males are jealous of the others. Jealous of the pure white elegance of the Great White Egret; the purple shimmer of the Sacred Ibis and the yellow legs of the Squacco Heron. With fierce determination our more humble birds collect treasure to adorn their bodies: long white feathers from the Egret woven into their own measly tails and shining purple ones tucked between wing feathers, fastened in place by gooey spittle squirted from their beaks. A daily harvest of tiny petals and leaves from the water plants pecked into their drab chests, almost compensate for thick legs that will always be brown.

With tails full and long, wings glinting purple in the sun and their floral chests, they are ready to find a female. She is more comfortable with her own body image but easily swayed by the sight of a long white tail and a pretty chest and so allows herself to be wooed. Her partner builds a nest among the reeds, small and scruffy but softly lined with fine, fluffy seed heads – a nest designed for a short tenancy. Four eggs, small and the colour of the river silt, soon occupy it and shortly afterwards the female flies off to be swayed by her next partner.

The Tattie Tattoo male bird stays on egg duty. He sits on the eggs for most of each twenty four hours, leaving them briefly during the late afternoon. By this time they have already absorbed the heat they need to keep them safe for a few hours. This is plenty of time to feed himself and collect the fresh grasses, young plant shoots and tiny water creatures that shimmer gold on the river. Sitting on the eggs once more, he separates his gathered material, one from the other. He diligently masticates his harvest with rows of tiny ridges lining his mouth and mixes each with his gooey spittle. Then carefully and artistically squirts dotty patterns of colour across and around each egg. The pattern is repeated on all the eggs but each has a unique combination of coloured spots.

After a further two or three days he lifts each egg in his ugly beak and flies off. One by one, he carries them to the nests of the grand and colourful birds he sees around him and places the, now beautiful, eggs gently alongside the offspring of the arrogant beauties. He is satisfied with his work. His sons and daughters will not be scruffy and drab.

When I visited Uganda I saw many hippos, lots of naughty baboons, crocodiles rather too close for comfort and what seemed like an everlasting exhibition of the most wonderful bird life. But I saw not one Tattie Tattoo bird – not sure anyone else did either, their camouflage must be so good…

THROUGH ALL MY PHASES
by Linda M. Crate

friends with matching tattoos
make me jealous

talked about it with my
bestie once,
and then it was just
forgotten;

i feel like no one i love
truly returns the sentiment—

why do i always have to be the one who
cares more?
why do i always have to be the one so
full of love and understanding
when no one reciprocates this for me?

if i could i would get matching
tattoos with the moon because she's the
only one that's been with me through all
my phases.

MAYBE THINK OF ME
by Linda M. Crate

my mother and my sister
got two matching tattoos
without me

& they said i could get one
to match afterward

once again brushed under the rug,
and not thought of;
so why would i bother?

i wish for once in my life
someone would think of me first,
and someone would ask me
with purpose what i wanted and
listen with all their heart instead
of only hearing parts of what i have
to say;

some people say you choose offense
but i think they try to excuse
their offensive behavior by saying they
didn't know it would hurt you—

how could some of things done to me
not hurt me? maybe think of someone
outside yourself, maybe think of me;

maybe think of me.

HAPPY BIRTHDAY
by Beck Collett

Friday, December 22nd 1995 is her seventeenth birthday. Horrible, even by normal standards. Not in college, can't find a job, nowhere to go and nothing to do. Depressed, isolated, all the great clichés of a teenage girl.

She is meeting up with her bestie that day; after 3:45pm when Bestie finishes college. She herself has no plans, but Bestie does. Bestie has studying to do, so can only meet briefly to drop off her presents and make Birthday Girl feel even more alone.

Clad in her uniform of shapeless black layers, Birthday Girl walks quickly for twenty minutes, Bestie a leisurely ten from college. Bestie lives down the road from their rendezvous point, so isn't going out of her way. Immaculate as ever, confident gaze, beautiful face, ebony curls bouncing merrily, full-lips slicked with Body Shop Kiwi lip-balm. Bestie wishes her a non-ironic 'Happy birthday!' and hands her a small red gift-bag, covered in hearts.

'Can't stop, sorry, tons of homework – you know how it is.'

No, she doesn't, not anymore, and surely, it's the last day of term? But she lets it go. Trembling with excitement, she proudly shows Bestie a wonky heart she tattooed onto her stomach two days ago – a razor blade and ink-cartridge job.

Bestie looks at her with undisguised disgust, 'Why?'

Bestie was her one and only hope of understanding why she'd marked herself – but she doesn't understand, does she? Birthday Girl is bursting to say something along the lines of, 'it was this, or just another scar,' or, 'because I can't cope, Bestie, and this is a better form of hurting myself, can't you see?' or, 'because, when I look at it, it feels like someone loves me,' but instead, she gives a weak smile, and shakes her head. Bestie envelops her in a hug, bestows three air kisses, and walks lightly away.

Standing alone, Birthday Girl fingers the still-sore carving through her layers, until the red starts to flow. 'Happy birthday,' she whispers, and turns to go home.

THE EDINBURGH TATTOO
by Elizabeth Eastwood

'Come on Gran.' Min shouted from the steps above her and Angela staggered to join her, feeling every one of her seventy-one years. The beat of the drums far below was just beginning and she still had several rows to climb. The musicians in their best military uniforms were ready to begin and she pushed on, wanting to be in her seat before they took to the parade ground. She flopped down heavily onto the plastic seat and took a moment to appreciate the backdrop of the castle, lit up by coloured floodlights. She felt the usual current of excitement tingling in her nerve endings as she heard the distinctive wail of the inflating bagpipes

'I don't know why you put yourself through this every year, Mum.' Martha had already settled in her seat and stowed her coat underneath it. Now, her arms were folded and her face drawn into a frown. 'Would you even recognise him now? And if you did, would you want to?'

How could her daughter ask? She'd recognise him anywhere. She knew she would. His hair probably didn't curl just over his collar anymore and the brown was likely to be shot through with silver, or perhaps it was gone completely. The smooth cheeks would be more crumpled than they had been, but his smile wouldn't have changed. His smile had dazzled her, blinding her to everything but the need to be with him. In 1967 she'd just completed her final year at Edinburgh university but had returned for a farewell trip to the Tattoo. Her first visit had been just before the start of her university life and it had become a tradition that she went to the last night of the festival. Even in the difficult years that followed, she'd always made it and it had become a kind of pilgrimage. When her daughter was old enough she'd been included in the trip and in later years, her granddaughter also went with them. Angela suddenly realised Martha was still talking.

'Why would you want to see him again anyway? We've always been alright, haven't we?'

Angela reached over and squeezed her daughter's hand. Dear Martha. Always so prickly. How could she possibly understand though? She'd only been with David a few months but Angela could tell her daughter was already getting bored. Martha never let anyone close to her for too long. Men were necessary for the procuring of a child and once she had Min she saw no need for further long term entanglements.

Martha's experience of being a single parent were vastly different to Angela's. By the time Min was born, single mums were no longer the social pariahs they'd been thirty years earlier. Martha had no need of the old brass curtain ring that still sat in Angela's jewellery box, nestled between earrings of semi-precious stones and silver bracelets. She hadn't worn it for years – eventually she'd saved enough to buy a cheap wedding ring and called herself a widow – but she kept it as a reminder of how hard she'd had to work to eke out a decent life for the two of them. Martha thought her mother was morbid to keep looking backwards, but how could she explain that she had no choice in the matter? Martha was such a different personality, constantly looking for the next new thing. How could someone like that possibly comprehend the tie that kept her bound even after all these years?

She'd known from the start there was no future in it, but she'd allowed herself to be carried along on the wave of love – there was a good proportion of lust mixed in there as well if she was honest – and not given much thought to the time beyond those magical few days.

'I hate the bloody bagpipes.' She'd laughed at the overheard comment and turned to see the man next to her scowling at the pipers far below them.

'Why on earth are you here then?' The words had escaped before she'd had time to think them through, but he grinned lopsidedly at her.

'I don't like wasting money,' he said. 'My wife was meant to come with me, but she changed her mind at the last minute and insisted I come without her. She's the one who likes all this stuff.'

Angela smiled sympathetically. She loved the pomp and circumstance of it all, but even she had to admit the bagpipes weren't her favourite part of the show.

'Marie can be… difficult,' he said, his mouth twisting with the words. 'That makes her sound awful, I know and I don't mean it to. It's just… complicated, I suppose. I'm Michael, by the way.'

Angela took his hand and shook it, introducing herself. They quickly settled into an easy conversation and talked all night, walking through the darkened streets of the capital long after the Tattoo had finished. Neither of them wanted to break the fragile threads that spun around them by parting and they saw sunrise from Arthur's Seat high above the city. The air felt fresh and clean and full of the promise of a beautiful late summer day. When he kissed her, just as the sun appeared above the horizon, she knew she was in love. She didn't believe in love at first sight. It was a ridiculous notion. But the truth of it was, there was no other way to describe how she felt. They walked back to her hotel, oblivious to the sounds and smells of the city as it came back to life. The last night of the festival was the culmination of weeks of events and there was an air of resignation in the flapping of abandoned leaflets and torn posters advertising the various Fringe acts. Edinburgh's time to shine had passed for another year.

She began missing him the moment he let go of her hand. A few hours later, he picked her up again and they had lunch in a tiny café tucked away behind Grassmarket. People chatted around them, but it was just noise. In their bubble there was only silence and they drank each other in along with the dry white. He held her hand while they ate and it was inevitable that their post lunch walk took them back to his hotel. They'd spent the next two days in bed, ordering room service to avoid separating for any length of time.

When the time came for her to leave he wiped her tears away and hid his own.

'I wish things could be different,' he said. 'I can't bear it.'

She told him she wished the same, but they both knew how things stood between them. Michael couldn't abandon his marriage – he owed Marie more than that – and Angela had no wish to become embroiled with a married man. Better for them both to pretend it was nothing more than a fling and return to their separate lives.

Martha had been born in 1968.

Angela's parents had been appalled and she'd moved back to Edinburgh. Away from their anger and their shame. Away from everyone who knew her. She found work and a sympathetic landlady in the same bed and breakfast and saved until she could afford proper childcare and a flat of her own. That was when she began calling herself Mrs Townsend and started working at the solicitor's office in the typing pool. Eventually she worked her way up the ladder and became secretary to the senior partner in the firm with responsibility for overseeing the girls in the room she'd begun in.

'Nan? Are you okay?'

Min's voice cut through her thoughts and she turned to smile reassuringly at her. Angela hadn't been sure about the name 'Araminta' when Martha had chosen it, but she liked it well enough now. It seemed to suit the wayward curls and slender form. Min was a talented artist and was off to art college in a few weeks. She had every ounce of her mother's drive and determination but there was a softer side to her as well and this came out in the beautiful things she created.

'I'm fine, darling. Just reminiscing.'

Angela's eyes scanned the faces of the people nearest to her. After all these years it was unlikely she would see him, but she clung to the hope that one day he might return. She'd often thought of Michael over the years. Wondering if he was happy; feeling sad and guilty that he'd never got to know his daughter and granddaughter. Coming back to the Tattoo was a ritual now. She'd long given up hope of seeing him there. Or at least, that's what she told Martha. A small part of her still clung to the idea of running into him again. It was a million to one chance, she was sensible enough to recognise that, but nothing could kill that tiny flame of optimism.

As the first triumphant march ended and the final notes died away, there was a tap on her shoulder and she turned. A man with thick grey hair stood in the aisle at the side of her. He gave her a lopsided grin.

'I still hate those bloody bagpipes.'

Angela stared at him for a moment, then rose unsteadily to her feet, a smile tugging at the corners of her mouth.

'Why are you here then?'

'Looking for a girl I once knew.'

Angela held her hand out to him. 'Well I'd hate for you to have wasted your money. Maybe we could look for her together.'

THE END OF DROUGHT
by Edward Alport

The rain danced and swirled and leapt.
The garden stood and roared its applause
At the massed drums thundering as we slept.
The earth sighed great choruses of petrichors.

And all for what? For what? The end of drought!
The end of water bowls and surreptitious hoses.
The end of the watering can's leaking spout,
Sneaking the odd pint under the neighbours' noses.

The rain! The blessed rain. Hammering a fandango
On the tin roof. Did we sleep? We couldn't sleep for
waiting,
Watching the weather app, the forecasts that come and go
The first shy drips and drops, like a virgin, hesitating

Before leaping into bed. And the world smells pink and
new,
Washed and fresh, though deafened by the rainstorm
tattoo.

A DEMON COME AMONG US
by Edward Alport

I reckon it's a demon, come among us.
He say why this skin so ice-cream pink?
I show you dreams of dragos dancing.
I show you angels' wings and stars shootin'.
I say your skin a message waitin' for the words that say,
And see your skin as white as paper.

He say a little scratch, a little cleaning pain
Cleanse your skin, he say, make it fiery pure.
It leave you light and airy as the clouds
It leave you light as feathers on an angel's wing
Tie up your heavy heart with the picture man
Leave your weighty business on the sidewalk waitin'.

Did anyone see him come? Or see him go?
I say I never saw this agony. Those bravo men who show
Me ink and say it never cost a tear? I curse them. Curse
them.
They never said a word about mutilation.
Wrapped up in clingfilm and a storm of pain.
My leg will never be the same again.

THE BALLAD OF DOVE AND NATE
by Beck Collett

In a fading time, in a faded place, lived a girl called Dove, and a man called Nate. Separated by classes and travelling shows, they met and they laughed and they kissed and love grew.

But Dove was a girl, not quite sweetest sixteen, and Nate was a man, far more life he had seen. Their friends and acquaintances smiled and refused to believe there could be a bright future for the two. But Nate and his Dove told them all they were wrong; their love was the kind crying out for a song. And if not for a song, then a permanent mark, but for Nate this would be no mere carving in bark of initials scored into the tallest of trees that would grow up and outwards and sway in the breeze. No, the carving in mind was with ink and with blade, the cartridge mixed blue with the red of his blood.

'Dear Dove,' he then begged, gesturing to his right, 'will you brand me as yours 'fore we leave here tonight?'

Poor Dove she turned pale, and she started to quake, far too young...far too soon...what if it's a mistake?

Nate started to laugh with his mouth (not his eyes) and he laughed until Dove would no more meet his gaze. And he said, 'you are mine, Dove, my own and my true, and my heart I have taken and laid before you, and now you mean to tell me you're having me on when I'm baring my soul in our very own song of our love that will last till the end of our days?' And he held up the knuckles he'd already razed, 'Pray tell, what's the purpose of left reading Nate when the right remains bare and would fill me with hate as the bareness reminds me of dearest Dove, who would use me and kill me by taking her love?'

Poor Dove (still just fifteen, remember this fact) felt no choice remained but to go through with their pact. So, she reached out her dainty young hand to his own and she clasped his scarred flesh 'gainst her cheek with a moan. 'Dear Nate,' she began, to her brooding sweetheart, 'you once told me you'd wait 'til I'm ready to part from my father and mother to become your wife, and stand firm by your side as your darling and wife. You told me you'd ask my dear father's permission to take me as yours if my life he had given to you to look after and cherish and love, as husband and wife in a home filled with love.'

Nate listened and bristled and started to pluck at the blood and the ink that had clot on his knuck till the blood flowed again, washed away all the blue, which seemed fitting to Nate as Dove's love wasn't true. 'I told you I would and I did,' old Nate said, and foolishly brushed his hands over his head. His overlong hair a pale shade until then, was daubed with wild colour from blood and from pen, but Nate cared not a jot, so concerned in his heart was he over the chance he and Dove would now part, 'I talked to your father already, dear heart, I told him how much I've loved you from start when I first saw you pass all those three weeks ago when you came with your friends to the travelling show. And you paid for your ticket and paid me attention and I paid you a compliment too coarse to mention again to your face, now your character I know, but I waited to see you 'gain after the show, and I told you right then I loved you, you recall? And I stole a first kiss from you against the wall of the chip-van while your dumb friends tittered and cried I was nought but a dirty old man to their eyes. But you stayed, dearest Dove, and we walked on the sand, the waves lapping our feet, your small hand in my hand and I told you right then that you would be my wife, that I'd waited for you my long forty-year life. And under the full-moon's stare I swore to gain your own father's permission 'fore making you mine.'

Dove waited with baited breath, full of confusion, three weeks was a lifetime to her, not a season to run against that of the travelling show, it would soon move along, surely Nate would then go? It had started as fun, she confessed she was flattered, at looks from a man whose words made her heart flutter, but as for her lifetime, her future? No way, so she silently prayed 'bout what Father did say.

But Nate, he stayed silent, eyes black in the sun, he was busy remembering the words of the man who had caused Dove to live, who had told poor Nate, No! Not you! Never you! Not for Dove, you won't do. 'I have you forever, my darling, my girl, I would lay down my life, I would give you the world if you'd just say you love me, and mean it this time, score your name in my flesh and be mine – please, be mine.'

Now Dove, though still childlike, was cunning and brave, and she saw in Nate's eyes that he meant to soon raise a balled fist to her face if she didn't comply, so she took a deep breath and Nate's blade and asked, 'Why do you feel there's a need to tattoo us together, when the truth is we never could last out forever with you a grown man, who knows better than I, and I still a child, yes, a child, Nate, that's why we must part, as you surely know in your heart, part as friends, not as enemies, when you depart.'

Again, Nate said nothing, but listened and sighed, Dove may put up a fight, but she would be his bride, So, he took back the blade and attempted to write Dove upon his right hand but the name was a sight of crook'd letters and gaps and a curious 'O' that looked more like an 'a' when Dove mopped up the flow of Nate's lifeblood. Yet he battled on with his art, even finishing up with thumb sporting a heart. Then he looked at his girl and commanded her, 'squeeze out the ink in my furrows now, don't think to tease, I am far too in lust with you to let it go, so please be a good girl and submit to your beau.'

Dove did as he asked but refused to defile her own body to please him, 'I won't, Nate, it's vile that you'd ask me to mark myself forever more, when you soon will be leaving here for a new shore. We have both had our fun, haven't we? Heaven knows I will treasure your kisses when you held me close, But. you know that we cannot elope here and now when I've school to attend, Father wouldn't allow.'

Then Dove smiled – like she'd seen older girls sometimes do – hoping Nate would see reason and just let her go. But she'd broke his poor heart, so he broke her poor face, and the blood from the two of them misted the place.

Poor Dove, she was lucky they were near the arcade and the boys on the bandits all rushed to her aid in the scuffle she freed herself – minus her blouse, hands held up where the red poured in streams from her nose while Nate kicked and he punched and he screamed shocking cusses at Dove and the bandit boys, screamed for the justice. For where was the justice for him after what Dove had done? Broke his heart, made a fool of this man for the name on his right – as was now plain to see – had a 'D' and a 'V' and an elegant 'E' but the 'O' that he struggled with earlier that day was as clear as could be a strange lower-case 'a.'

Yes, the love for this girl had now turned to pure hate, for his knuckles were branded with DaVE and with NATE.

Dove ran off to her home, exposed, bloodied, unnerved, knowing Father would think her lot all too deserved. He had warned her off tangling with such a man that had poor reputation, that lived in a van that would travel through England and each time they pitched Nate picked girls – never women – to paw and bewitch and then take all he wanted and leave without thought, leaving children alone, in tears, truly distraught. 'But not I,' young Dove argued, 'I'm clever and shrewd, for he won't be forgetting me now he's tattooed with that etched on his knuckles, I swear he'll behave, he's a marked man forever, with that blessed name Dave.'

ARCHIE'S BOLERO
by R.E. Loten & H.D.W. Loten

0:00-0:29

The drumbeat kicks in. Dum de de de Dum de de de Dum de de de Dum. The two figures draped in purple kneel on the ice, their faces almost touching. The music starts and they sway apart, keeping time to the beat. Elegant movements defying the pulse that underpins them. The rat-a-tat-tat of the snare continues to sound.

The man's body is slumped on the sofa. His eyes are trained on the small television set in its wooden cabinet. But his mind is over a thousand miles away. His fingers drum the familiar rhythm on the pink velour upholstery. He tries to bring his mind back from the hillside. He knew they were skating to this tune. Why wasn't he prepared for it? He wasn't prepared then, either.

<u>Italy, 1944</u>

'Move it!'
The man beside him stumbled, the weight of his equipment propelling him forward. He shot out a hand and steadied him.
'Thanks, mate.'
Archie grinned, his teeth startlingly white against the mud-spattered face.
'Honestly, Drew. I've never known anyone with as much ability to trip over their own feet as you have.'
'Proper talent, innit? Not my fault I've got no coordination. We can't all be bleedin' Fred Astaire.'
Archie sighed.
'Astaire's a dancer. I'm a music teacher. Not quite the same thing.'

'Yeah, but it's all music innit. You've gotta have some sense of rhythm to play. Stands to reason it translates to yer feet as well.'

Archie shook his head. They'd had this conversation before. Drew was convinced Archie's musical talents in some way explained his reputation as the best soldier in the platoon. He didn't usually try too hard to persuade him otherwise. It was nice to be admired for a change. When he was younger, his musical abilities had marked him out as different. He was the quiet boy, not interested in football or girls and too often he'd had to fish his music case out of a puddle while other boys laughed at its sodden state.

He and Drew had met at their training camp. They'd shared a lift on the back of a truck going into the village near their base. A dance had been advertised and they'd been given permission to go. They'd arrived and left together, separating only to dance and a friendship had been forged. Archie sensed he'd found a kindred spirit in Drew. It was something about the way he held himself when he danced, as though he was holding a part of himself back.

On their return, they were told that their orders had come in and they were shipping out to the Med at the end of the week.

0:30-1:50

Finally they are on their feet. Their bodies move in perfect synchronisation – two halves of the same person. First one leads, then the other. Always connected. Always supporting. And still the drum beat beneath driving them on.

It had been like that back then as well. Archie and Drew. Inseparable. Even in the valleys below Castle Hill. The rest of the platoon used to joke that they'd been separated at birth. One excelled at spotting the hidden German forces, the other at shooting them. Except, he thought, One of us only pretended to excel. One of us made a mistake.

Italy, 1944

The slope of the mountain reared above them, the castle at its peak almost invisible from where they crouched.

'How the bleedin' hell are we supposed to get up there?'

'Slowly.'

'Carefully.'

'Can we call a taxi?'

The whispered answers all came at once and the platoon's laughter was quickly smothered. They knew from bitter experience that sound travelled further at night and somewhere above them were German soldiers with machine guns.

' 'Ere, Archie mate. Didn't you say you 'ad a technique for hillwalking?'

'I hardly think this is the time –'

'Nah mate. Anything you can do to make this easier, you go ahead and share it.'

Archie sighed.

'Do you know Ravel's Bolero?'

'Yeah mate. Course. Me ma used to sing it to us every morning.'

Someone sniggered. Archie ignored it and demonstrated the rhythm of the drum.

'On each heavy beat you put your right foot forward. It takes your mind off the fact you're going uphill.'

'Anything's gotta be worth a try.'

01:51 – 3:15

The woman lies prone across the man's leg — they're obviously at a difficult part of their climb and he takes her face in his hands, reassuring her of his love. He lifts her. She checks they are still heading for the top of the volcano and they continue onwards. She leans on him and he is always there, taking her weight. Supporting her. The volume of the music increases as the dance continues. The drum is more insistent now.

The memories are flooding through him. Insistent. They want to be heard. Richards had been their first casualty that night. He missed his step and twisted his ankle. Archie and Drew had moved back from their customary position at the head of the platoon to support him. One each side, his arms looped over their shoulders. He told them to leave him. If he recovered, he'd catch them up. If he didn't, he'd see them at the top when the rest of the men caught up. He doesn't want to remember but still his fingers move, stabbing a tattoo into the plush fabric.

<u>Italy, 1944</u>

The looming hulk of the castle was silhouetted against the murderous firework display that greeted them as they approached the higher ground.

'Jesus H. Christ.' Webster ducked as another shell exploded somewhere above them.

Archie grinned.

'It's not that bad. You've obviously never experienced a First Form music lesson.' He looked at the teenager's blanched face and touched his arm gently. 'Listen.'

A mortar fired somewhere off to the right of them.

'There's your cymbals.'

A machine gun spat bullets that flew harmlessly over their heads.

'The snare drum.'

An artillery piece boomed to their left.

'There's your bass drum.' He gestured with his rifle. 'And now we add in the high hat.' Webster nodded, his face now determined.

Archie scrambled forward, joining Drew at the head of the men.

'Ready? You spot 'em, I'll down 'em. Just like always.'

3:16 – 4:35

The couple take little running steps, eager now to reach their destination and meet their fate. They cling to each other, faces upturned, reassuring themselves they are doing the right thing. The music is getting steadily louder, the tempo increasing as the end approaches. He lifts her off her feet, twisting her in mid-air, almost flinging her. The mouth of the volcano is in sight. The music rises to a crescendo, the drum beat loud and persistent. Has she reconsidered? Is he angry with her? No. She has complete faith in him. The doggedness of the thudding drum knocks the couple to their knees and together they give themselves over to the mountain. In life they could not be together. In death they cannot be parted.

He knows he doesn't have long left. The doctor made that very clear. She broke the news gently, but she didn't know he welcomed the news. Forty years is a long time to be alone after all. There'd been no-one else. How could there be? He'd been too sad at first. Then there had been the law to consider. By the time it changed it was too late for him. He didn't want to share his life with someone who wasn't him. He can feel his heart giving up. He's not surprised – it's been hardened with grief for so long it was bound to wear it down eventually. He can almost feel the arteries folding in on themselves and he smiles as he closes his eyes. I'm coming, he thinks. I won't be long.

All attempts at a silent approach were forgotten as the platoon surged towards the castle. The snare drum accounted for Webster and continued to spit out its unforgiving rhythm until Morris' grenade silenced its steady beat. Bullets ricocheted off the medieval stone. Staccato shots rang out around the hillside. Archie and Drew led their men onwards, taking out enemy troops on all sides.

'Fall back! There's too many of them!'

Wheeling around, the men withdrew back over the hard-won ground, tripping over bodies as they went. They were focused on covering the retreat and no-one saw the arm rise over the low stone wall. An egg-shaped lump of metal landed with a dull thud. Archie and Drew saw it at almost the same time. The muffled explosion was almost anti-climactic: the sound deadened by the body that contained it. The platoon froze in shock. Another of their men was gone. They looked to the other half of the pairing for instructions. He turned and almost without aiming, took out the owner of the arm which had wreaked such devastation. His men urged him to run. He didn't hear them. Eventually, they took his arm and pulled him away with them, leaving half of him behind.

4:36 – 7:42

The couple in purple are back on their feet. They skate over to acknowledge the crowd. Flowers clutched tightly to their chests, their faces are wreathed in smiles and they embrace as the marks are announced. Twelve perfect sixes. Two skaters. Two halves of the same whole in perfect unison.

The pain in his chest is severe, but he barely notices it. He rises from the chair with more ease than he has done in years. He is there. He has come for him. He has waited.

They never spoke of it back then. They couldn't. He was never completely sure if his feelings were returned. Now he knows. Now he is complete. The television is replaying the routine and the rhythm sounds again in his head. He smiles.

'On the heavy beat, you put your left foot forward?'

'You never could get the hang of it, could you? It's your right foot, you twerp.'

His smile becomes a grin. It's time to go.

Background To The Story

In September 1943, following a successful invasion of Sicily, the Allied Armies landed in Italy. The British Eighth Army advanced on north via the Adriatic Coast, whilst the American Fifth Army advanced up the western side of the central mountain range towards Naples. The two armies had three routes to Rome. One was flooded by the Germans, another had an initial breakthrough by the Canadians but had ground to a halt with the onset of winter blizzards. This left Highway 6, through the Liri Valley with Monte Cassino at the southern entrance. The German defences in the area were well fortified and it took four assaults to finally capture Castle Hill. On 17th May 1944, Polish troops captured Monastery Hill and the Battle for Monte Cassino was over.

In 1984 Torvill and Dean won gold at the Winter Olympics in Sarajevo. Their score of twelve perfect 6.0s and six 5.9s made them the highest scoring figure skaters in Ice Dance history. The routine was danced to Ravel's Bolero and the pair have talked about how they came up with a story to inspire them. The story was of two star-crossed lovers who, because they couldn't be together, decided to ascend the volcano and throw themselves to their deaths.

ETERNAL SUNSHINE OF THE SPOTLESS SKIN
by Dini Armstrong

'When will you get a tattoo, mum?' my daughter asked me. I hesitated. All three of my children have tattoos. I say children. My son turned thirty-one this year. He's a bear of a guy, just grabs me for a big hug, Covid be damned. My daughters are talented artists and have both offered to design something special for me. I don't doubt that they would be able to create something unique, something fitting, something I would love forever. And still, my answer was:

'I don't think I'll ever get one, Schnuffie.'

She scoffed. We were sitting at a socially distanced table in Portobello's finest seafood restaurant. It was my daughter's birthday, and this was our first meal out since the easing of lockdown. Our masks were folded carefully and placed on the edge of the table, just beside the QR code for 'Scan and Protect'. I moved my chair a little to the side, the bright sun was shining through the windowpane, directly into my eyes. Squinting, I could make out the silhouettes of children playing ball on the white sandy beach. An elderly woman was walking her dog. If it hadn't been for the little reminders, bottles of sanitiser here and there, arrows on the floor, wide spaces between tables, we might have been able to forget there ever was a pandemic.

'Why not?' my daughter asked.

'Huh?' I had forgotten the question.

'Why don't you think you'll ever get a tattoo?'

I paused and reflected for a while.

'Well, there are very good reasons.'

'Name one.'

I had visions of someone pouring the contents of a glass of explosive little marbles onto our table. Touch one and they will blow up with a bang. My daughter has many tattoos. She had started with a couple of small ones, professionally done, selected with care, followed by others that she had designed herself. A couple of years ago, she had bought her own tattoo gun and invited her friends to 'doodle' on her skin.

'I can't afford them.'

She laughed. 'You know I have a gun. I'll do you one for free.' I swallowed. Hard.

'You can't have MRI scans when you are tattooed. I hear the iron in the ink gets sucked out by the magnet and it rips open your skin and everything.' She smiled at me with an air of triumph, and I knew then that I had engaged in a losing battle. Eventually I would have to tell her the truth.

'Mum, that is for CT scans and only for black ink. And even then, it causes burns or incorrect results, not aliens ripping out of your chest. I could use a colour that doesn't contain iron particles.'

'Ready to order?' I jumped at first, because the woman had spoken from the space behind me, but as soon as I realised it was the waitress, I was ready to hug her. Not that I would, of course, even if she wasn't a stranger.

'No, sorry,' my daughter replied, 'we need a minute.' The waitress nodded and walked away. I studied the menu with the intense focus of a gannet about to dive and spear a fish.

'Isn't it lovely,' I began, 'that luxury of having someone else cook a meal for us for a change. It's been so long.' She murmured assent and declared she wanted the risotto. It was the only vegetarian option, so I ordered the same. Get her on my side. It didn't work. As soon as the waitress had placed a jug of ice water and two glasses between us, my daughter asked:

'So, if it were free and you could get it done with CT scan friendly ink, what would you get?'

'Nothing,' I said. 'I have always wanted to travel to Japan again.'

'What has that got to do with anything?' she asked, puzzled.

'Well, they don't allow you into certain places if you are tattooed, like the public Onsen, the bathhouses. I hear it is something that they find offensive because it is associated with members of the Yakuza.' I raised a glass of water and took a large triumphant gulp.

'You never went to an Onsen last time you were in Japan.' She grabbed the jug and started filling her own glass. 'You said you felt uncomfortable being naked in front of strangers.'

'It's not really the done thing on public transport there either.'

'Wear a cardigan.'

'What if it's hot?'

'Wear a really thin cardigan.'

'I am not good with pain.'

'You gave birth to three children without so much as an Aspirin.' She pronounced the last part of that sentence with a mock German accent, an impression of me. Had I really used that boast in front of the kids?

'I need the toilet,' I exclaimed and reached for my mask. It was still moist from collecting my breath during the day. Maybe she would have forgotten the topic by the time I came back. I dawdled in the bathroom, washed my hands well over the recommended twenty seconds, then studied the posters of Victorian sea vessels along the corridor, before finally making my way back into the main restaurant area.

'Are you okay?' she asked, 'You were gone for ages.'

'I guess the coffee finally kicked in,' I offered. No takers.

'You didn't have coffee.'

'There you go, ladies.' I was beginning to develop serious affection for the waitress, who carefully positioned the two plates of Risotto in front of us. For a while, we were both munching away, savouring big mouthfuls of the deliciously creamy dish.

'I wonder what mushrooms they used?' I made a show out of sniffing the next bite, inspecting the tiny brown pieces among the white.

'You never answered my question.' Oh, come on, just when it was beginning to feel safe. Maybe it was time to come clean.

'Listen,' I said, 'I just don't think I am that kind of person.' I could see the eye roll coming before it happened. 'Hang on,' I tried to stem the flood of judgement, 'let me finish.' She cleared her throat, as if to expel a half-formed sentence that had already lodged itself there. 'What I mean is, I am just not the kind of person who holds on to things. I am much better at letting go.'

She looked surprised.

'Well, you know about my, well, my shitshow of a childhood. I had to be like that, you know, let things happen to me and then go to school and just, sort of, let it go, so I could laugh and play with the other kids. And then when I got older, I wanted to forget all about it. And then, when I got divorced, I wanted to move on and it just sort of continued like that. I am not the kind of person who wants reminders of the past. I want to be a blank slate, a blank canvas, I want to look forward to my future.'

She was silent for a little.

'Was everything okay?' asked the waitress. We both nodded, which encouraged her to add: 'Do you want to see the sweet menu?' We both shook our heads. I had made a birthday cake, a vegan coffee and walnut sponge, which was currently waiting in my daughter's kitchen, next to her new espresso machine.

'What about us?' She looked about eight years old then, not twenty-seven, looking at me with big wet eyes. The weight of her question hit me square in the stomach, knocking the wind right out of me. When I felt the breath coming back into my lungs, I managed to say:

'I don't need to tattoo reminders of you guys onto my body. I see my stretch marks as lots of little signatures. You all lived in that belly. All the letters of my DNA are inscribed into your genetic code, for all the future generations to come.' I quickly added: 'If you choose to have children, that is. I don't need to tattoo your names or your birthdays onto my skin, I will never forget them anyway. But when I think of my time as your mum, yes, if I am honest, I cringe. I remember all the things I did wrong, all the times I should have chosen a different path, found better words.' I paused. 'Like now probably. I don't think I am explaining this well.'

'Mum,' she said, in her softest voice, 'I didn't have that kind of childhood. I had friends and siblings and I travelled, and I created art. I had a mum who made me a birthday cake every year and I never had to forget and move on. I like to look at my arms and my legs and see all those little reminders of all the people and all the places I love.'

I placed my hands on the table and she placed hers next to them. I haven't been able to touch my girl very often. Not since she was little, not since she declared 'I don't do human contact' and wormed her way out of my embrace. Not since we accepted that this was more than just a teenage quirk and that I had to let her have her own space. So this, this was her way of letting herself be touched?

'I am sorry, we only accept contactless,' said the waitress, when I tried to hand her a bundle of notes.

'That's fine,' I said. 'Makes perfect sense.'

STORIES
by S.A. Pilkington

I saw the story you told today.
You read it out loud on your skin.
I saw the story written on you.
Your feelings seeped out from within.
The girl with the insects,
And vivid rose briars.
No one looks at the scars on your face.
Celtic knots on your arms,
And dragons as charms.
Say that you're sure of your place.
The man with the whirls,
Unusual curls,
Tells of the cultures he's seen.
Another with marks,
Overcoming the parts,
Of the hurt his life has been.
The love of a mother,
Shown on your calf.
That hand print where he first stood.
The mark of my own,
Shows I have grown,
And tells all the world I did good.
Tell me the story of you today.
Let me read it out loud on your skin.
Let me see the story written on you.
Your feelings seeped out from within.

THE BUTCHER'S TATTOO
by Jane Langan

Thud, creak, squelch. Thud, creak, squelch. Thud, creak, squelch. It is so methodical and practised. He's done this before.

I feel like I am going to be sick. I can't move, I can't speak. My pores have opened, and salty sweat is seeping out of me, yet I can't look away. My dry eyes are unable to blink. The worst part is the sound: First the thud as metal hits the body, then the pull, a swift swish, then creaks as the wood of the handle resists. Finally, the squelch as the axe's exterior is drawn in by the flesh like a suction cup. A butcher's tattoo. Blood is everywhere, coagulating in and around the bodies. I watch him slip slightly as he moves amongst the bodies on the plastic sheeting. I want him to fall, but he rights himself quickly and continues. Thud, through bone, muscle, arteries, veins. Creak as he tries to detach. Squelch, a resistance of fibres. Thud, creak, squelch. Thud, creak, squelch.

~

The day starts bright, I open my eyes, then squeeze them close again, quickly, as the sun sneaks through a gap in the curtains straight into my face.

'Uh…' I rolled over.

'Here, coffee.' There she is. My beautiful girl. The woman who loves me and brings me a coffee to wake me up in the morning, before she has to go to work. She leaves it on the bedside table, knowing full well the sweet aromas will draw me to them like magic beans.

As I get downstairs she is at the door, keys in hand, ready to leave. I kiss her.

'Thanks for the coffee.'

The kiss is the kind that should make her stay. She pulls me closer and returns the favour. We linger by the door until eventually, she pulls away,

'I'll be late and so will you. I'll see you later…love you.'

'Love you too.'

I look at the door as it closes for a second longer than I should, half expecting her to come back. I know her professionalism and dedication to her work will stop her, but I can't help but hope. This is our last kiss.

About ten minutes later Murphy turns up, 'Alright Ma'am?'

'I have told you before and I will tell you again if you call me Ma'am one more time, I'll have to kill you.'

'Yes, Ma…Ms Thomas.'

'Fuck's sake, Murphy. How long have I known you?'

'Nearly six months, Ms Thomas.'

'That's right, so call me, Cara.' I get in the unmarked police car. Murphy starts to drive. 'Any updates?'

'Yeah, we got the mobile reports for Jessie Tennyson and Sarah Underwood. Both had their GPS on, and we can see that their phones lost the signal around Harlington Woods. We have the dogs there now seeing if they can sniff anything out.'

'That's the best lead we have so far. Anything else?

'Yeah, we compared the numbers dialled and received. We got a match.'

'Good work. Have we got a name?'

'We have, but you're not going to like it.'

'Why?

'It's Doctor Jansen.' An image flashes into my head of our forensics man. He's a big friendly bloke, always the first to offer to buy a round at the pub. He doesn't seem the type, but one thing this job has taught me is you never know anyone completely.

'Fuck.'

When we arrive at the station, Murphy drops me off before he parks up. I walk through the busy Police station to my windowless office at the back. Murphy joins me a couple of minutes later and sits at the desk opposite me.

'OK, run through it again? We know both girls had a side-line in online porn. Jessie hasn't spoken to her family since 2018, but Sarah still lives with her mum on the Sherringham Estate. Remind me, where does Jessie live?'

'She's in Burston.'

'Right.'

I stand up and looked at the whiteboard behind me. The map is stuck on with Sellotape. I circle where the girls lived and draw a line to the girl's mugshots. They have both been arrested for soliciting in the past.

'So, Sarah was reported missing about a month ago and Jessie disappeared last week. Have we double-checked further back for any other missing women with similar...em... attributes?'

Serial killers always tend to have a type. In this case, both women are petite and large breasted and look younger than their age. Jessie reminds me of Nick. I brush that thought away as quickly as it arrives.

'No. Nothing recently.'

'OK. Good. Let's just double-check the phone records again and see if there are any other matches. I don't want to go and speak to Doctor Jansen without due diligence.'

'Right yer are Ma...Ms...Cara.'

~

Thud, creak, squelch. Thud, creak, squelch. Thud, creak, squelch. It is almost hypnotic, the sound, the way he works. When Murphy is killed first, then slowly dismembered, I am sick. The smell of stagnating vomit fills my nostrils but doesn't hide the tang of iron at the back of my throat. The room looks like a butcher's shop.

Limbs, heads, guts, all hanging from metal hooks above me, almost unrecognisable as human.

I feel behind me, my fingers stretching, practically numb from the tight plastic cord around my wrists. I'm beyond fear now. I want to live. I need to escape. I cast my eyes around me. Is there anything that could help me? I will be next - once he has finished with her. My love…I can't think about you now, I need to get away.

~

'I've found another match,' says Murphy, looking up from his screen. I quietly thank the police gods; we can't afford another one of ours going off the rails. 'It looks like a professor. Your girl…, Ms…em'

'Spit it out, Murphy.'

'Well, I reckon Ms James would know him. He works in the same department of the University as she does. He's a Professor of Archaeology.'

My head spins at the thought of Nick anywhere near trouble. I keep my voice calm.

'What's his name?'

'Professor David Hammond.'

Shit. I know him. Nick has introduced me. She and I laughed at his clumsy attempt at making a pass at her. He is large with a ruddy complexion and bad skin.

'Yeah, I know him.' I look at the clock, 'It's four 'o'clock. Lectures will have finished so he may still be in his office, or we try him at home? I don't want to give him a heads up.'

'His home's nearer, close to Harlington Woods.'

~

Thud, creak, squelch. Thud, creak, squelch. Thud, creak, squelch.

~

It's the normal routine. We turn up, ask a few questions, get a feel for the man and his situation, and take it from there. To begin with, it's exactly that.

'Hello Professor, I'm DCI Thomas and this is DC Murphy. Any chance we could come in and have a word.'

'Of course,' He looks at me intently, 'I know you, don't I? You're Nick's…'

Why some men have such a problem saying girlfriend or partner is a mystery to me. I help him.

'That's right. How are you, Professor Hammond?'

We follow him to his kitchen at the back of the house. The blinds in the living room are down so I can't see the road where we parked the car. The house is dark, and the atmosphere feels heavy. It's like there hasn't been fresh air in the house for a very long time. I make a mental note.

'A cup of tea… coffee?'

'No thanks, this shouldn't take long, we just need to ask you a few questions.'

Next to the kitchen island, I perch on one of those uncomfortable stools people have, where there's nowhere for your knees to go. Murphy remains standing.

'Is it OK if I make myself one? I've just got back from work.'

'That's fine, we can talk as you make it.' I look at Murphy and nod for him to begin. He tugs at his collar briefly, a nervous habit I have noticed before. He fidgets from foot to foot, as he takes out his black notebook and pencil.

'Right.' He clears his throat. 'Forgive me for asking Professor, have you ever used the website BabesXBabes?'

Professor Hammond has his back to both of us. I watch as he continues to pour hot water into the cup. For a fraction of a second, the flow of water stops, and I think I see a slight tensing in his shoulders.

'No, I don't think so. Is that one of those porn sites?' He turns around and smiles. His face looks odd like he doesn't smile much.

'Yes, that's right. You make a call, and a girl will talk to you live.'

'Interesting, but not my cup of tea, so to speak.' He puts his head down and hides his grimace at his attempted joke. Murphy nods and notes Hammond's response.

'That's a little odd as we have your number calling the website.' I say as I watch his reaction closely. He doesn't blink.

'I had my phone stolen.' He has stopped making tea, his arms hang loosely by his side. He is bigger than I remember, he looks like a ginger ape with acne.

'Really. When was that, Sir?' Murphy grips his pencil ready for the response, holding eye contact until Professor Hammond looks away.

'Oh, I don't know. A week or two ago?'

'One of the calls was a month ago.'

'Maybe it's been stolen a month. Who remembers these things?'

I am watching him unravel. His eyes are all over the place as if looking for a quick escape. He blinks more rapidly,

'I reported it. Let me just get the bit of paper. It'll be in my office.'

He moves past us quickly, his head down, disappearing through a door just behind Murphy, off the kitchen. We hear him scrabbling about. Murphy raises his eyebrows at me and half smiles, as I give him a nod. We know we are onto something.

I watch Murphy collapse in front of me like a concertina: knees, body, head. He is down. When I look up the professor is there, his eyes wide and wild, his mouth open and his lips wet with saliva. He is laughing as he grabs me. My police training kicks in and I try to defend myself, but he's too quick. He slams something into the side of my head and I blackout.

When I wake up, I can't move. Murphy and Nick are lying on the floor in front of me. Nick is naked. She fought. There are bruises, welts and cuts on her breasts, her thighs, and her beautiful face.

~

Thud, creak, squelch. Thud, creak, squelch. Thud, creak, squelch. The butcher's tattoo.

Why has he left me until last? Why Nick? Above me, I recognise Jessie's head attached to a hook; maggots have started to maw on her eyes and around her mouth. Bile rises in my throat. I look away quickly.

I tried screaming earlier. The professor just laughed and muttered something about soundproofing and no chance, he is in a rhythm that cannot be interrupted. Thud, creak, squelch.

I have watched his process; I know how he butchers a person. I know he is nearly finished with Nick. I'm next.

Thud, creak, squelch. Thud, creak, squelch. Thud.

WILDING

by Jayant Kashyap

After we first kissed and my hands reached your thighs — your
eyes a quiet *yes* and you — warm, gradually — like the

earth, I thought of a fox, perhaps because drunk, once, you'd decided
to get a tattoo: *What if this earth that's already so much water*

drowns? Perhaps I'll then have this comfort of being
apologetic — the idea of getting buried with an animal I've had

my fair share in killing. It was then I had fallen in love with the
idea of *you*; the way we, as a species, have always loved the sun

painting our ceilings orange, and the sheer impossibility
of writing about happiness. That night, we hadn't gone too further

because, overwhelmed, you had thought of asking what love is
instead — and, quietly, I'd said *nothing* and you wouldn't blink,

so I added *not if you don't want it.* You: *And what if you do?*
It's like craving for the idea of rainwater trickling down our naked

backs in midwinter; the idea of kissing a cigarette with burnt lips; the
idea of getting a tattoo of another animal we're sure to end up

killing; the ambiguity of almost. You say *if the world were already*
too much water, would there still be love?

Yes.

UNIQUE
by Lily Lawson

Your tattoos tell your story,
people and things you love,
the expression of who you are,
even stripped naked
there you would be,
with your unremovable individuality.

MONGOOSE (FIFTEEN POINTS
by Toby Goodwin

Ever since the age of fifteen, Zoe Fenway has been quite certain that she is dying. A slight, almost imperceptible pain in the jaw. Sore muscles. Feelings of tiredness, apathy. A sinking sensation every morning. A breadcrumb trail to a certain and indomitable truth. The truth of her impending doom. No diagnosis was necessary, Zoe was more than capable of looking up the symptoms herself. She knew it in her bones, or rather she knew it in the lymph node just below her jawbone on the right-hand side. Hodgkin's lymphoma, most likely. A likelihood that hung over her every day. A longing to name the serpent, but fear of its definition. Zoe Fenway is quite certain that she is dying, and Zoe Fenway is also totally pished.

She's standing outside a nondescript pub in the Glasgow city centre wearing dungarees and a striped tee-shirt. In a way, for Zoe, the pandemic was a relief. "Nae fear if yer no gawn oot." Or that's what she thought, at first. The thing with fear is that it doesn't just go away. It takes on a different form. Fear needs tae be clawed to smithereens. You've got to sink yer teeth intae its scaley fuckin flesh and tear out its throbbing gizzard.

Jessie Fenway is rocking back and forth thinking about sickness, squiffy. Her toes hang over the curb and her frizzy hair flaps across her face. There used to be days when Zoe's parents would take the day aff when she was sick. Sit and cuddle her up in bed with a hot water bottle and read her a book, but those days are gone.

The street is lined with cars. Pedestrians lope lazily along. Snakes. Cobras. Vipers. Slithering, tasting the air. Behind Zoe stand two bouncers wearing black t-shirts and white masks. One is a man, and the other is a woman. Both have short hair, and the man has a set of slithery, snaky, tribal tattoos covering one arm. Shortly to the left of them is a sprawling beer garden. Rows of six-seater wooden benches expand across a cordoned-off road. People are chatting, enjoying the sunshine.

Zoe looks down at her forearm, at her own tattoo. Her wee, mongoose pal. Petey the mongoose, she calls him. A flowery, art-nouveau design, like a tarot card. His weaselly body arches back and bears his teeth. In Zoe's opinion, Mongooses are the most fearless animals in nature. She got him for her eighteenth, six years ago, and he's served her well. "They wee bastarts think nuhin ae fightin a king cobra, nae bother. Poison that'll turn yer blood to jam and they're like 'sound, I'll eat that.'" That's what Zoe wants from life. Not a resistance to certain types of venom, but to live without fear. Fear that grips her every morning. Fear that has her feeling at her neck for inconsistencies every hour of the day. Fluttering fear that's so bad sometimes that she can't even leave the house. It's not a fear of death itself. She fears people. She fears what people will think of her when she's finally diagnosed. She fears the doctors. She fears the knowing looks, the pity. This is why she's so pished. That and the discount on daiquiris on a Wednesday afternoon.

Zoe's favourite book growing up was Herb Montgomery's, Mongoose Magoo. A picture book about a mongoose who was to be deported from an American zoo, and so had to find a way to prove his value.

"What's wrang with Mongoose Magoo?" wee Zoe said, cuddled up in her bed.

"There's nothing wrang with Magoo. It was the people in suits who wanted rid of him." Da-po said, wearing a fisherman's jumper and a ginger beard. "They didn't know how brave he wiz. He had to show them."

"I'll show them tae," her da's name was Paul. Her maw called him Po, so Zoe did too.

On the street, she whips around, "Everycunt's afraid these days, man. There's poison in the air, man. There's poison in yer fuckin phone, man."

"How's she so pished?" the male bouncer says. Posh accent, barrel chest. Prick.

"No idea," the other bouncer says. She's got a friendly, Weegie accent and she's about the same height as the posh one. "She was only in fer two hours."

"Dunnae talk aboot me lit am no here!"

"Aye, she's wasted."

"I'm no wasted. You're a fuckin waste, man. I've never seen hings so clearly, man. I'm talking aboot bravery, man!"

Da-po couldnae be brave. When her maw wanted a divorce, he just said, "Aye." A low, sighing, aye. She heard it through a crack in the door.

"Off you go, hen. You're not getting back in," posh-bouncer says. He turns to his companion, "Seven o'clock and they're all pished like it's 3am."

"It's the pandemic, man. It's the fear, man. We need tae jist stop bein afraid ae everyhin."

"Right, you've had enough. Move along, hen. Your pals left ages ago."

Zoe stumbles and the female bouncer steps forward, "C'mon, deary."

"Don't touch me!"

Zoe'd been drinking with a few friends from a degree that she never got round to finishing. They'd left after an hour, leaving Zoe with two choices: either go home, still sober and play a game of scrabble with fuckin Kyle, or get maer pished. The latter proved to be the more attractive option, or at least it had been until she took herself for a smoke and wasnae allowed back in. It never occurred to her that she could smoke in the beer garden, but they were strong fuckin daiquiris. She steps forward and pokes the posh bouncer hard in the chest, pushing him back slightly.

"What you doin?" he says.

"A'd fuckin cream you at scrabble. I ken aww the words. Here's wan, mongoose; fifteen points and that's wi nae doubles. I fuckin love mongooses. I'd cream ye, custard cream. Nae abbreviations, nae initialisms. Zymology, define that. Can you? Didn't think so. It's the chemical study of fermentation processes. The fuckin, paranoia process. How about cortisol, ten points; define it."

"Whit?"

"Define cortisol. Ye cannae can you? You cannae use a word if you cannae define it."

"Right, I've had enough of you. Get gone or I'll radio the polis."

"Take a step back and think aboot it," that's what Da-po used to say. He always used to help wi Zoe's homework, but that stopped after the divorce. She even used to try to get bad grades on purpose, but it never worked.

"C'mon."

"Right, right, fuckin hell. Cannae take a joke." Zoe raises her chin and starts towards the taxi rank. She looks down at the mongoose and slaps it, "Good old Petey." It was a nervous moment, a rite of passage. Sure, she'd been fluttering more than on most days and sure the pain had been brutal. Like a humming, hot pencil dragged through flesh, but that's what it was all aboot: conquering fear.

There's a white cab at the front of the rank. Zoe marches up and raps her knuckles on the window. "You free?" she says through the glass.

The driver waves the back of his hand at her.

"Crossmyloof!" that's where her maw and Kyle stay. She cannae fuckin stand Kyle.

The window comes down. "No the day," the driver says.

"C'mon."

"Have some food and try a different taxi." Does he no know she's a deed girl walkin?

Zoe stumbles back across the pavement. A handsome couple stroll up and get straight in the cab. High heels, a suit, and a wall of perfume. They look brave. Nice hair, nice clothes. It's the same thing. They've spent hours in mirrors, and from where Zoe's standing it's all ootae fear. She catches a glimpse of herself on the side of the taxi. Dungarees, frizzy hair, mongoose.

"Queen's Park please," the girl says. That would get Zoe pretty close to home. The door slams and the engine shudders. Zoe looks down the street. A small queue has formed at the front of the pub, distracting those impudent (thirteen points) fuckin bouncers. There're also a few pedestrians, but naebody's looking. Zoe can see the cabby typing in directions on his phone. A split-second decision.

Fuck aye, mongoose. She runs to the back of the car, keeping her head down. There's a button under the boot and in one smooth movement she opens it and rolls in. She waits for a "The fuck're you doing?" that never comes, and the cab starts to move. The boot is spacious, dark. Zoe cannae stretch her legs, but she puts them to her chest, comfortable enough.

"I'm sorry, you'll be staying here this weekend," her ma said. Zoe was fourteen, and she was meant to go to Da-po's house. "I'm really sorry, but he's died, Zoe."

"Whit? How?"

"It was a blood clot. Didn't realise till too late."

That's a good word, clot. Low score (six points) but there's a certain onomatopoeic quality to it. "What?"
"C'mere," Ma put an arm around wee Zoe. "Sometimes life can be shocking. Sometimes there's no way to prepare yerself, understand? What matters is how we deal wi these things."

The cab turns a corner and Zoe's head is bumped against one side. She can hear the couple nattering away in the back.

"And then I was like, 'You're too short, Robert,'" the girl says.

To which the boy laughs daintily, "I love it when yer bein facetious, Chantelle." That's another good word, facetious (fourteen points), but he's just used it incorrectly.

Zoe's mother's boyfriend, Kyle, sits about with a face like a slapped arse watching pre-recorded daytime TV, playing scrabble. She remembers the last game they played. A build-up that he said was illegal. First stand – then understand – then misunderstanding. It was a thing ae beauty. Kyle's no got a beard, he's gawky. Never had any kids of his ain and he's made no attempt to get to know Zoe or her older brother, Tam. She can feel it in the fear. It's not a fear of Kyle himself. It's a fear of what he thinks, of what he says when she's not there. He's smart and successful and she can tell he thinks she's a waster, a permanent squiffy. That's a big scorer, squiffy (twenty-five points): to be mildly pished, drunk, shit-housed, hammered, floored.

Kyle wears khaki shorts, and he talks down to her. The man loves Scrabble, loves tae win, and Zoe just cannae have that. Over the pandemic, this has been her only resolution. The only thing to keep the fear at bay. She got her ain board and she spent hours working out winning combinations to beat that facetious fuck. Just to be smarter than him at the slightest thing. That's what any good-hearted mongoose would do.

"I hope you told him where to get off," the guy in the back says.

"Oh, well I then proceeded to be even more facetious. I said that he's ugly and that he should go away."

"Actually," Zoe says, sitting up. "Facetious is an adjective describing a phrase that is intended not to be taken seriously, like if I said, 'I love the smell of this car,' and I was takin the piss, then I would be being facetious."

"What the hell?" the boy says.

"Who's there?" Chandelle says, and then she goes, "Excuse me, excuse me!"

"What is it?" the cabby says.

"There's someone in the car boot!"

The cab stops, flinging Zoe hard against the back seat. "Who the fuck is in the boot?"

"The fuckin mongoose!" Zoe shouts. A door slams and there's a sound of marching. A crack of light appears and the boot swings open. Zoe's knees are still at her chest.

"Get the fuck out of my cab."

"It's a misunderstanding. I'm a bit squiffy." She puts a hand at the edge of the boot and heaves herself out. The cabby slams it behind her and gets back in the driver's side.

"Away tae fuck," he says before driving off.

Zoe shakes a fist, "Aye, slither away ya bastarts! Your use of facetious was spot on."

Zoe looks around, she's in Pollockshields. Not too far. She knows that in the morning she's gonna worry about everything; the conversations, the gland on her neck, the ache on her back, her impending doom, but if she keeps trying things will get better. Mongooses don't give up. She turns south and starts to walk. Fuckin squiffy, man.

TIT FOR TATTOO
by Amit Parmessur

As you already know, this earth is cold. There
are many poisonous snakes in its grass. So, she
has coiled a couple of them around her areola.
They guard her on the nights her favourable
stars are getting drunk in a bar. They are

her faithful fireflies. People laugh at her. I guess
they must laugh at their mirrors first. She does
not need religious demons to paint
the tapestry of her life. I wish someday you
could see the blue octopus sprawling its

seven toxic tentacles over her breast.
I am sure you would ask about the missing
tentacle. I wish you could see the tiger
consumed with anger under the octopus.
She often shares how she had broken many

a costly shoe to find the right path. How she
had bruised many a frail finger to find
the right punch. She has fought from tip
of her toenail to tip of her hair, the countless
emotional cicatrices keeping her virginity.

How about that dragon on her other breast?
Each time the invisible butterfly clock
on her beige wall chimes midnight, the time
when she makes secret love with the shadows
in her room, it springs to life and vomits fire.

As you already know, this earth is cold, very cold.

AN INCRIMINATING TATTOO
by Ron Hardwick

'Robert Frayn, you are charged with the theft of a satellite navigation system from a Citroen car on the twenty-third of October last. How do you plead?'

    'Insanity.'

    'That is not a recognised plea in this court. You must enter a plea of 'Guilty' or 'Not Guilty.'

    'Your Honour,' interjected the Defence Solicitor. 'I must inform you that my client is illiterate.'

    'No I'm not. I just can't read or write.'

    'Enter the plea that we agreed on,' whispered the Defence Solicitor to the defendant.

    'Not Guilty, missus,' said Robert.

    Thus started the trial of the hapless Robert Frayn, a twenty-two-year-old petty criminal who had been in and out of prison since he was a teenager.

    Copthorpe's Magistrate's Court was a smart modern affair. The three magistrates sat high up on an imitation teak bench and looked down on rows of other similar benches that housed the rest of the assembly. The walls were white and the place reminded you of a chapel of rest. Copthorpe's large and extravagant crest, a testament to its rural past, if not its less promising present, was pinned to the wall above the chief magistrate's head. The crest comprised three sheaves of wheat, a tractor and a lion rampant with a quotation in Latin - Discite Justitiam Moniti - "Having been warned, learn justice." Robert had been warned many times but had signally failed to learn justice.

    'Call the main witness for the Prosecution,' said the Chief Magistrate, a fearsome middle-aged woman with blue hair who rejoiced in the name of Catherine de Bruyn.

PC Blacklock shuffled into the witness box. He was on the verge of retirement and appearing in any court case caused him great annoyance.

The Prosecuting Solicitor started his questioning.

'Can you describe the events of the evening in question?'

'Yes.' A pause of several seconds.

'Well, go on then.'

PC Blacklock dug out his notebook and riffled through a few pages before clearing his throat and speaking.

'I was on duty at the Police Station on Isis Road at nine in the evening of the twenty-third of October.'

The Defence Solicitor, an eager young chap called Lamb, interrupted.

'How do you know it was the twenty-third?'

'Because there was a calendar on my desk. I cross out each day as I leave work.'

'Can we get on?' asked Catherine.

'I was observing the closed circuit television,' said the policeman. 'It was trained on the car park in Kendal Rise. We've had a lot of car thefts there.'

'Go on,' said the Prosecuting Solicitor.

PC Blacklock did so.

'The Inspector had the idea of placing an unmarked car fitted with expensive satellite navigation equipment in a prominent position in the car, where it could clearly be seen on video. He chose a Citroen because they are the easiest to break into.'

'Objection,' said the Defence Solicitor, 'There is no evidence to support the proposition that a Citroen is the easiest car to break into. I own one myself and no-one has broken into that.'

'Mr Lamb, may I remind you that this is not the set of an episode of Perry Mason. I frown on these ridiculous interruptions,' said Catherine. 'Carry on, Constable.'

'I seed that film,' said Robert to Lamb. 'Funny, it was. Black and white. I like Sid James.'

'Mr Lamb, can you please tell your client to cease talking, otherwise he will be charged with contempt of court,' boomed Catherine.

'Your honour, my client suffers from talkaholism.'

'He suffers from what?'

'Talkaholism. It's a form of neurosis. He is a compulsive talker. He cannot help himself.'

'Well, you had better gag him, then. PC Blacklock, please continue.'

'While I was watching the screen, a young man came into view. He was carrying a screwdriver. I saw him insert the screwdriver into the driver's door handle, twist it with some violence, and open the door. That caused the car alarm to go off. He wrenched out the sat nav in his panic and had it away on his toes.'

'I beg your pardon?' asked Catherine.

'It's an expression, Your Honour. It means he ran away with some despatch.'

'I see,' said Catherine, who didn't.

'Was the area well lit?' asked the Prosecuting Solicitor.

'Very brightly lit. We had positioned extra arc lamps so that we could better identify anyone who attempted to break into the car.'

'How did you know it was the defendant?' asked the Prosecuting Solicitor.

'He had his surname and date of birth tattooed on the right-hand side of his neck.'

'He had what?' asked Catherine.

'His surname, Frayn, and his date of birth, the nineteenth of May, 1999, tattooed on his neck.'

'These modern young people,' said Catherine, 'off their heads, if you ask me.'

'That's what I pled - insanity,' interposed Robert.

'Mr Lamb, please tell your client to remain silent.'

'Better do as the old bat says,' whispered Lamb.

'Mr Lamb, I have excellent hearing. I would advise you to keep your insults to yourself.'

Lamb flushed to the roots of his hair and nodded his acquiescence.

'Let us return to the matter in hand,' said Catherine.

'You are sure that the name was Frayn, and not Frawn or Frine, for example?' asked the Prosecuting Solicitor.

'It was most definitely Frayn,' said PC Blacklock, 'with a capital "F."'

'Thank you, Constable, with a capital 'C,' quipped the Prosecuting Solicitor, who fancied himself as something of a wit. 'Your Honour, that concludes the case for the Prosecution. You may cross-examine PC Blacklock, Mr Lamb, if you so desire,' he added.

Lamb got to his feet.

'I most certainly do desire. PC Blacklock. There must be dozens of Frayns in Copthorpe.'

'No there aren't. There's just one family,' replied the Policeman. 'I know them of old. They live on the Penge estate. Bunch of villains. I know the father well - he's the worst of the lot.'

'Constable, I suggest that you are biased against my client,' said Lamb.

'Too right I am,' said Blacklock. 'All the paperwork that family has caused me - more pages than a telephone directory.'

'I must ask the Clerk of the Court to strike that remark from the record,' said Lamb.

'See to it,' Catherine told the Clerk of the Court. The Clerk did as he was bid. 'PC Blacklock,' added Catherine, 'Please desist from making such inflammatory remarks.'

'Sorry Ma'am. My emotions overtook me. I'll keep my opinions to myself in future.'

'Very well. Mr Lamb, you may continue.'

'In what font was the wording of the tattoo written?' asked Lamb.

'Font?' replied the puzzled policeman.

'Was it Garamond, or Times New Roman? Ariel, perhaps?'

'I haven't a clue,' said PC Blacklock. 'I know nothing about fonts, except you christen babies in them. The writing was in italics.'

'Ah, so you couldn't see the tattoo clearly?'

'Yes, I could. It took up most of his neck.'

'I don't suppose you have any definitive evidence?' asked Lamb.

'That's where you're wrong. I have evidence here in my bag,' replied PC Blacklock.

The policeman opened a folder he had brought with him and extracted a sixteen by twelve photograph. He flourished it in front of Lamb's face and said:

'There's the evidence. Taken from the video. You can see the time and date in the bottom right-hand corner. You can see the defendant Frayn inside the car with the satellite navigation thingy in his hand. You can clearly read his tattoo, and also see his small pugilist's ears, dyed blond hair and lack of chin. He's got less chin than a squirrel.'

Lamb took hold of the photograph and looked closely at it. His body sagged like a collapsed soufflé.

'Your Honour, I would now like to call Robert Frayn to the stand,'

'Is there any point?' asked Catherine.

'Certainly. Your Honour will understand the shambolic life my client has had to endure thus far, and will doubtless be moved by his plight.'

'Very well. PC Blacklock, you may step down.'

With alacrity, the burly policeman did so.

Robert walked to the witness box and seated himself.

'Mr Frayn, would you describe your home life as rewarding and motivational?' asked Lamb.

'Eh?'

'Let me rephrase that - are you happy at home?'

'I'm not at home.'

'What do you mean, you're not at home?' asked Lamb.

'My old man threw me out. Said I wasn't pulling my weight.'

'You mean you weren't engaging in enough criminal activity to suit his needs?' asked Lamb.

'I mean, I kept getting caught.'

'And where are you living now?' asked Lamb.

'I'm dossing down in Copthorpe Park. Third bench from the left.'

'Your father beat you regularly?' suggested Lamb.

'No, that was my Ma,' replied Robert.

'How did you progress at school?'

'What school? I never went to no school. That's how I can't read or write.'

'Why did you choose to have your name and date of birth tattooed on your neck?' asked Lamb.

'In case I forgets who I am, of course. Cost me fifty quid, that tattoo. Joe's Tattoo Parlour on the High Street. Had to rob a ironmonger's to pay for it.'

'Quite so,' said Lamb. 'Your Honour, that concludes my questioning of the defendant,' said Lamb.

'About time,' said Catherine. 'An open-and-shut case if I ever heard one.'

'Your Honour, could I make a statement in mitigation?' asked Lamb.

'If you must,' said Catherine. 'Tempus fugit and I do not want this court's valuable time wasted by your seemingly pointless perorations.'

'Thank you, Your Honour. You see before you a tragic case. A hopeless, damaged, utterly unsatisfactory member of the male gender...'

'Steady on,' said Robert. 'I ain't all that bad.'

'...A petty criminal, in and out of prison. Introduced to cannabis resin at an early stage, which has led to further confusion in an already addled brain. Cast out by his father into the wilderness...'

Mr Lamb, this is not a bible class,' said Catherine.

Lamb ignored her. He was now in his element.

'...And beaten senseless by his mother, who is Copthorpe's answer to Ma Barker, the infamous murderous American matriarch...'

'Here, Ma didn't murder no-one - at least I don't think so. Mrs Pearson did disappear, though, sudden-like,' said Robert.

'...Deprived of an education, an illiterate but not very artful Artful Dodger, stealing handkerchiefs and wallets with impunity...'

'I never stealed handkerchiefs - you can't get nuffink for handkerchiefs these days,' protested Robert.

'A prison sentence would be the wrong thing to do here,' said Lamb. 'What we need is compassion, understanding. My client is prepared to come clean, to give up drugs and alcohol, and return to his partner, who is expecting her first child by him.'

'I thought he slept on a park bench?' asked Catherine.

'Not all the time,' interjected Robert.

'Is that your summing-up finished?' enquired Catherine.

Lamb nodded and resumed his seat.

'We will now retire to the ante-room and discuss this case. You will wait here until our deliberations are finished.'

They were back in less than ten minutes. Catherine gazed sternly upon Robert.

'Mr Frayn, your counsel has done his best to mitigate for you, and we have some sympathy with your situation, although we consider you an utterly loathsome individual. It is clear from Police Constable Blacklock's evidence that you are Guilty as Charged. We consider the theft to be a heinous crime, and because you had the temerity to plead Not Guilty...'

'I only done what he told me,' whined Robert.

'...You will go to prison for nine months. Take him down.'

'You could have at least worn a polo-necked sweater when you broke into the car,' said Lamb, as the court emptied.

'Don't have one,' replied Robert.

'I mean, you must be the most gormless crook I've ever come across in my career.'

Robert's face brightened.

'Really? You mean I'm good at something? Wait till I tell my cell mates that I ain't got no gorm. It's the best thing anyone has ever said to me.'

Lamb raised his eyes to Heaven and put away his papers. He thanked goodness that his next case was concerned with the keeping of a dangerous dog. He could cope with animals.

INVISIBLE

by Karen Honnor

My tattoos are not inked into my skin
yet there they remain, just the same,
if you know where to look.
To me, each bump and blemish
is a reminder to cherish,
marking both the best and the worst of times,
but telling the story of me.

The stretch marks unfaded,
mapping out motherhood,
along with the emergency C-section scar,
a story of survival,
a tribute to care.

One look at my hand
and I see both youth and age reflected -
the permanent bump of my fountain pen finger
taking my thoughts back to school days,
while alongside, age spots creep
and drying skin holds peaks in a pinch.

Wrinkles on my face carry worries,
weaving between dark circles under my eyes,
where tear tracks betray the silent cries
and hint at nights lain awake,
while others focus on the freckles
and the smile I sometimes fake.

If I were brave enough, I'd get a seahorse tattoo,
a symbol of the soul I'd like to be,
not always seen -
creative and yearning to set that free.
Perhaps one day I'll be bold enough,
to add ink to that expression,
to realise that intention,
before the moment passes and I'm too old.

Still, I know all that is there.
The seahorse and the mermaid with flowing hair,
beneath the skin,
hidden within the middle aged woman,
where there's nothing to see,
nothing - but everything I have done and have been,
obvious to me, but maybe to you -
all of it, an invisible tattoo.

LUCKY, LUCKY ME
by D.H.L. Hewa

People tell me I'm really lucky. Lucky to have been sent to the best school. Lucky to have wealthy parents. Lucky to have made a love match. Lucky my parents adore him. Lucky he's besotted, lucky he grants my every wish.

Lucky, lucky, lucky, lucky, so lucky.

"Thunk thung, thetha thung thung, thaka thaka thunk, thuk, thuk. thunk, thunk, thunk."

Strumming of drums on my parents' drive, announces the arrival of Laskhman's family. Opening my wardrobe, I take out my white mini dress, pulling it on over my head. Not for me the sequinned sari shimmering, glistening in the shaft of sunlight. Leaving it in its clear dust cover, I bang the cupboard door shut, dragging a comb through my hair. Ignoring the make-up and jewellery cluttering my dressing table, I slip on my white stilettos, chosen for a special occasion so carefully, months ago. Covering my eyes with sunglasses, I put my head in my hands, blocking the sunshine streaming in. Wish I could just sit here. Wish I'd never carried on with this day. What on earth made me do it?

'It's time darling.'

My mother stands framed in the bedroom door. Dressed in a white sari, she holds a garland of white jasmine. Standing up, I stumble towards her, feeling her arm stemming my fall.

'Stay strong Dhuva,' she says softly.

Clinging to her, I inch forwards, as she guides me along the landing, to the top of the stairs.

'Can't do this Amma,' I hiss, looking down at the crammed, open-plan lounge.

So *many* people.

Upturned faces, looking at me.

So many eyes.

Boring into me.

All quiet.

Just watching.

What *are* they all waiting for?

'It's OK. I'll stay with you darling,' Amma whispers, tightening her hold.

Tottering, I hang on to the bannister. Watching my feet, I prise one leg at a time off the cement floor. One step, then another, one step, then another. At long, long last, Amma and I reach the bottom. The large gathering parts, clearing a path towards a line of Buddhist monks. A splash of orange in a black-white sea. A thousand feather strokes brush my hand, as others lightly touch my waist. Muffled words float in the air. I pass through them all, my heart pulsating to the Kandyan drums now reaching a solemn crescendo in the garden. The smell of coriander, cumin and garlic makes last night's meal of dry toast churn, churn, churn inside me. Belching, I swallow back the vomit rising to my mouth. Fixing my eyes on a small table covered by a white cloth, I walk towards it, holding on to Amma. I can hardly bare to look, but yet, yet...I have to look. Look, look, look at the black and white photograph resting on the table. Reaching out, I run my free hand around the face looking back at me with its oh, oh so familiar smile.

So Cold.

Hard.

Still.

The carefully gelled hair unruffled by my fingers today. The face no longer changing to a pretend scowl for messing it up. My whole body *aches* for that scowl. Amma places the jasmines around the photo frame, gently guiding me to a cushion on the floor, next to Lakshman's family. I know they're looking at me, wanting to draw comfort, but I keep my head bent down.

The drums stop.

Pulling at the hem of my mini dress, I draw my legs underneath me, rubbing at the goose pimples on my thighs. Should have worn a white sari like Amma, or maybe a pair of bell bottoms.

Stupid. Stupid. Stupid.

A loud rustling like a large forest jostled by a huge storm tells me, that everyone in the room is now sitting down.

Waiting.

Deathly silence.

Suddenly broken.

Broken by regular rhythmical chanting. Monks starting the celebration.

Lifting my head, I search the room. The only place I see him is in that photograph—squatting proudly—one arm over his new pride and joy—his beloved Triumph motorcycle.

Shuddering, I cross my arms. Close my eyes. Take a deep breath.

'Come on slow coach,' Lakshman shouts above the crashing waves.

'Don't go so fast,' I yell back.

Running along Galle Face Green—the wind on our faces—we laugh—watching Laks's latest purchase—a red and yellow kite flying ever higher and higher towards a turquoise blue sky. Finally, I catch Laks up when he stops, puffing, bending over, letting the kite drop back down. Twisting the string round the winder, he picks up the kite.

'You'll be such a wonderful father,' I say, linking my arm with his.

His glistening chocolate brown eyes look intense.

'I wonder what it's like? What's up there?' he says, nodding his head upwards.

'Apparently heaven,' I laugh, 'long time before we have to think of that Laks. Come on, let's sit.'

Knocking me softly on the head with the kite, Lakshman follows me to the sea wall. Dangling our legs over—we sit together—kite by our side—listening to the hoarse roaring of waves frothing and rolling on to the shore. Putting his arm around my shoulders, he draws me into him. The minutes tick past until the sun turns lobster red, sinking itself into the horizon.

'Gosh, look at the time. Amma will be going mad,' I shout, jumping off the wall, dusting myself down.

Stepping down from the wall, Lakshman picks up the kite, handing it to a young beggar child.

'This is for you,' he says.

The child's face lights up like a car headlamp on a dark night.

'Ahhhh. He'll be blessing you a long, long life,' I say, squeezing Lakshman's hand.

'We couldn't have taken it back on the bike could we?' Lakshman shrugs.

Arm in arm we walk to where the Triumph motorcycle is parked. Riding pillion, I put my helmet on as Laks revs the engine. Resting on his shoulder, I wrap my arms around him.

'Ow. Too tight,' he says.

Relaxing my grip a little—I close my eyes—following his body movements with mine—swinging around like on the waltzer at a funfair—the bike throbbing—twisting, turning, through clamouring—bustling streets of Colombo—finally grinding to a halt.

'Home, Mali,' Lakshman says.

Letting go of Laks's waist, I stagger off, standing on jellied legs, removing my helmet.

Thank God.

'Staying for dinner Laks?' Amma leans over our balcony.

'Thank you. Better not. My Amma says she never sees me these day...' Lakshman replies.

'Oh. OK. Mali, don't be long now,' Amma says, going indoors.

'Better do as you're told young lady,' Lakshman winks.

'Yes Sir,' I salute.

'Hey, the funfairs on. Shall we go this week?' Laks says.

'Yes, but no fast rides,' I reply.

'OK Miss,' he says, pecking me on my lips, putting his helmet back on.

Getting on the Triumph—he waves—starting the machine—driving off in a cloud of dust. Standing at the top of our drive coughing, I wave and wave as I always do, until he becomes a small spot at the end of our road.

Until he's gone.

In three weeks, we won't need to be apart. We won't need to be in separate houses. Everything is ready.

In a short three weeks.

The three weeks have passed, and we are celebrating today, but not the celebration that Laks and I were expecting.

What was that someone once said? Life is a tightrope, one loss of balance and you're off? Laks and I walked our tightrope, and one of us fell off. How lucky is that? I only found out when the phone trilled and trilled—waking the whole household at first light—the morning after the kite-flying day in Galle Face. I'm not sure what happened. Don't think I ever will be. Will only ever know what I've been told.

Apparently, Laks went home as he said he would. Apparently he felt tired, was getting ready for bed when his friends called. Apparently he said he wouldn't go to the fair, but changed his mind. Just go for a couple of hours. Which is why he took the bike. Told them not to pick him up. Apparently, on the way, a lorry turned out of a side road. Laks and the bike hit the lorry, then a lamp post. Apparently, he wouldn't have felt a thing. How do they know? What would he have been thinking? All alone, in the dark? Without anyone he knew? What made him do it? No one seems to know.

Oh.

The chanting has stopped. I open my eyes, and watch the masses, hands together, bowing to the monks. The ceremony is over. Aroma of spices mingles with the scent of incense and, coconut oil from the burning wicks of clay candles floating in large bowls. Scrabbling off the floor, I take Amma's arm. Seating me on a chair, she fetches a cup of tea, placing it in my hand.

'Will you be alright Dhuva? Just need t…' she says, moving her head backwards.

'Be fine Amma. Thanks,' I reply.

Sipping my tea, I look around. Aunts, uncles, cousins, Lakshman's parents, brother, friends, neighbours. My father and mother move around each small group. Shake hands. Nod. Shrug. Look towards me.

So many people. The only one I want, the one that's missing.

No one approaches me. My sunglasses keep me from catching anyone's eye—I see them looking at me—giving me a wan smile—glancing quickly away—shuffling.

So alone.

Very, very alone.

'Come. Everyone. Eat,'Amma calls.

The crowd ambles forwards, forming an orderly line into the dining room. The clatter of plates accompanies the sound of chatter and laughter. Hearing the drums re-start, I carefully place my cup under the chair. Standing up, keeping my eyes on the cement floor, I make my escape into a garden of sunshine.

Finally free of sympathetic glances—muttered words—gentle touches—shake of heads—tearing eyes—trembling lips—I trudge past the bright red anthuriums fluttering in the gentle breeze—a birthday present from Laks last year. Moving past the drummers and the smoking few on the drive, I make my way to the white garden wall, straddling it, looking up the road.

He's here. On his Triumph.

Stopping next to me, he turns off the throb, throb, throb of the engine. Hopping off, grinning, holding out his hand.

I hold out mine.

The single solitaire gleams as it catches the light.

He's here with me. Always will be. My heart fills, and I smile, smile, smile at the empty road.

Today—today—our planned wedding day—when we should have been celebrating two lives—we celebrate just the one. Three weeks after Lakshman went ahead of me as always, I'm once again left to follow.

The drums on the drive continue to beat, beat, beat. Lucky, unlucky me. Lucky, unlucky me.

Amma means mother
Dhuva means daughter

THE BALLAD OF BLACKTHORN
by Jane Langan

She had a crow painted on her chest,
with raven black feathers o'er each breast.
The beak, as black as night,
sat snuggly in her sternum tight.
The beady eyes gazed wisely out
and saw all that went about.
And with each beat of happy heart
The girl and crow became one part.

The crow so black and she were born,
She named him, the mighty Blackthorn.

She was of whimsy and of magic.
Her tale so ancient, a real classic.
A suitor came, he drank some whisky.
Her beauty, he claimed, made him frisky.
She didn't like it, and made it clear,
but the boy intended to interfere.
Blackthorn felt a sloppy hand upon his wing,
and pulled from her body like a spring.
The suitor didn't expect a feather,
much less, to see a bird without a tether.
With alacrity of claw and beak
His eyes were gone before he could speak.

The crow so black and she were born,
She named him, the mighty Blackthorn.

The blind boy bled and wailed before her,
she held him still and said, 'Listen sir,
you must know your lesson learned,
you paid the price to be spurned.
So, tell your tale to all who'll hear.
A lady has a choice, make it clear.
If she says no, she means those words.
Be warned, who knows whom else has birds?'

The crow so black and she were born,
She named him, the mighty Blackthorn.

TATTOO
by Louise Wilford

With a noise like a dying goose, Beck surfaced from a nightmare in which she'd been chased down a railway track by a horde of tooled-up clowns with runny face-paint. Her mouth felt like she'd been drinking glue and her head was pounding.

She'd never liked hen-parties, even in her twenties, and they were no more fun now she was thirty-eight. All that alcohol-fueled innuendo - mindless, raucous laughter - stupid games involving bright pink dildos and strippers dressed as police officers. At least she hoped they'd been strippers. A sudden memory of snapping the elastic on a young man's thong, after pushing a tenner between his butt-cheeks, made her groan again.

The memories were now queuing up, each more excruciating than the last. An indistinct recollection of mincing down the middle of a road, at one point – in the rain – holding her shoes in one hand and singing 'Single Ladies' at the top of her voice made her grimace.

Why had she agreed to go? She knew she couldn't hold her drink these days. What if someone had taken a photo and put it on Instagram or Facebook? She could lose her job. Primary school teachers in their late thirties aren't supposed to go on pub crawls dressed as sexy nurses.

It was all Diana's fault. It was her hen-do, and she never knew when to call it a day. She was always leading Beck into these situations, thinking up new ways of pretending to herself that she was still a fresh-faced teenager rather than a supposedly respectable Head of Department. And she never got hangovers herself, did she?

Beck couldn't remember getting home, though she had a brief flashback of Jane barfing in the back of an

Uber and Ruth calling the driver a wanker. The last bar she remembered being in was Crazy Joe's down by the canal. And then the whole hen-party, all seven of them, had staggered out into the night, giggling and holding each other up, and Diana had spotted something nearby and started squealing and pointing.

What had it been? Oh, yes. A tattoo parlour a few doors down from the bar. Still open. Festooned with fairy lights, in fact, and its door standing open as if welcoming passing drunks in.

And then...Oh, no...

As she turned over onto her back, gingerly, a sudden burning pain across her shoulder blades made her squeal and sit up, twisting round in a fruitless attempt to examine herself from behind. As she did so, a wave of nausea rose and she had to pause in her contortions until it passed.

She staggered to her feet and stood in front of the mirrored wardrobe doors, looking over her shoulder so she could see her upper torso in the reflection. Bloody hell! Spread out over the shoulder blades was a large monochrome tattoo, still pink and swollen. She couldn't quite make out what it was supposed to be - possibly a picture of Tower Bridge - but one thing was for sure: it wasn't a transfer, or a picture hand-drawn with a water-soluble felt-tip – it was the real deal!

"How could you let me get a tattoo?'

Diana was wearing her standard 'I-don't-understand-why-you're-upset' expression. She lived in the flat two doors down and they were standing in her kitchen. Beck had her shirt off and Diana was examining the tattoo with the air of a visitor to an art gallery, contemplating a masterpiece.

'I've never believed in standing in the way of my friends' dreams,' she said. eyes wide and innocent.

'Dreams? I've always hated tattoos! You know I've always hated them.'

'Mmm,' said Diana, at last. 'It looks like Tower Bridge – unusual design, very well-drawn. Must've taken hours. Some real talent went into that.'

'I don't care if it was drawn by bloody Grayson Perry, I want it off my back!' Beck paused, making an effort to keep her voice calm. 'How much do you think it'll cost to get it removed?'

Diana ignored the question, peering closer at Beck's back. 'There's something falling off the bridge,' she said, tracing something with her finger.

'Be careful. It's still sore, you know!'

'You've just pulled the skin a bit, sleeping on it. Bit of Savlon'll fix that.' Diana's optimism made Beck grind her teeth. 'The tattooist must have a sense of humour.'

'What do you mean?'

'Well, it looks like he's drawn someone jumping off the bridge into the Thames!'

'It'll take a few days to heal fully,' said the tattooist, that afternoon. It wasn't the actual tattooist who'd inked the drawing into her skin. Beck and Diana had revisited Crazy Joe's but could find no tattoo parlour nearby. They'd asked in the pub, but none of the bar staff knew of such a place. In the end, they'd concluded that the hen-party must have wandered much further than they thought after leaving the bar.

The first name that came up when they googled 'city-centre tattoo parlours' was only a few streets away so they'd decided to pay it a visit, but they knew straight away that it wasn't the place they'd been the previous evening. The tattooist, a middle-aged woman with a sleeper in her nose, was friendly and sympathetic, however.

'You'll need to keep it covered for a few days,' she said.

'That won't be an issue,' said Beck, grimly.

'Interesting design. I've not seen that one before. Real artistry. Must've cost a bit?'

Beck rolled her eyes. She hadn't even considered how much it had cost.

'Bit of a dark subject, though,' said the tattooist.

'What do you mean?' asked Beck.

'Well, the body floating in the river, face down – looks like a a suicide. Odd thing to choose. Is it a scene from a film or something?'

'No, you've got it wrong,' said Diana. 'There's no body in the river. It's someone jumping off the bridge.'

'It definitely looks like a body floating face down in the river to me,' said the tattooist. Diana peered round her, staring very closely at Beck's back.

'Look, will one of you take a bloody photo so I can see it too?' said Beck, grumpily.

On the bus, the women stared at the photo on Diana's phone. It seemed odd to Beck to see her own back from this angle; the tattoo gave her flesh an alien quality that sent a shiver down her spine. She could see, however, what the tattooist and Diana had meant by its style. It was a simple line drawing, rather cartoonish but definitely more Da Vinci than Schulz. Somehow, those simple lines seemed to contain more life than you'd expect. It reminded her of some Aboriginal art she'd seen on a documentary once, though it was very clearly a picture of Tower Bridge.

'I must have seen it wrong, earlier, somehow,' said Diana. 'I mean, it's obvious, looking at this, that there is definitely a body in the water. It's a picture of a suicide.'

'Who the hell would draw a suicide on a drunken stranger's back?' Beck's headache was returning. She was trying to check her online bank statements but could find no record of any recent unexpected debits. 'We need to find the git who did this to me and get him to remove it.'

'At least you can't see it.'

Beck glared at her friend.

'Every time I go to the beach or a swimming pool, I'll have to reveal I have a picture of a bloody bridge-jumper etched onto my back! What about when I have a man staying over?'

'Well, that won't be a problem, will it? Not with your love life!'

'It's just a bloody joke to you, isn't it?' Beck pressed the palm of her hand to her forehead in an effort to stop herself crying. There was an awkward pause while she stared, unseeing, through the bus window, then she turned back to Diana. 'I've been violated, because of you. You made me go on your juvenile pub crawl, got me so bloody drunk I didn't know what I was doing, and then let some big sweaty bloke stick his big needle in me.'

The woman in front of them put her hands over her child's ears, and an old man across the aisle gave them a startled look.

'It wasn't like that,' said Diana, loudly, for the benefit of the other passengers. She lowered her voice and addressed Beck directly. 'No one made you get a tattoo, did they? You're a grown woman. And how do you know it was a big sweaty bloke? It might have been a sweet little woman like that girl earlier.'

'There should be a law against tattooing people when they're drunk.'

'There probably is,' said Diana. 'Look, let's ring the girls. They might remember the place. And, if not, we can take this photo round every tattoo parlour in the city until we find the right one. Ok?'

'Ok.'

To be fair, the women who'd accompanied them on Diana's hen night were – at least after their initial giggles and expressions of teasing outrage – sympathetic. They were also keen to help. They divvied up Diana's list of city-centre tattoo parlours between them, so that soon virtually every tattoo-artist in the city, and a few outside it, had been visited by a woman flashing a photo of an unusual tattoo and asking if a group of drunken women had been in their shop late Friday night. No one, it seemed, recognised the picture or any of the women. Many claimed they didn't open in the evening and would never tattoo a drunken person.

'But they would say that, wouldn't they?' said Ruth, with a cynical frown.

'They don't want to be sued,' agreed Jane, shaking her head in a resigned way.

'It looks like it's a dead-end, hon,' said Devi. 'And they all say it'll cost at least a thousand quid to get a tattoo of that size removed.'

'Looks like you're stuck with it,' said Diana. 'At least for now. Maybe you'll get used to it.'

After this first flurry of sympathetic energy, the 'girls', as Diana called them, seemed to lose interest. They were Diana's friends, after all, thought Beck. She'd met most of them for the first time at the hen-party. And Diana's wedding also distracted them from Beck's tattoo problem, of course. Months ago, when Diana had first asked Jane and Ruth to be her bridesmaids, Beck had been vaguely annoyed that she hadn't asked her. Diana had known them since her schooldays, of course, and it was only random chance that she and Beck had become friends in the past few years due to both working in the same school and living in the same block of flats. Anyway, who wanted to be a bridesmaid aged thirty-eight? But still, she'd felt vaguely disappointed, even a little jealous, at the time. But now she was relieved: it meant she wouldn't have to wear one of those low-cut bridesmaid frocks and reveal the hideous tattoo to the congregation.

Beck had hated tattoos for as long as she could remember. Her father's arms had been covered in them. Ever since he ran off with her babysitter when she was six, she'd associated them with fecklessness and betrayal. She remembered her mother telling her never to trust a man with a tattoo.

'Pikeys,' she'd say, curling her lip as if there was a bad smell. 'Unreliable chavs. Steer well clear, Rebecca. Don't make the mistake I made.'

At least her mum, who'd died five years earlier, would never see the monstrosity carved into her daughter's flesh. Beck could imagine her reaction. It would be just one more thing for her to be disappointed by – not only was her daughter still unmarried aged thirty-eight, not only had she recently been overlooked for promotion at the school where she worked, not only was she living in a poky little flat in the middle of the city with very few friends – but now she had a bloody great tattoo across her back!

It was a fortnight after the hen-party when Beck noticed the tattoo was changing.

After the initial soreness wore off, Beck found that Diana was right: because the tattoo was on her back, she couldn't see it easily, and she found she could forget about it for hours at a time. However, every morning and evening, when she dressed and undressed, she would catch sight of the black marks in the mirrored wardrobe doors and a fresh wave of revulsion and anger would sink into her soul.

At first, she wasn't sure that the image was actually changing. It just seemed a little wonky, a few lines seeming finer, paler than they had been, others curving slightly when they had been straight. She assumed it was an optical illusion caused by the awkward twisting movement she had to make to see the picture, or even a distortion caused by the mirror.

After a few days, however, the changes became unmistakable.

'Compare it to your photo,' she told Diana, who had now returned from her honeymoon in Sicily. But when Diana opened up the photo on her phone, she found it looked exactly the same as the picture on Beck's back.

'But it was a picture of Tower Bridge before, wasn't it?' said Diana, mystified.

'Yes. You saw it and the woman at the tattoo parlour saw it too, because you had a debate about whether the figure in it was falling or in the water, remember?'

Diana was silent for a while, staring first at her phone and then at Beck's shoulder-blades. 'This is so weird,' she said at last. 'I could have sworn it was a picture of Tower Bridge, but it now looks more like a train.'

'It's changed, hasn't it?' Beck's voice was urgent and fearful.

'It can't have,' said Diana. 'Or my photo of it would be different. We must just have somehow seen it wrong before.'

'Or your photo has changed too.'

'That's insane!'

They called the others, but none of them could help. Devi, Sue and Ruth had deleted the photo from their phones, and the pictures on Jane's and Fiona's phones looked exactly like the one on Diana's, which looked exactly like the tattoo: a cartoon-like but skillful line-drawing of a tube train moving at speed towards the viewer, its destination 'Piccadilly', the darkness of the tunnel down which it was travelling cross-hatched around its edges. It was definitely no longer a picture of Tower Bridge, and Beck noticed that Diana and her friends soon seemed to believe it never had been. She began to wonder whether she needed her eyes testing, or whether she was herself delusional.

Then, one morning about three weeks after the hen-party, Beck saw that something had been added to the picture which made her freeze in shock for several seconds, before she rushed round to Diana's flat in her dressing gown.

'Oh my god!' said her friend when she saw it. There was a human figure in the picture now, her falling body silhouetted by the train's headlights.

Beck suddenly stepped away from Diana. 'It's you doing this, isn't it?' she hissed.

'What do you mean?' Diana's face was pale with shock.

'You drew this on my back while I was asleep, didn't you? Did you drug me? Is it some kind of sadistic prank?'

'Of course I didn't!'

But Beck was slamming the door and running back to her own flat.

She showered for a long time but there was no sign of the ink fading. It must be indelible, she thought, through angry tears. All that day at work, she avoided Diana, ignoring the texts her friend sent her. In her calmer moments, she suspected she was being ridiculous. Why would Diana do something like this? Was she trying to gaslight her? It seemed like some mad thing out of a beach novel, not something that would happen in real life. But she could think of no other explanation for how the tattoo had changed.

That evening, Diana rang her doorbell.

'Did you see the news?' she asked, her face drained of all colour.

Beck nodded, mutely. The two women clutched each other's arms, both trembling. The main story on the evening news had been about a junior minister in the Conservative government who had thrown herself under a London tube train during the evening rush-hour.

'So, are we saying the tattoo is somehow predicting tragedies?' asked Diana. They were both sitting on Beck's sofa, holding tumblers of the brandy Beck's mum had given her years before 'for emergencies'. Beck had never opened it before as she hated brandy, but it was the only alcohol in the flat and they both felt like they needed something to calm their nerves.

'Not just tragedies,' said Beck. 'It's more specific than that. It's suicides. The man jumping off Tower Bridge, the woman jumping in front of a tube train.'

'Both in London.'

'Yeah. Is it some kind of...of magical predictor? I mean, that's super-crazy, yeah?'

'It sounds completely bonkers, but it has to be true. Tattoos don't change! Not in the normal world!'

'So I have a bloody magical tattoo on my back?'

The two women stared at each other.

'It could be a good thing,' said Diana, slowly, at last. 'It might be so you can prevent people committing suicide? Like a super-power.'

Beck stared at her friend, incredulous. 'And how exactly would that work? How could I save the poor sod who threw themselves into the Thames? And how could I be expected to know which tube station to hang around in on the off-chance I'd spot a woman who looks like a politician and realise she was going to take a dive right under a bloody train?'

Diana shrugged helplessly. 'Maybe you could get help – you know, tell the police?'

'Oh, yes, I can see them taking me seriously...'

'But they'd have to. They could see for themselves.'

'How? The bloody photos change just like the tattoo itself! There's no evidence! They'd just have to take my word for it!'

'Our word.'

'Then they'd just think we were a pair of lunatics, or crackheads, or secretly filming them for TikTok or something…'

The next change happened only a week later. Over a period of four days, the tattoo's lines shifted themselves into an image of an old-fashioned roll-top bath. It was a view from the side, with water slopping over the edge to form a few puddles on the floor. It was still drawn in that distinctive style, like a high-brow graphic novel, the simple black lines somehow managing to convey the essence of what was being portrayed.

Diana took snaps of Beck's naked back every morning and evening, but each time they looked at the photos they showed only what the tattoo itself looked like at that moment, even though the women knew it was transforming daily. It was as if there was some kind of link between the tattoo and the photographs of it, so they both metamorphosed in tandem. And – even more alarming – Beck noticed that Diana too started to forget the previous images after a few hours. She remembered the tattoo's existence and she accepted Beck's explanations of how it changed and how it seemed to be connected to real-world suicides, and the importance of her daily photographs, but her knowledge of the actual specifics of earlier images seemed to drift away.

On the fifth morning, a figure appeared in the bath – a man, head lolling to one side, mouth open, hand and forearm draped over the bath's side, blood dripping from a slit in his wrist.

Beck and Diana scoured the papers for any news of such a suicide; two days later they didn't have to look anymore. The day's big story was how a Russian oligarch had been found dead, in his penthouse suite in London, having killed himself by slitting his wrists and slowly bleeding to death in a hot bath. He'd left a note, in which he'd explained his belief in what he called 'the Roman method'.

'I thought Romans fell on their swords,' said Diana. 'That's how Mark Antony does it in Shakespeare.'

Beck didn't respond. She was thinking of David's painting of The Death Of Marat. She'd studied Art History at university before switching to a teaching degree at her mother's insistence. Marat had not committed suicide, however – he'd been murdered. But the tattoo's composition reminded her of the painting's shocking realism. There was something almost obscene about these lines on her flesh predicting such deaths – deaths that she could prevent, if only she knew who and where and when. Without any means to find out these details, it was as if the tattoo was mocking her, sneering at her impotence, her fallibility.

Beck drew out all her savings and paid for a series of laser treatments to remove the tattoo. A week after the final session, the lines reappeared and, within days, they were as vivid as before. This time they showed the gates and fence outside Downing Street, number ten just visible beyond. A day later, a figure appeared, spreadeagled against the fence, presumably in the act of sliding down to the floor, his chest peppered with bullet-holes.

'That's not suicide,' said Diana, a note of triumph in her voice. 'That's murder!'

The news story the following evening was how a suspected Islamist terrorist had been killed by police outside the Prime Minister's London residence. It soon emerged that the man hadn't been a terrorist at all but an ex-soldier suffering from PTSD.

'It was Death-by-cop,' said Beck, in a flat voice. 'Basically suicide.'

With each change in the tattoo, and each accompanying suicide, Beck became more withdrawn. She could no longer cope with her job and was given extended leave. She spent every day searching news broadcasts, papers and the internet for stories about suicides in London, examining her tattoo in the mirrored wardrobe doors every hour to see whether there were any changes. As soon as Diana returned from work, Beck would bang on her door, begging her to take another photo, though she knew it was hopeless.

It was only a few days after a teenager was found hanged in his cell in a Detention Centre in Lambeth [the tattoo had depicted him as seen through the grille in the metal door] that a Deliveroo driver banged on Diana's door.

'Delivery for Number three,' he said, nodding down the corridor. 'You're her nominated neighbour.'

Diana knew that Beck rarely left her flat these days. Carrying the parcel, she banged on the door but there was no response.

'Anyone at home?' she called through the letterbox.

After a while, she used the key Beck had given her years ago, so she could water her plants when she was away. The flat was oddly silent and Diana felt a spasm of dread.

She found Beck lying, motionless, face-down on the bed, head twisted to one side. Several empty pill bottles and the spilled remains of the bottle of emergency brandy lay beside her on the mattress. The bedsheet was draped over her buttocks and thighs, and wrapped round one leg.

The tattoo on her back showed a naked woman lying on a bed in exactly the same position.

Diana sank down beside Beck. She felt her friend's wrist and neck but there was no pulse. She hadn't expected one.

She rang 999, and, while she waited for the emergency services to arrive, she flicked through the photographs on her phone. She wasn't sure why, as there were none there of any interest.

When, finally, she heard footsteps on the stairs, she turned her wet face towards Beck again and saw that her naked back was now smooth and pale, with no sign that it had ever been the canvas for a tattoo.

Makarelle Autumn 2021: 'Twisted Tales'

If you would like to see the visual art of this magazine issue, you can access the flipping book for free by scanning this QR code:

MIMBA'S HANDS
by Ioney Smallhorne

At the start of hurricane season, when the sun sinks into the horizon, Mimba searches for her hands. Her arms bleeding at the elbow where Miss Violet's cutlass amputated her crushed bones. Clean-clean, quick and sharp. The mill tek weh her hands but Miss Violet saved her body, bound her arms tight with rum to prevent infection.

Mimba was a mill-feeder. She guided cane into the greedy, grinding mouths of the wooden rollers motivated by the whirring sails that revolved; steady and constant proclaiming wealth and industry.Pushing and pulling cane back and forth extracting every last penny of juice. The skill was knowing when to let go, but skilled people get tired.

Now, Mimba encircles the old mill, like how oxen once did; pulling treadmills in harvest season to aid production when the wind was down, their hoofs a muted metronome beating the ground.

The wind carries her voice as she laments the old cane cutters song;

Mi waan guh a river lawd,
river run free,
work never done oh lawd
river run free
cut t'rough eart' and stone
river run free
flow and find its home
Oh river tek me

Her truncated arms leaving a bloody trail, with a bullet lodged in her forehead, Mimba circles and searches, circles and sings.

The other enslaved people on Pleasant Hill would leave kerosene lamps burning to help her search and cups of rum to ease her efforts. They did not fear Mimba, for she was one of their own. It was Overseer John who had to fear.

"Old slaves weed the fields, picini slaves catch rats that eat the samplings, the strong plant and harvest, the skilled work the mill and curing house. What use is a slave with no hands?..." is what he said before shooting her; despite Mimba having his child, May.

The trouble started for him after Mimba died. Each time he rode his horse-drawn-cart to check field workers, he saw hands instead of cane. The long stalks like the bones of fingers; their knotted nodes like knuckles. The cane cutters chopping them, leaving short stubs and her blood would spill, over and over in his mind.

Madness began to feast on him like maggots in a starved mongrel dog left out to rot in the day's heat. He'd wake up in the dark belly of night digging with hoe, searching for her hands. Then, he started digging, bare face, in the day, under the ferocity of the sky's fire, like a field slave. Mimba his overseer, and she mek him wuk.

"...And I hear her singing, and the beat of the oxen hoofs, and the whirring sails... day and night they don't stop..."

Mi waan guh a river lawd,
river run free,
work never done oh lawd
river run free
cut t'rough eart' and stone
river run free
flow and find its home
Oh river tek me

He would cry to the Doctor, whose prescriptions proved no remedy for Massa John's mind.

Suspicious that May and Miss Violet were working obeah; he ordered fifty lashes for Miss V, and May was sold to the Doctor's friend. Soon, he started to see Mimba's hands on his plate instead of the nice-nice food he so accustomed to eating. So, he stopped eating. Until he was found dead in the mill with no hands.

The old mill on Pleasant Hill, with time, disappeared under creeping vine. Its stone walls crumbling; a fragmented structure, like passed down memories of home, like families of enslaved people, like the languages they forbade us speak.

THE STING
by S. A. Pilkington

Bright, hot summer's day,
They sat out of the sun.
Snuggled together, daughter and mum.
Albums and books scattered around.
Radio playing familiar sound.
Told tales of what had been.
Of what was to come.
Looking at pictures, daughter and mum.
Grandad asleep Christmas hat on his head.
The cat and the dog asleep in her bed.
They laughed at the picture, Jack in the mud.
The cake and the time, did them both good.
They told of the future and summer in Wales.
Believing in fairies and other wild tales.
But the twist in this tale,
Brought a sting of great pain.
Her mother looked up.
And asked, what was her name.
The horror of time dragged them apart.
Not merely breaking, but smashing her heart.
Bright, hot summer's day,
They sat out of the sun.
Snuggled together, daughter and mum.

MIMICRY
by Ben Lisle

It had seemed like such an amusing little jape. Buy a
parrot, one with a real talent for mimicry, and teach it a
few key phrases.

"I miss my hands."

"Never break a promise to a witch."

"Please, you have to help me."

The young avian learned fast, motivated by a steady diet
of praise and treats, and soon it would happily squawk out
its party pieces without prompting. From its cage in the
corner of the cluttered room, surrounded by mystic
curios, the sound of its voice would startle and unsettle
visitors, often leading to nervous laughter at the absurdity
of it all. After all, it was just a mimic, right? No real magic
here, no such thing. The sigils around it were fakes, and
so what if there was a pentagram just visible at the bottom
of the cage? The whole thing was absurd. And yet… The
experiment was a great success, a triumph of a prank.
Each bonus detail added over time just increased the
hilarity, and it wasn't as if the patterns and shapes did
anything anyway. Until they did.
You can't really remember how exactly it happened. There
had been a… book. And chalk, yes, tracing some new
arcane rune. Something that had been in the paper, a new
kind of sorcery. It's so hard to remember now. No flash,
no blinding light, just the space of a blink and now you
were looking out of the bars. Your body had vanished,
disappeared without trace. And now you were in here.
You'd tried squawking, screaming at those who'd come.
But they'd known the tricks you'd played and written your

shrieks of panic off as a more advanced effort to get to them. Your disappearance was noted, and a detective had visited once.

You'd screeched and flapped to get his attention until the world had gone dark when the cage was covered. You'd croaked your new voice to exhaustion, but no-one had cared. No-one listened to a prankster's parrot. And soon afterwards you had been sold, sent away to live in a new house. Your owner had been warned about your heritage, and paid no heed to your cries for help, and soon you'd stopped trying. There was no point anymore.

And then there was The Bird. The Bird was always there with you, scratching at your thoughts. The Bird wanted a peanut. The Bird wanted to play with the tinkly bell. The Bird wanted to imitate the dog because the sound confused the cat. The Bird wanted to be back in control. At first it had been easy to ignore it, to dismiss that part of your shared mind. You were still a person trapped in a mental net, one that you would soon escape. But as the months and years had passed your resolve had weakened, your confidence dimming with each new sunrise. The Bird would steer your thoughts, make you want what it wanted, to hit the bell with your beak so the Bird could listen to the ring. Slowly, you forgot yourself. Your friends' faces went, and now you wanted seed cake. Your schooling disappeared, and in its place, you enjoyed a turn on your little swing. Your children's voices faded, and you learned to copy the telephone. You just want to hold your wife...Want your wife...Want...

Polly wants a cracker.

GLIMPSE
by Jane Langan

I stare back at the old woman,
I glimpse in the shop window.
She is round where she was once flat,
slow moving.
Is she sick? Her face bloated.
She looks tired, her hair all angles,
sprouting.
No one sees her.
People bump and jostle.
She is like a stout bollard
all width,
in the way.
Eventually, she moves,
eyes down, floored,
knees aching, arms heavy,
carrying shopping not for her.
I move quickly to avoid my eyes, but then,
there is just a glimpse.

'TAROSVAN' OR THE LEGEND OF LOGRES
by R.E. Loten

'Are we nearly there yet?'

I groaned. Arthur was awake.

'No, sweetheart.'

'How much longer will it take?'

'Would you like a bacon sandwich?' My husband interrupted and I smiled gratefully at him.

The offer was accepted, peaceful silence settled over the back of the car again and I resumed listening to Bill Bryson's Notes From A Small Island. This was exactly why we'd set the alarm for 3am and begun the long trek down to Cornwall at 4 o'clock in the morning. We were well over halfway and our youngest son had only just woken up. I calculated that once he'd eaten the sandwich, we'd have a maximum of ninety minutes of him and Henry squabbling. You'd think that at sixteen and almost six there'd be enough of a gap for long car journeys not to descend into 'stop poking me', 'keep it on your side of the car' and my personal favourite, 'Muuuuuummmmm, can you have a word.' However, if you did, you'd be wrong! Most of our family holidays begin in this way and so we've learnt over the years that if we set off in the middle of the night, we stand at least half a chance of getting there without James and I needing to reach for the gin bottle the moment we arrive!

This year, however, was going to be a holiday with a difference. A month earlier we'd completed on our holiday flat and this was the first time we were going to make use of it. I'd spent the last month driving between North Essex and Cornwall every week, taking deliveries, assembling furniture, cleaning and generally getting the flat ready so that we could actually use it over the summer. Doing that whilst still trying to ensure that everything ran smoothly at home had been 'interesting' to say the least and I was ready for a break.

We decided that if we were going to make the most of both the flat and the area, we needed to learn more about Cornwall and its history. James and I both love the county and would love to move there eventually and we felt strongly that we needed to have as much of a sense of Cornish heritage as we could. Although it is part of England, there is also a feeling of separateness about it. It has its own language for a start, although we were both surprised and alarmed to discover that there are less than a thousand people who are fluent in Cornish and only a few thousand more who could have a basic conversation, or know the odd word. However, when you consider that the last person who claimed Cornish as their first language is traditionally believed to have died in 1777, perhaps it is more astounding that it has survived at all and is now a growing language. James decided he was going to add to the numbers, bought himself a book, downloaded an app and started learning basic words and phrases. I took on the task of learning about the history and folklore of Cornwall and this is where the twisted tales come in.

Until quite recently, whenever I thought of Cornwall in literary terms, it was usually romantic comedies set in quaint Cornish villages, Winston Graham's Poldark or Susan Cooper's Over Sea Under Stone and Greenwitch. I'd read Rebecca years ago but had no idea it was based on a real house in Cornwall. I stumbled across Jamaica Inn by accident when I was looking for an audiobook set in the county – I did a virtual walk from Land's End to John O'Groats and listened to books set in the counties I was walking through – and fell in love with it straight away. The haunting opening lines so perfectly captured both the scene and the essence of the book that I knew immediately this was an author whose writing I was going to adore.

However, it seems that romantic as Cornwall is portrayed – and it truly is – its real literary heritage may lie in the slightly less prosaic ghost story. There are literally hundreds of these things, as I discovered when I bought Michael Williams' Ghosts Around Bodmin Moor.

'Did you know Jamaica Inn is meant to be haunted?' James was reading leaflets in preparation for the 'flat folder' we were putting together for when family and friends used it.

'Pretty much everywhere in Cornwall seems to be haunted,' I said, waving Ghosts Around Bodmin Moor at him. 'And yes, everyone knows Jamaica Inn is haunted.'

'Well I didn't,' he said, looking a little put out.

'It was on Most Haunted years ago. We should watch it.'

'I don't like scary things, Mum.' Henry suddenly took an interest in the conversation.

I smiled at him. 'It'll be fine, honestly. Come on, it'll be fun.'

He looked doubtful, but I found the episode on YouTube and we settled down to watch it. It was hard to take it seriously when the mediums generally just repeated the stories we'd already been told but with a few added embellishments. None of us completely dismiss the idea of ghosts, but it wasn't massively convincing. The only bit that was a little bit spooky was when they were in the boiler room and that was destroyed for us by the very northern accented exclamation of, 'Something touched me side!' before they all sprinted for the exit. The boys have always taken the mickey out of me for being northern and this became the catchphrase every time we went to Jamaica Inn for a drink. Someone would get poked and have to exclaim, 'Something touched me side' in an exaggerated northern accent so we could all fall about laughing and pretend that we weren't a little bit spooked by the fact we were in a place with such a ghostly reputation.

'You know they do ghost hunting nights here?' I said.

Henry nodded. 'I like the idea, but I think I'd probably be heading for the door as soon as there was a noise!'

Towards the end of the holiday, we decided to take a hike up Roughtor – a mere 400m climb over rocks to the top.

'Why this walk?' James asked.

'What do you mean?' I frowned, puzzled.

'All your walk suggestions have an ulterior motive. There's always something you want to see, or a story you want to be at the location of. What's this one?'

In fairness, he was perfectly correct. I dragged the family across Fylingdale Moor in pursuit of Dracula, we climbed up a huge hill in Bath because I wanted to walk in the footsteps of Catherine Morland and Henry Tilney, we'd visited Jamaica Inn more times than I could count simply because of Daphne Du Maurier and the last time we'd been in Cornwall I took them all on a very muddy route march around Frenchman's Creek in search of La Mouette and her captain. Henry has still to forgive me for the loss of his Skechers in the mud on that walk! Roughtor was no exception. At the base of the Tor is the memorial to Charlotte Dymond, probably one of the most famous of Cornwall's ghosts.

The eighteen-year-old Charlotte was murdered near Roughtor Ford in 1844, allegedly by her lover, Matthew Weeks. He was arrested and hanged for her murder. His conviction seems to have rested largely on his written confession. However, there is some doubt about whether or not it was actually written by him. Local people were outraged by this vicious attack on a young girl and collected the funds to raise a memorial to her, which still stands near to where she was found. The day of our walk was beautifully sunny with lots of people around. We saw the memorial, but couldn't get near it as it was fenced off. It was hard to imagine such a brutal act taking place in this stunning location – whether Weeks was guilty or not, someone slit Charlotte's throat that day – but I would imagine that in winter, at night, the moor might take on a different feel and Charlotte's ghost is still said to walk the ground where she was murdered. The impact of this tragic tale is still felt today – as recently as 2015 locals raised money to buy a headstone for her and the trial of Matthew Weeks is one of the star attractions at Bodmin Jail, where visitors get to vote on his guilt.

Over the holidays, we had several more encounters with the supernatural – or at least with stories of it – including at The Cathedral of the Moor in Altarnun. I'd wandered away from the boys to have a look at the graves and ended up inside the church on my own. I've been in a lot of empty churches over the years and generally they're quite peaceful places. In this one, however, I definitely felt the weight of history pressing down. I had the distinct feeling that it was waiting for something and although I wasn't aware that the church was haunted – I thought the ghost was in the old rectory which we'd yet to locate – there were patches of the church that felt much colder and when I stood at the back I felt decidedly odd – as though both the church and I were waiting for something to happen. It's not a feeling I've often had before. The sunlight outside was a welcome relief and I was greeted there by an incredibly friendly local who took me around the churchyard and pointed out the graves of the vicar and his servant, who she told me are said to haunt both churchyard and old rectory. Her son, who like her is a sceptic, once told her he'd seen a figure in the doorway when he'd been on his own in the church, not far from where I'd felt the cold. I'm still not convinced, but it was an uneasy feeling to hear the coincidence in the location.

The most interesting thing for me about all these ghost stories, is that in the summer holidays I always know I'm not going to get any writing done. It's just too difficult to find the quiet time I need when all three of my boys are at home and wanting my attention. This summer, although I didn't get any actual writing done, I did make copious notes about ideas for new stories and novels based in Cornwall and using many of the ghostly tales I'd read about as a starting point. I reckon I've probably got enough for a collection of short stories and at least three novels, which should keep me going for a while! All I need now is to find the time to write them all, which reminds me of a conversation James and I had on the car journey home at the end of the summer.

'I've managed to sign Arthur up for Kid's Club, so if we need to use them before or after school now, we can.'

'That's good,' he replied absently. 'Does that mean we'll be okay for when you go on the writing retreat in March?'

'Yes.' I paused a moment. 'Of course… you do realise it also means that if I want to have a few days to crack on with some writing in peace, I can book him into it and go down to the flat on my own and have my own mini retreat.'

Out of the corner of my eye, I swear I saw his skin go a shade paler and a slight sheen of perspiration cover his face.

'Erm… are you planning to do that soon then?'

'Not really, it was just a thought. Why?'

'Arthur.'

The boy in question piped up from the back of the car. 'You said my name. Did you want me?

'No, darling. You carry on watching your film.

'OK. Are we nearly there yet?'

THE LINEAR FAMILY
by Ken Smith

I can't remember when I first noticed them.

I see them from my first-floor window: The Linear Family. Always they walk in line, a thin, jagged procession; each member several yards apart, forming a broken column. Always at the head is the mother: a short woman in too-tight clothes. She walks quickly, an expression of urgency on her face, suggesting that it's important for her to be in control of what follows her and of where she's going; and that she's afraid that control will slip away. She leans back a little, as if an unseen hand is pushing into the middle of her spine, propelling her onwards.

Behind come four small girls in identical pink dresses and oversized spectacles. They follow their mother in descending order of height and seemingly age. They run to keep up, a mixture of cheerfulness and despair in their voices as they call out their thoughts and enquiries about the world and their eager requests. Once or twice, their mother twists back towards them and shouts a brief response; but mostly they are ignored as she determinedly leads the way, setting out the trajectory they must follow.

At the end of the line walks a tall, lean man, roughly textured like sandpaper, carrying a heavy bag in each hand. Their reluctant father. His hair is cropped and his nose sharp. On his face is a half-smile, making him appear cheerfully distracted, though it's a smile that tells you he is someone it's best not to cross. He's nervous. Behind that smile, he balances on the edge of anger. Around his left arm, a dragon tightly winds itself, painted in green and burnished brown, hungry like a devouring charm.

Every day through the year, in the late afternoon, they come. The seasons change around them; but their procession never ceases – the Linear Family. I can't say if they are on their way home or looking for a new destination. They pass out of view, behind a tree that stands at the roadside a little way down the street, from which they never emerge. I tell myself that I am getting used to seeing them and to seeing them disappear, but I never quite manage to forget them, never quite get used to their fleeting appearances. Expecting them, watching them, is unsettling, like waiting for a broken clock to stop. Every day they come. And as the seasons change, so the light of the day dims earlier and earlier, until they process along the street in darkness. And as the darkness transforms what was afternoon into evening, I notice how the Linear Family takes on a curious luminosity, more than the light given to them by the streetlamp under which they pass. They seem to glow and in the dimly shining spaces between them, I can see now that they are not alone.

Entwined among them, but unseen by them, walks a second procession, formed of skeletal figures. Each of these figures wears a costume, at the extremities of which protrude the fleshless bones of feet and hands and neck and skull. They are dressed as priest, policewoman, barrister, soldier, nurse, some in less formal clothes that suggest other humbler or more ambiguously defined occupations. As they become more visible, I can hear a very faint music, fracturing the winter silence, to which they skip and gyrate. Together they form a random sample of privileges, aspirations and misfortunes that convey, in the mix and struggle of their dance, a sickening futility.

Seemingly infected by the motion of the interweaving figures, the Linear Family starts to sway. Mother, girls and father begin to dance. Perhaps they have always been dancing and I've just not noticed before. The light they shed shines on their skeletal companions, whose darkness draws out their light and sucks it away, so that all the figures start to ebb and flow in and out of visibility. Next to the mother another skeletal form appears, in bow tie and tails, waving a baton in the air to mark the time. He is joyful and laughing and urges them all on. The sound of the music brings back a childhood memory, of pipes and drums, another unnerving procession seen through a different window. As I watch them, time becomes for me at once halting and endless, uncertain, circular, monstrous.

They dance briskly, the Linear Family, in their ever-repeating procession, oblivious of unclaimed futures and mislaid pasts, always returning; they hurry towards their inexorable, unknowable fate – just like us all.

DON'T TELL THE PRIEST
by Jonathan Willmer

'Who did you tell?'

'No one. You said not to.'

There it came again, the rapping at the door. Louder this time. Loren shrunk away from it, to the wall at the back, where the light from the fire didn't reach. There was light there, but only in thin shards, in the gaps between the timbers. It was the only sign it was day. Isaac's eyes drifted again to the thing in the corner of the hut. Every time he looked, there was the same shock as the first time he saw it. It never got normal.

'Might be Peter,' said Loren. 'Might be Carol. Carol said she'd be bringing some onions round.'

'It isn't Peter or Carol,' hissed Isaac. 'It's the priest.'

Loren flinched at the word. 'I never told the priest.'

'You said you never told no one.'

Too long passed before Loren said anything, so Isaac knew.

'Doesn't matter who you tell,' he said. 'People talk.'

Third time now, the knock came.

'Why must it be the priest then?'

'It's the tapping. It's a ring or a staff on the wood, it isn't skin. Peter or Carol haven't any rings or staffs. It's the priest.'

There came his voice now, through the wood. 'Isaac? Loren? It's Father William. I didn't find you on the fields so I thought you must be here.' The priest's voice was assured and kind. 'I'm concerned.'

'He knows we're in. Smoke's coming out,' Loren whispered.

Isaac walked over the hard mud and straw and pulled the door open. After the dark of the hut, the white daylight around the priest made him look holy. Isaac blinked and squinted.

'Father,' he said.

'Isaac.' The smile on the priest's fat ruddy face was broad. 'I was starting to think you didn't want me here.' The priest laughed.

'Oh no,' said Isaac. He looked down at the floor. 'No, not that.'

'Well?'

Isaac looked up at the priest.

'Will you let me in?'

Isaac tried to smile but he could only grimace. He stepped back into the hut and let the priest pass.

The priest stood in front of the fire. The fire was in the middle of the hut, under the hole in the roof. Not all the smoke got away through the hole. The hut was smoky, and the light didn't get all the way to the corners. There was no need to panic. The priest wouldn't spot the thing in the corner. Isaac wanted to say so to Loren, but he couldn't with the priest there. He wondered what the priest knew.

Isaac was still standing near the door. He wondered whether he should go and stand right in front of the thing in the corner, to block the priest's view of it. Or whether he should stand across the room from it, to draw the priest's eye away. For want of deciding, he didn't move an inch.

Loren came forward from the back wall and into the light. 'Hello Father,' she said.

'Loren! I haven't seen you around the village lately. You're all right I hope?'

'Yes Father. I'm well enough.'

Maybe he knew nothing, maybe that's all he came for.

'Good. Good.' The priest looked into the fire for a long time. He didn't move. He looked like he was deciding how to say something.

He drew a breath. He held it for a moment before he spoke.

'I was talking to Ruth yesterday.' He said it like it was only small talk.

Isaac looked over at Loren. Of all the people in the village she might've told.

'I said to Ruth I hadn't seen you in a while. Said I was worried. And Ruth said she'd seen you, Loren. Said she talked to you not long ago, at the well.'

The priest looked through the fire at her. His face, through the flames and riddled with grog blossoms, looked perfectly red.

'Said you're in a bit of trouble.'

Loren didn't talk and neither did Isaac.

'Something I might be able to help you with.'

The priest looked about the hut. Casual, like he was looking around for a child who was hiding out of shyness.

'I don't know what you mean, Father.' Loren couldn't keep her voice breezy like the priest could. It wavered a bit above a whisper and it didn't fool anyone.

'Haven't seen your cow out on the pasture for a while, Isaac.'

'Cow died two months back.'

'Ah yes. I remember. Good age, wasn't she?'

'Decent. Twelve or so.'

'Hmm. Two months.'

The priest started to make a very slow circuit of the hut. He walked around the fire, but his attention was on the walls. Isaac watched the priest. There was a chance he would walk past the thing in the corner without seeing it. There was still a chance he didn't know.

'Long time to go without milk. Henry's had calves. Month or so ago. He's been looking to get rid of a couple.'

'Not looking at the moment.'

'No? You're looking thin.' The priest paused his circuit to look at each of them in turn. 'You're both looking thin.'

When the priest came round to Loren's side of the fire, she saw that his heavy black robe was crusty with mud from the knees down. The fire showed up in the fat gold ring on his right hand, so it looked like his finger was ringed with flame. And on top of his head, his thinning white hair thrust away in all directions. He looked frightening, and Isaac had told her he was a dangerous man, but when he spoke, his genial baritone still put her at ease.

'I spoke to Henry as well. Week or two ago.' The priest paused, and when he wasn't speaking, there was only the cracking of the fire and the soft shuffling of his feet on the mud and straw. 'Said you took one of his calves. Week after it was born.'

'Ah,' said Isaac. 'Ah, yes. We did. Had to give it back.'

'He told me that too. You know it died?'

'Ah. No, Father, I didn't know that.'

'Never the same, so Henry said. Wouldn't eat or sleep or sit down even. Henry says it wouldn't blink. Died a few days later.'

'I am sorry to hear that.'

The priest stopped walking and then there was just the crackle of the fire. 'Is this where you kept the cow?'

Isaac couldn't get a word out. Instead he did a sort of grunt.

The priest looked into the corner for a long time. Isaac and Loren looked too. Because they were used to it being there, they knew what to look for. It took the priest longer to make it out, in the darkness.

Isaac could only see the back of the priest, but it was enough. He saw his shoulders arch, and he saw him step back a pace, and he knew that the priest had seen it.

The corner was dark, but the shape of the dead cow was black. It was black even at night, when there was no light at all, so that Isaac and Loren had realised they had never seen black at all, before the cow died.

They should have killed the cow a year before, when its udders started to dry up, but Loren was attached, and so was Isaac, if he was honest. So they left it, and they woke up one morning to find it dead in its bed in the corner.

There had been no confusing it for a sleeping cow. It was twisted and contorted. Its neck was thrown back. Its eyes were wide and its mouth was open. Its front legs we thrown forward and its hind legs were splayed, and its back was arched terribly. It looked like it had died violently, but nothing had woken Isaac or Loren in the night.

The two of them had carried the dead cow out into the grey dawn. It was stiff like it was frozen. They buried it in the copse. There was something about the cow they didn't want anyone in the village to see.

When they came back to the hut, the cow was not gone.

'My God,' whispered the priest. His voice now was neither kind nor assured. He looked round at Loren, and then at Isaac, and then back at the black form of the cow. It was the shape of the cow when it died, but all black, not like a shadow, but an imprint, like the cow was stamped on the air.

Neither of them had slept much since. Loren said she was scared of it getting inside her. Isaac said what will it do, go up your nose? Neither of them had laughed.

The priest moved a step closer to it. 'Devil's been at work here.'

This was why Isaac wouldn't tell the priest. Maybe the priest could get rid of it, but he knew he'd say they were devils and witches, and they weren't. They farmed their patch, like everyone else.

The priest turned away from the thing in the corner. His head span between both of them, and his face, already red from the heat and the light of the fire, looked crimson. Isaac thought that it would certainly explode.

'Devil's work,' the priest said again. The compassion in his voice was gone. There was only fear and anger. Fear and anger, sitting one on each shoulder and whispering one in each ear. It was what he spat from the pulpit at every Sunday sermon, and it was just behind every kind word he spoke.

'I never thought it of you, Loren.' He turned to Isaac. 'And you,' he said. 'Harbouring a witch.'

Neither of them said anything. There was no point defending themselves. No point telling him they had nothing to do with it. The priest's mind was made up. Loren had tried to bring the cow back from the dead, and it went wrong. People in the village had been drowned for less.

A good priest would have tried exorcising the thing in the corner. But theirs was a bad priest. He preferred to use his power on people.

He looked at Loren.

'You'll be hanged,' he said.

He turned to Isaac.

'Both of you.'

The two stayed quiet. The fire cracked and threw a cluster of sparks into the room. At the noise, Loren lunged forward and pushed the priest with both arms. She wasn't strong, but the priest wasn't ready for it. He didn't fall, he only stumbled back a step. Not even a step, but his right foot landed squarely in the black form. He stood there like that for a second, one leg behind the other, his right foot lost inside the black gloom. His eyes opened wide and he drew a breath sharply. He shifted his right foot out of the black. The black swirled around like it was mist, and settled back as it was. It had done the same when they tried to put the new calf there.

The priest stood straight. He looked dead ahead. There wasn't any fear or anger in his eyes any more. There didn't seem to be much of anything.

A BUMPY RIDE TO HEAVEN
by Alain Li Wan Po

The one-line cryptic WhatsApp message read, 'Have you heard about Paul's wife?' No, I had not heard about Virginie! When I did, I needed fresh air, time to recover, time for reflection. It was about 5.30 pm that October day when I walked down the concrete steps that led straight to the beach from the Mauritius villa where I was staying. The sun, which had lost its searing daytime fire, wrapped its balmy arms around my shoulders as if to say it'll be alright. The sun worshippers had mostly decamped to get ready for dinner. Those left were waiting to see the final crescent of the sun dip into the shimmering sea against the psychedelic orange of the sky; a sight to stir the soul. Here and there were people praying, some to the sun, others to gods or spirits, some alone, others in small groups.

'I saw Jesus rise in the horizon in a brilliant white silver-lined shroud,' my friend Paul told me once.

The last time I visited the island before the WhatsApp's message was a year earlier. I had come to act as best-man for Paul's wedding to Virginie, a mutual friend, one of the prettiest girls on the island. They were well matched; both intelligent, both in well-paid jobs, both with inherited wealth. There was a nice, beautifully located, freshly redecorated and spacious house, ready for the groom to take his bride across the threshold. At the wedding there was an embarrassment of good things to say about them. There was no need to invent, no need to add fiction to reality. My only slight embarrassment was when I was standing in church witnessing their exchange of vows in the name of God, in whom I had long stopped believing. From the intensity with which they looked at each other, it was clear that Paul and Virginie were deeply in love, that any god and any spirit would look after them, and that they would have an idyllic life together, and they did, at least for a while.

The sojourn in heaven can be transient sometimes. Paul and Virginie were readying themselves for their first wedding anniversary, planning a long overseas holiday including visiting me in England, when tragedy struck. Sudden death, the coroner said. Young women do not die of heart attacks. Virginie did.

Paul became unhinged. He was naked and had a distant stare when he opened the door to the ambulancemen. They helped him dress. He refused to return to his house, once of idyll, now of too much pain. He would not allow anyone to intrude, locking his house up for good. He rented a small cottage, perhaps better described as a wreck, not too far from the villa where I was staying.

'We sometimes see him. He refuses to speak to us, and does not even seem to recognise us,' one friend said. 'Scruffy looking, and so sad,' said another. 'You'd think he was one of the beggars in town near the marketplace.' Dishevelled and almost emaciated, Paul would sit staring out to sea in a fathomless world of his own. My emails remained unanswered, as did those of my friends.

As I was walking along the beach on this second visit, I was gripped with a sudden desire to see my old friend. Lonely pensive walks do such things to you. I cut my walk short and jumped into my car heading for his cottage. It was no more than ten minutes away but as it was set back from the road, I had to walk another five minutes before I saw the hut, much shabbier than even I had imagined from my friends' descriptions. The wooden battens that served as a door appeared unhinged, and the thatch had slid down to the ground in some places.

'Paul? Paul?' I called, some ten yards away from the door, hesitating before I proceeded further by slow steps. I looked through the gaps between the loose battens. It was dark inside, darker than the dusk that was closing in. When my eyes adjusted, I saw some matting on the floor, an old wicker chair, a DIY pine table with two dented and encrusted aluminium pots, a chipped enamel dinner plate, a pock-marked metal mug, and a half-stick of bread.

'Hello. What are you looking for?'

The voice that came from behind startled me. I turned and saw Paul, haggard, dirtier, face unshaven for long, clothes tattered, but him for sure, flesh and bones, mostly bones.

'Paul!' I exclaimed, loud enough to scare the whole neighbourhood of tropical birds, as I rushed towards him, but then stopped abruptly for fear of knocking him down to the ground as he showed no reaction or sign of recognition. He had none of the smile that used to lighten his face permanently when I saw him at his wedding five years earlier. He had aged fifteen, maybe twenty, years with thinning grey hair, almost bald. He lifted his right arm slowly and placed it on my left shoulder.

'I am glad you came. I have a favour to ask. I have been waiting for four years.'
As there was not enough sitting room in his hut, we sat on a log just outside. He stood up again almost immediately heading for his hut.
'Would you go to my house and pick up something for me?' he asked. 'You were my best man.'
I promised to go the next day. Friends had told me that his house was haunted, so spooky and of such terrifying repute that even burglars had kept away from it. On the paradise island, empty houses were ransacked within days.

Paul's had been unvisited for four years. Believing in neither god nor ghost, I would have gone to Paul's house that evening, but it was dark, and the house was a good hour and a half drive away.

The following day, I set off after lunch when the traffic was less dense as I needed to cross the capital, Port-Louis, before reaching the house in Rose-Hill in the middle of the island. It was three o'clock when I got to the gate, once painted in shiny black enamel, now chipped and rusty. The path of granite blocks was overgrown with weeds and the two patches of lawn on either side had merged with the flower borders. A rose bush with hips of many a year was defiant with its fungus-infested leaves and thorny, bendy stems. Dandelions were juggling for space with nettles and brambles. Some of the wooden tiles had fallen off the roof to beat down the weeds. Threatening Black Widows were spinning their webs on the thorny blackberries and flashing their shiny, black, red-spotted bulbous bums. Layers of paint, once brilliant white, now mossy brown, black and grey, were flaking off the frames of the door and windows to leave cracks that sank deep into the bleached wood. A huge badamier with its large leaves shaded the house to add to the gloom. Hitchcock would have been happy with this setting. As I unlatched the gate, a neighbour poked his head out of his stone-walled gate some twenty feet away but immediately rushed back without saying a word or waving, as if I were a ghost. I slid the key into the lock, surprisingly still smooth as I twisted, but the door was jammed. The frame had swollen with the moisture that had seeped into the naked wood. I pushed hard, once, twice. It yielded on the fourth heavier shoulder. It was dark inside. All the blue velvet curtains were drawn, and the side windows were shut closed with both layers, the outer usually only when cyclones threatened. I still remembered the lay-out of the house from my previous visit in happier times. The living room came first. The sofa was still as I remembered it, but the leather was dusty and had cracked and lost its shine. Cobwebs were in all corners. Two empty cups and Albert Camus' La Peste were on the teak coffee table. The musty smell was invasive, an odd mixture of mushroom and sawdust. It was then that I sensed the sepulchral chill of the room.

'The envelope is in the left-hand side-drawer of the bed,' Paul had said.

I headed for the master bedroom right at the back. I remembered that you could see the mountains through the large sliding door that led to the garden. The storm shutters were drawn making the bedroom even darker than the living room. Near the door was an expensive wheel-on travel bag. Samsonite. I went to my right across to the left of the bed towards the side-drawer. On the floor near the foot of the bed were a scarlet silk bathrobe and a black lacy bra; a little further along, matching knickers and some men's briefs; Pierre Cardin. On the bed, sex toys. The remains of a wild morning of pleasure that ended so tragically, I thought to myself. I recalled being told that Paul was naked when, distraught, he opened the door to the ambulancemen. I sidestepped the clues and opened the drawer to find the envelope, exactly as Paul had described it – Thin white glossy cardboard wallet with IATA and its blue logo printed on it. Out of respect, I slid it into the inside left breast pocket without looking inside. The room grew even colder. I could sense a presence. Did I leave the front door open? Had somebody walked in? I closed the drawer and was making my way out when I saw a sleek woman with long shiny black hair sitting on the other side of the bed, clothed in a white satin dressing gown, looking the other way.

'Would you be kind enough to put my undies in my travel case?' asked the woman in a gentle voice without turning towards me. It was unmistakably

Virginie's voice. Surprisingly, her voice made me less tense, easing the pounding of my heart.

'Virginie?' I enquired. There was no answer, but I could hear thunder in the distance. Weird, I thought, as the weather was not bad when I first arrived. I gathered all the trappings of desire into the case and zipped it shut. I was going to carry it to Virginie when a sudden blinding flash lit the bedroom, as if a blade of fire had seared through the roof. When I readjusted my eyes, Virginie was gone. There was no damage to the ceiling.

I was shaken but not frightened. Tricks of imagination, I said to myself when I carefully locked up the house, closed the gates and headed north. The dull late October sun was still trying to peek through the grey sky, but only succeeded to throw some lighter patches. No sign of stormy weather though. It was still light when I got back to Paul's hut. He came to greet me at the door and thanked me without inviting me in or joining me outside. He flicked the wallet open, and I could see what looked like some air tickets. There was a hint of a smile in his weathered face.

For the next four evenings, I went back to Paul's hut armed with sandwiches for us both. He was nowhere to be found. No one remembered seeing him. The assistant at the local shop he visited occasionally for his meagre needs had not seen him. She knew the 'poor man.' I went to the local police station but again drew a blank. I drove to his old house to check if he might have moved back, but it looked as abandoned as when I last saw it. I rubbed the dust off one of the window panes to peer inside. The sitting room was in the same state. The two cups and Camus were still there.

My holidays had come to an end. All good and bad things have an end. I had just been waved through passport control at Heathrow Terminal Four when I was stunned by Virginie's commanding voice. I looked back and, in the distance that would normally have been beyond earshot, saw Paul and Virginie as smartly dressed as in their happier days. I waved and wished them bon voyage, smiling to myself. Virginie had her travel case with her; the one I helped pack.

THE ART LOVER
by Maggie Small

A psychologist once asked me: 'If you were a colour, which would it be?' I had no trouble with that one: the colour of blood. Not the bright, arrogant scarlet of arterial blood, pumping a body dry in a matter of minutes, garish and vulgar, but the more subdued shade of a darkly oozing wound, veering to a rich maroon as it dries. Beautiful. Of course I haven't had the pleasure of observing and comparing these nuances at leisure for many years now.

My lawyer, a court-appointed boy fresh out of law school and full of abolitionist zeal, wears green socks with a lozenge pattern - hideous. He means well, but I clearly have no mitigating circumstances at all, unless you count a weakness for artistic innovation. 'Why did you do it?' he kept asking. I couldn't remember any other reason.

There's the warder peering through the spy-hole again. His job is to make sure I don't deprive them of the ultimate spectacle: the family arrayed behind the glass on those cheap chairs, the starched-white figure of the attendant doctor standing to one side, the pale glint of a syringe… they're all like me; interested in killing. They're going to get to do it soon, too. The show opens tomorrow morning, before dawn.

It won't be a festival of polychrome, though - merely another second-rate study in black and white, uninspired and over-rehearsed; a tableau vivant of no aesthetic merit whatsoever.

VIOLATION
by Suzanne L. Burn

A beautiful afternoon in early September, saw Ellie picking a careful route amongst ancient graves. She wore a high necked black maxi dress which gave little concession to the late summer heat, with her blond hair scraped back severely into a tight bun. She would never gratify a man again.

Her expensive camera felt heavy as she reached a newer headstone set close to the church wall. She paused, and gazed up at a winged creature carved high into the blackened façade of St Mary's. The Gargoyle screamed silently into the void, its face frozen into a terrified rictus, mirroring the tragedy of her youth.

'You can do this.' Her brother Nathan's voice echoed through her mind. 'You haven't built a career in investigative journalism by shying away from challenges.'

She knelt down and gently touched the small headstone in front of her, the granite cool against her skin, the inscription simple:

Baby Johnson
2am 10th October 1988 – 3.15am 10th October 1988.

Nobody had given her the choice of where he would be laid to rest. Nobody cared. They were all complicit in her suffering, shaming her almost to breaking point. She couldn't cry anymore, there was just a hard knot of anger in her chest which made her catch her breath. She was just sixteen when Father Liam violated her trust and her body inside the Church, only four yards from where she now knelt. The memory of that night was ingrained on her psyche, Father Liam's cruelty was perpetuated through her baby's grave, and she raised her head towards the Gargoyle once more.

'He used to tell me that you would protect me from sin' she whispered, and then checked her watch, confirmation class would soon be over.

Young female voices drifted towards her, as she took the lichen covered path round to the West door.

'Ellie? Ellie Johnson?' Two teenage girls approached her, but kept glancing back towards the West door.

'Yes, oh Caitlyn and Sara, I'm so relieved to meet you both at last', said Ellie, 'are you sure you're ready to go through with what we've discussed by phone? The last thing I want to do, is to put any sort of pressure on you.'

'We're more than ready,' said Sara, 'that bastard needs to be brought down!'

'Wait for me around the corner, stay out of sight,' said Ellie softly, and she prepped her camera as she strode towards the door. Father Liam appeared in the doorway with his arm around another girl's shoulders.

'Still acting inappropriately around your pupils Liam? You don't remember me, do you, but you will when my testimony and those of two more of your victims, are read out in court. Smile for the camera.'

THE JUNGBOTS OF FRONTIER SCOTLAND
by Dini Armstrong

"Where the hell have you been?" Duncan wiped the sweat off his forehead and briefly tapped his wrist implant. The release mechanism buzzed the door open, just long enough for Alban to join him inside the lab.

"I was stuck in the cupboard," he said. "Couple of randy co-workers. Tried not to look but that was some freaky stuff. Thank Christ he didnae last long. No sure I could've stomached any mair."

Duncan raised an eyebrow. Now a cleaner, Alban had access to the Frontier Scotland building. However, he had no permission to enter the nanotech lab, and any attempt to use his own implant would have triggered an alarm.

"Glad to hear you are able to stomach drilling a hole in my forehead," Duncan mumbled.

"Nae worries, pal," Alban retorted, "not much in there to damage anyway."

They had to finish the trepanning procedure before the night shift arrived at eleven pm. That gave them exactly forty-eight minutes.

"I don't want to come across as thick, like, but have you considered just injecting the little buggers into your veins?"

Duncan explained. The Jungbots had to be injected directly into the brain tissue. Other methods had been tried but failed as even nanotechnology was too large to pass through the blood brain barrier. He took a swig of malt whisky straight from the bottle, the peaty kind, twenty-six years old. Alban stretched out his hand, but Duncan refused, clutching the bottle.

"You've got to be kidding me, pal."

"Fair enough," Alban said. "I'd rather have some real Irn Bru anyway."

Duncan laughed. "Fat chance."

The other employees of the Frontier Scotland lab had left at six pm, giving Duncan enough time to sterilise a drill bit, only marginally thicker than the needle on the syringe he had prepared. He walked over to the sink and washed his hands. He had learned the procedure from re-runs of Scottish Superhospital, an old TV series in which surgeons still had to prep for surgery. He scrubbed each arm first, then worked his way over the sides of each finger, before cleaning his nails with a small file. The doctors on TV would then ask a scrub nurse to help them don the sterile gown and gloves. No nurse for Duncan. No anaesthetist either, for that matter. Alban was standing by the window, observing tourists on Freedom Square, meandering in T-shirts and short strapless sundresses; the blistering summer heat would linger on until much later. Most locals would have returned home by now.

Frontier Scotland had begun human trials three weeks ago, and all participants, all diagnosed as terminal, had volunteered, enticed by the promise of a fat cheque for the families they left behind. The procedure of inserting nanobots was quite safe and had been successfully trialled on primates.

"Pass me the …," he began, but, hesitating, he put the gloves on by himself, struggling to pull the thin biodegradable material over his moist skin.

"Wash your hands," he commanded.

Duncan had tried to carry out the procedure by himself last night, without success. He had looked into the mirror, raised the drill like a gun and pointed it at a spot he had just cleaned with an alcoholic swab, half a centimetre above his eyebrows. It was difficult to keep the point steady at this angle and he'd decided instead to support the drill with both hands and work the on-switch with his right thumb. He'd thought of Mhairi. Fifteen years old, smiling, dressed in her Taekwondo kit. She would have been furious to know that this was the photo the media had circulated for the past six months, since February 25th, 2030. He'd been surprised to find that he no longer had any emotional response to the image and was incapable of conjuring any other. He had started to shake uncontrollably, forcing him to go back to plan A and involve Alban. What if he passed out? What if he didn't find his way back?

"Talk me through this," Alban said.

"I've programmed them to take me to the day before she disappeared," said Duncan.

"February 23rd," stated Alban without hesitation.

"Exactly. If this works."

No one at Frontier Scotland had any idea that he had adapted their precious nanobots, originally designed to connect the human brain with a super-cloud, allowing it to not only upload thoughts but to also download an unlimited amount of knowledge, creating a collective unconscious. Hence the brand name: Jungbots. It was considered a minor setback that seventy-eight percent of the volunteers had committed suicide within a week of the trial. Duncan, senior nanotechnologist, was the first to spot the potential of using bots to seek out specific memories within the brain and reactivate them, essentially allowing the user to relive a specific moment from their life. He was aware of the commercial ramifications of his discovery, but for now, he had to keep it secret, avoiding medical trials and stringent procedures which would inevitably be enforced to protect the patent.

"So how is this going to work? Like watching a movie or something?"

"No, we perceive the world around us as real because our nerves take in sensory information and our brain puts the whole thing together as our reality. The bots will activate all of the sensory information as well, so it should feel and smell and taste just like a real experience."

"Fuck," Alban stated, matter-of-factly. "You've just gone and invented time travel, old man. Can you change what happened? Can you, you know, can you …?"

"Bring her back?"

Alban nodded.

"No." He paused. "The bots can only activate what's already in my memory bank. I think it will be a bit like time travel, but I can't do anything new. What I can do is pay attention."

With any luck he would be able to observe details with much more care than he did the first-time round. When he thought he would have an entire future with Mhairi. When he took it all for granted.

"And can you come back any time you want?"

"Ah, now there's where you come in. I need you to 'hang up' for me, so to say." He handed Alban a small device. Alban inspected it. It was a taser, the label read Strathclyde Police.

"You are kidding me, really? Is this from the twentieth century?"

Duncan nodded. "I am afraid it's the only way I could think of. Hopefully I will come up with something else soon."

He sat down on the reclined chair, bum first, careful not to touch anything with his gloved hands. Next to him he had arranged the drill and syringe on a clean towel.

"Get on wi' it, lad," he joked, "quit cuttin' aboot the toon aa day."

The vibrations of the drill in his skull made him feel nauseous but, somehow, he managed not to throw up. There was a brief cracking sound and then a pulling sensation when Alban tried to pull the drill back out. Just put it in reverse, he wanted to say, but then he noticed the beautiful light flooding in through the window. It shimmered on Alban's black hair, he wanted to stroke it, so soft, so smooth.

"Haud still just now," Alban commanded. You are beautiful, he wanted to say, you are so shiny. Alban lifted the syringe, it glistened in the light, just full of clear fluid, lovely clear silky fluid. He wanted to drink it. He wanted to …

"So, can I?" Duncan heard Mhairi plead, before he noticed that his eyes were already open. His vision was surprisingly sharp, more acute than in real life somehow. His hands were on a steering wheel. Funny how long it had taken him to stop doing that and let the auto drive take over. It was not until after the worst had happened that he was finally able to let go of the controls, plus he wanted no distractions in case his communicator was activated. That didn't mean he trusted the new vehicles, if you could call them that. Especially since they were no longer using electricity pods but instead generated the charge from thin air, using a tank full of geobacter. After the Coronavirus pandemic in the early twenties, many had been wary of using bacteria in their tanks, but it had been the breakthrough that had given Scotland a place on the table as one of the richest EU nations. Thankfully, they had already broken away from Westminster at that point, just years before England had been taken over by the totalitarian regime of the WhitBrit party. Duncan called them the Shit-Wits. That, and Scotland's continued EU membership, had enticed business away from England. In addition to this, President Sturgeon had made the right choice in focussing on the development of renewables and IT; she had cleverly noticed that Scotland, other than drier countries, would be able to provide the moisture rich-environment that was necessary for the geobacter-drive to work efficiently.

Oh god, there was Mhairi, on the passenger seat, her eyes wide open, mascara still clumsy, eye shadow too thick and too colourful, an unsettling contrast to her school uniform. You're beautiful as you are, he wanted to say, I miss you, I am sorry I wasn't there. Where are you? Instead, his lips, throat and jaws formed the words:

"I don't know, girl. Who else is there?"

Mhairi shrugged. "Just a couple of my pals, I guess."

"Any boys?" Duncan asked.

"Dad, you are so old-fashioned!" He had forgotten how often they had argued this point. Binary gender definitions were no longer used, and yet she had come out as cisgender. Choosing one side over another, there was a stigma to that. Maybe it was because when her mum died, Mhairi had inherited her wedding dress, and Duncan had one day caught her trying it on. Not that many people married anymore. Most opted for that new-fangled cohab agreement, which automatically expired after five years, unless it was renewed.

"So, can I go? I promise I'll be home before eleven." Duncan noticed that Mhairi seemed nervous. Her hands were in her lap and she was fiddling with her communicator scar, running her index finger over the bump under her skin, as if she was expecting it to activate. Handheld mobile devices had been banned in 2025, when it was found that their addictive properties were too damaging for productivity, health and relationships. Even birth rates had plummeted to a dangerous low. A different part of his brain remembered the look of the bloodstained chip in the evidence bag and shuddered. It was all they found.

His head turned and he noticed a woman crossing the road. She had long shapely legs and her skirt was just a little too short. Focus, he wanted to shout at himself, focus!

"Da?" he heard Mhairi's voice. "Oh, sure, whatever," he heard himself say. The woman was wearing a blouse and a gust of wind exposed her breasts for the fraction of a second. But Duncan was prepared for this. He had replayed and replayed this memory in his mind long before the bots were inserted, ever since he woke up on February 25th, noticed that Mhairi had not come back, had cursed himself for falling asleep, had searched for her, in the city, in the country, in the world, in his mind. He was determined not to miss what his daughter was saying this time.

"Uncle Al will give me a lift."

A piercing pain in his heart, ice-cold, metallic, jolted him back into the present, before he had a chance to process her words. He looked down at his blood soaked shirt, then up at Alban, holding the drill, eyes wide open like back in the day, when he was just a wee boy, who had kicked a football through the neighbour's window, and he couldn't help but smile at him, before he slowly drifted out of time, forever.

BILE
by John K Ellingsen

Pick that up for me, will you? That's your universe you're holding in your hand. To find something like this, here. In a Seven Eleven of all places.
Lucky you.

You take the universe, a milky bar, and hold it up for the cashier to scan. Then you notice it. The black ooze. All over the card terminal. Black fingerprints on the number pad. A streak of black bile across the NFC screen. You freeze. The beep of the scanner snaps you back. You jam the candybar down into the pockets of your red barbour jacket. Did the scanner touch it? No, you would have noticed.

"Hey, are you gonna pay for that candy, or what?" The cashier says. As you scramble around in your pockets, your bus ticket falls out. You consider a moment to pick it back up, but no. It isn't safe. Not with the ooze already here.

"I'm just, I'm gonna pay." You say, and take out a bag of surgical gloves.

"What the fuck?" The cashier stares at you. It's routine by now. First one hand, then the other.

"I just gotta be safe. Gotta be safe, you know?"

You know he doesn't, you see the ooze already on him. It's in his long scruffy hair. You can almost see the ooze seeping into his follicles. He's done for, for sure. He doesn't even know it, but he's done for. At least he didn't touch you with that scanner. That would have been it, game over.

You stare into his eyes, hidden behind his glasses. He can't see what you see. You hope he sees you're sorry for him.

You take out your debit card, hold it carefully over the NFC pad. The first two lights light up, the beeps of the card being recognized ring in your ear. You're hyper focused, time crawls to a stop. Your heart thumps once, it feels like it wants to punch its way through your ribcage. You peer at the card terminal, just in time to see the streak of black ooze across the NFC area bunch together, like tiny army ants. It wants to reach your card. It's a way in. It could get you like this. It won't reach it, you pray. Please don't reach it. The third light flicks on, and another sound rings loud in your ear.

You have to make a choice now.

Can you do it, can you sacrifice your debit card for safety? It's your only source of cash, but in another couple of milliseconds it's nothing but a worthless plastic piece of trash. You're going to have to get rid of it. Burn it. Along with the gloves.

You let it linger.

Just as the final light lights up on the terminal, and the final "Beep" drones out. Just as your sensory world reunites with real time. Just as your heart once again yearns to break free of your body, your card gets touched. It's just a tap, but it's enough. A small dot of black ooze in the very corner of the card. Shit.

You hold the card extended outwards, and run out the store.

"Hey, kid! What the… Are you okay?" The cashier, dumbfounded, stares at your back as you stumble outside.

Shit, shit, shit, shit. You've got it on your card. You dumb fuck.

You only bought a milky bar, you idiot. You're fucked. All this for a milky bar.

"But no," you think. "Not just a milky bar. The only part of existence still clean. Still pure. And I have it. I Have it in my pocket."

You look around you. The Seven Eleven you just left is remote. A long road leads in both directions. Some gas pumps, but no cars. You look at the card and panic. The ooze, it managed to reach your glove. Somewhere around here you have to make a fire. Burn the card, burn your gloves. Quickly before it spreads.

Look, around you, what do you see?

Quick! Tell me!

"I see the forest, that's all." you say to yourself. "Just trees. But that's good. The forest is calm, nice, and clean."

You move into the forest.

Idiot. What are you doing? You're contaminated, you'll just bring it with you, into the forest. You'll ruin it as you ruined your home. You got to dispose of the card and the gloves first.

Now!

You look at your hand, holding the card. A small black line slowly crawls over your thumb, reaching for your knuckles, you imagine the line burning your skin, and you feel it. A searing pain, like your thumb splitting open, dividing in two.

You scream.

Just let go of the card, just drop it here, and the gloves, and run away. Drop it here, at the edge of the forest, and run away. The opposite direction. across the road again, and into the fields beyond. It's probably safe.

"No, I can't just drop it. Who knows, if it reaches the roots then..."

You're right, what will happen if one drop of that black ooze touches the roots below you. Will it just contamine a single tree, or are you trapped in a cage of nothing. Imagine it, eating away everything around you. Eating the trees, the brush, all of it. The very thing now eating your hand.

"But it's not." You say to yourself. "I only imagined that part. It's just on my glove, see?"

You hold up your hand grasping the card. The black bile still runs across your one time use latex glove. Runs down to a small tear between your thumb and forefinger.

Oh shit.

What have you done?

How could you not have noticed this?

How could this even be worth it? Leaving your home like this, with no plan, no future. Nothing to return to.

It's all burned. All of it torched.

Along with Szymańska, the old polish woman on the second floor. She had a broken hip, damnit, she never got out in time. You burned her too.

But that whole building was done for. Touched by this damned ooze. She was better off dying like thi…

Shut up. You killed someone, someone who didn't deserve to die. You ended that old lady, burned her to death. You deemed your place of home unsafe and unclean and set it on fire and ran. To hell with the consequences.

You stare at your hand. You know what you must do.

You look around you, for a sharp rock, or something to tear and break your bones. There is still some lighter fluid left in your bag. If you're quick you can still just cut that dead hand off, then torch the ground where it lands and run.

With your right arm raised high above your head, you crawl along the ground, looking for something, something to chop your own hand off with.

Sweat crawls into your eyes, it stings, and as it reaches your mouth, you taste it, that salty taste of fear and panic. You must look like such a mess, crawling in this weird crablike position, with one hand held high. What a fool you are to end up like this. You could've just stayed home, just kept to yourself. Just live alone, in your apartment.

"I tried that." You think to yourself.

It only took one mistake. One failed delivery. Your package, contaminated. Who knows what or who touched it, it doesn't matter. You left it in the stairway, and ran to your apartment. You needed to clean the stairway. Fire should do the trick. You open your Kitchen closet. Three bottles of lighter fluid, saved just for this. You drench the package, the carpet. the stairs, everything. As the wooden floor burns you run. Through your apartment. Through the kitchen. Out the window. The emergency stairwell. It only took one mistake. You panicked. Burnt down an entire building. You panicked. You coward, you big, dumb coward.

Fucking coward, do something! You just lost precious seconds wandering in your own thoughts. Just fucking grab something, you idiot!

Your left hand grabs hold on a long, oval shaped granite rock.

Now do it. Chop it off!

You put your right hand down on an exposed root.

Coward, just do it! Just fucking get rid of it now, while you can still escape!

You smash down, landing a direct hit on your wrist. You feel the bones splinter inside, and a pain like a thousand needles all at once piercing your skin, spreading up your forearm. You scream again, tears well up in your eyes. You lift your hand again, and prepare to strike.

"You idiot," you think. "What am I doing?"

"What is wrong with me?" you whimper, as tears flow freely down your chin.

Hold on. Think for once. What are you doing here? You're cutting off your own hand here. Self amputation. Do you even know how to treat wounds this big?

"God, it has to be done though." You say, and sniffle. "Fucking Christ!"

You yell out and strike again. And again.

And again.

The root gives way, and by reflex you try to brace yourself by your weak right hand. A pain like a thousand needles tear through your forearm. You still feel it, as you lay on the ground, screaming. Through tears of pain you inspect your work. The wrist is blue and black and tender. It's twisted and torn, and blood flows from several ruptures. The bone is fractured, and skin and tendons and muscles torn in several places. Nothing but minced meat.

Twist it off, just twist it. You can do that much at least. Twist it off right now.

You grab it with your left hand and after a quick breath, twist as hard as you can. The skin starts to tear, rending open. A fourth time you let out that familiar scream, a scream of prey. That is what you are, prey. Running from the blackness, forever just running. What did you think you could do, really? Wouldn't it be better for you too to just let it run you over, like it has everyone else. When was the last time you visited your parents? Or had friends over?

They are all gone into that vast black emptiness, touched by the ooze. Contaminated. Dead.

You say that to yourself, in your head. As you tear off your hand, in anger, in pain, in desperation.

Now toss it. Toss it away.

You pull back your left hand, and prepare to toss.

Wait.

Wait!

Your eyes open wide, you have lost your debit card.

Shit, oh shit, oh shit.

Where is it? You have to find it.

Fast, quick, find it! We have to get rid of that as well, or all this has been for nothing!

Through searing pain, you turn yourself over on your side. You see it, it's laying on the ground beside you. The black ooze is there also. Your makeshift chopping block is the same, you see it now. It glistens with your blood, of course. But also with that darkness. And as you notice it. You see the trees around all become black.

You did it. You trapped yourself.

"What now?" you ask.

Now you die. You lay down your head, on the ground, and die. Just like the rest. It got you too, in the end.

Then you grab it, that universe in your pocket. A small wrapped milky bar. And as you close your eyes, you drift into it. Safe, finally, from that enveloping dark.

You stare back out with your mind's eye, to your dying body, slowly eaten alive by that black bile. You can almost feel it eating your flesh. You can almost feel the cold loneliness of this madness still. But that's someone else lying there, dead. That's not you.

You are here, wrapped up and safe. Hidden away in a red barbour jacket.

THE TALE OF THE RED BARON
by Henry Loten

A clear April sky.
Burning orange flames.
A plane swivels. It falls falls falls from grace
in an inelegant tumble: it
twists and turns.

His adversary in the machine - The King of the Air -
twists in a corkscrew. Through
the clouds. Turns
above the barren fields hunting
His next victim. Tossing his frame high.

Red as the blood of his prey,
His Lordship locks his target. Toils
behind him. A flurry. A flutter. Then the spin begins.
Round and round: sparks swirl in a
great leaping flame.

Machines up high, rising into an arc. Target in sight.
Breath held. The thrill of the kill.
It falters. It roils. Then
comes the gyrating fall to
the snaking trenches below him.

The fourth plane is downed
by The Baron in His Red Machine. His name made.
His legacy secured. Enough for one day. The Squadron Leader's
swivelling engines and rotating propeller roll Him home
Bloody April's savage scourge.

His Flying Circus of Death entertains the ranks on the ground
as planes pirouette in their domain.
A month of infamy and fear.
Enemies curl through His land up
high and He fells all that come before Him.

A clear April sky.
Burning Red flames.
His plane swivels. It falls falls falls from grace
in a final inelegant tumble: he
twists and turns.

Gnarled remains of Reddened burning wood and steel.
Ousted from his throne, no longer
King or Baron.
His twisted reign of eighty kills ends
with his own. His ruthless tale still swirls.

EAGLE ONE, EAGLE TWO
by R.E. Loten

I need to write this down. If I don't, I'll forget it happened. Forget it was ever more than a story. I'm a writer by trade, but the truth is far stranger than any fiction I could ever invent. Isn't it always though?

I walked past the hotel and shuddered. They were doing it again. Looking at me. I mean, obviously they weren't. How could they? They were made of stone. Stone can't look at you. So why did it feel like that's exactly what they were doing? I gave myself a metaphorical shake. They were just decorations. Nothing more than stone statues designed to make the hotel entrance look grander. And as for the one on the roof, well that was pure eighteenth century patriotism at its very best. The hotel was originally a mansion, built by the wealthy mayor of the town in the days of George III and the architecture was typical of the grandiose posturing such people preferred, with eagles guarding the gates, Britannia on the roof and an abundance of columns and white stucco adorning the smart red brickwork. Everything about it screamed wealthy, imperial Britain. It was a truly beautiful building, but those statues gave me the creeps. I'd only lived in Launceston a few weeks and already I didn't like walking past them at night. Deep down, I knew it was only my over-active imagination having 'fun' with my nerves, but still.

As I reached the opening in the wall which gave access to the outdoor dining area, a woman dressed in black and with a veil covering her face, passed me on the other side of it. A faint waft of lavender drifted behind her and the scent made me turn, as I always do, to inhale it again. It's such a soothing smell: it reminds me of my grandmother.

The woman had disappeared. She'd had no time to enter the bar or the hotel. She was just… gone.

Not giving myself time to think, I turned on my heel and almost sprinted through the old gatehouse and onto the green of the castle grounds beyond. I was mistaken. There was no woman. Or if there was, she was simply hidden behind something. The sun was beating down and I'd been busy all morning building furniture. I was just hungry. That had to be it. Just my tired, hungry brain misinterpreting the signals it had been sent.

I bought myself a pasty from the shop on the High Street and sat by the war memorial to eat it. I know, I know… I sat in the sun in Cornwall eating a Cornish pasty, but honestly, I don't care. The ones from Malcolm Barnecutt's are so nice it's worth being a walking (or in this case, sitting) cliché. I closed my eyes, allowing the glorious weather to chase away the last of the fear that insisted on lurking in the furthest recess of my mind. I scolded myself. How could I have let my imagination run away with me so badly? I'd been in the hotel for several drinks and a meal. I'd spoken to the owners, who were lovely by the way, and on not one of these occasions had there been any hint of ghostly old women. In the short time I'd been in Launceston, I'd realised that one thing the locals were always happy to tell you about was any hint of a ghost. Even if they claim to be completely sceptical themselves, the Cornish know their local history and the accompanying ghosts and I'm pretty sure that one of their favourite past-times is scaring the emmets. Technically, I no longer count as an emmet as I live here and am doing my best to learn the language, but I'm also clearly not Cornish born and bred, so I'm probably still fair game when it comes to the spooky stories. My next door neighbour certainly takes great delight in sharing them with me.

Wiping the last flakes of pastry from the corners of my mouth, I stretched and rose from my seat. For a moment I debated whether to take the longer route back to my flat, past the church and down the narrow path that ran alongside it. It was steeper but it would mean I didn't have to walk past the hotel again. Deciding I was being ridiculous, I jammed my sunglasses firmly back up my nose and headed towards the castle.

'Dydh da.'

Two voices made me jump as the contrast between the shadowy coolness of the gatehouse and the brilliant sunlight momentarily disorientated me. I squinted at the two small figures before my brain processed what they'd said.

'Dydh da.' I smiled apologetically. 'That's about the extent of my Cornish, I'm afraid.'

The two fair haired boys grinned at me.

'Emmet?'

'No, I live here. It's the first time I've heard anyone speaking Cornish though. I'm guessing you must be local. Are you fluent?'

The boys nodded and broke into a stream of Cornish, taking it in turns to gabble away at me.'

I laughed and held up my hands. 'Very impressive boys, but I didn't understand a word!'

They looked at each other and smiled.

'You saw her, didn't you?'

I frowned. 'Who?'

'The old lady.'

I felt my feet root themselves to the ground even as I felt the urge to flee.

'We were sitting up there and we saw you react.'

'Did she say anything?'

'Did she look old?'

I held up my hands. 'I thought I'd imagined her.'

'No, she's real. Well, as real as a ghost can be. She's the old owner's mother. He killed himself, you know. She haunts the house looking for him.'

That caught my attention. It certainly hadn't been in the potted history of the hotel I'd been given.

'That's terrible.'

The boys looked at each other again.

'They say it's because he had his heart broken.'

'He fell in love with a woman and they got engaged. Then she just disappeared. Left him all alone and he drowned himself in the Kensey down by the packhorse bridge.'

I had a feeling I was being wound up. At that point the river is barely more than a stream. The boys seemed to sense my scepticism and hastened to assure me of the truth of their tale.

'Apparently, he just lay down with his face in the water one night. They found him the next day.'

Poor lady, I thought. I said goodbye to the boys and continued down the hill, resisting the urge to check if the eagles were still watching me. Just before I turned the corner I glanced back. The boys were gone, but the eagles were there, heads turned away from each other, watching the hill in both directions. I walked quickly round the bend and back down the road to my flat.

A few days later, I decided to go for a drink. It was a beautiful summer's evening and the view from the hotel terrace was glorious at sunset. I'd been cooped up inside all day and felt I deserved a treat. I walked slowly up the hill, anticipating the cold notes of blueberries and raspberries in the Eagle One gin I'd promised myself if I stayed at my desk all day.

As I sat watching the sun sink slowly behind the trees, I noticed a dark figure alone at a table in the corner of the terrace. For a moment, I looked at my glass: it was still almost full. I looked over again. She was still there. As I processed this, she caught my eye and nodded an acknowledgment. Tentatively I smiled and she beckoned me over. I picked up my drink and took the few steps across the terrace.

'Do I present such a fearsome picture?' she asked.

Her face was deeply lined with age, but now I'd established she was flesh and blood, it held no horrors for me and I shook my head, half-laughing at myself.

'Not in the least. It's only that I caught sight of you a few days ago and you seemed to just vanish and then I was told you were a ghost. A joke, I realise, but it was a bit of a shock to see you sitting there.'

Her answering laugh was dry and brittle, like the rustle of old paper.

'I'm old but I'm not dead yet.'

'My imagination runs away with me sometimes. I'm a writer you see, so it's mostly an advantage, but it does mean I'm easy to frighten. I don't particularly like statues at the best of times and this place is old and it's Cornwall and there's ghosts everywhere. You get the idea! My neighbour thinks it's great fun to torment me with ghost stories.'

'And was it your neighbour who told you I was a ghost?'

I shook my head. 'No. That particular gem came courtesy of two little boys. I bumped into them just outside the gates and they took great delight in telling me the story of the old lady whose son had killed himself, because the woman he loved left him. They said you were his mother still haunting the hotel and looking for him.'

My smile faded away as I took in the expression on her face. Her hand clamped over mine, her grip surprisingly strong given her frail appearance.

'That's no story. My son did kill himself many years ago for that reason, but there's none left alive now who would remember. What did the boys look like?'

'Very like each other. Blonde curly hair. Twins maybe?'

The hand gripping mine convulsed and she made a choking sound.

'One of them had a scar on his cheek.'

Now she mentioned it, I remembered the mark clearly and I nodded.

'That's right.'

'You can't possibly have spoken to them. Those boys are dead.'

I stared at her, feeling the perspiration slide down my back.

'Dead?' I echoed.

'Murdered by a madwoman over a hundred years ago.' I took an unsteady sip from my glass as she continued. 'Local witch. Didn't like the fact her beloved son had taken up with a woman who already had two children. He didn't care, loved them like they were his own, but the witch knew what the woman was really like. On the surface she was loving and kind, but the witch knew. She knew the woman was only pretending. Her son was wealthy. Owned a beautiful house. The woman had nothing. The son wasn't a good-looking boy and he was quiet and shy. Some said it was because his mother had too firm a hand over him. She'd cast a spell on him to keep him close to her. The spell wasn't strong enough though and he fell for the woman. His mother was mad with jealousy. The woman was going to take her son away from her. She was going to hurt him. The witch gave her fair warning. She told the woman she knew what she was about. The woman protested of course: said she truly loved the witch's son. But the witch knew better. She had to protect her son. She cursed the woman and her sons, but the curse went wrong. When her son saw the new statues on the house, he knew what his mother had done and he swore he would never forgive her. She told him he was overreacting, that she'd done it to protect him. The woman had never really loved him, but he wouldn't listen. The witch was worried, so she renewed the spell that kept them bound together, but her son escaped and they found him the next morning, face down in the river.'

I swear I didn't make a sound, but she must have felt my hand twitch, for she tightened her grip on it.

'The spell worked though. The statues remain so the son remains, still wanting to be close to his love. And because the son remains, so must the mother. I've been here a long time, my dear and will be here a while longer.'

She released my hand abruptly and left me alone at the table. The hotel's owner suddenly appeared at my elbow.

'Are you alright?' he asked. 'Mrs Kendall can be a little intense sometimes, but she's generally harmless. Has she been telling you ghost stories about this place?'

I nodded. 'Who is she?'

He frowned. 'She came with the hotel when we bought it. She's a permanent resident and has a suite on the top floor. We only ever really see her for meals.'

I handed him my now empty gin glass, feeling the need to return home to the safety of my flat. Had she been telling me the truth or was she, like my neighbour, entertaining herself at my expense?

As I walked past the hotel entrance I glanced up at Britannia, then my eye fell on the eagles. I stared at the nearest one. It gazed back, unblinking.

This story was inspired by the Charles Causley poems, Eagle One, Eagle Two and Miller's End.

THE STRANGE INCIDENT AT HONEYMAN COTTAGE
by Ron Hardwick

'Tom, what's that noise?'

'I don't know. I'm a dentist, not a mechanic.'

'It's a clattering noise.'

'I can hear it.'

'What is it?'

'Mary, it could be the clutch, the big-end bearings or the sun-roof, for all I know.'

'Don't you think you'd better stop and have a look?'

'Mary, it's January, ten o' clock at night and it's raining cats and dogs. We'll press on.'

Mary sat back in her seat, her mouth in a tight line, arms folded across her lap, her usual stance when her husband defied her wishes.

A mile further on, the car gasped, groaned and breathed its last. Tom brought it to a halt.

The pair sat in silence for several seconds before Mary spoke.

'Better ring the breakdown people.'

'What, out here? We're on the edge of Rannoch Moor. The nearest place for a phone signal is probably Aberfeldy, God knows how many miles away.'

'You'll have to get out and find shelter.'

'On a night like this? I'll get hypothermia before I've gone twenty yards.'

'Well, I'm not going to sit here all night. You're my husband. If you think anything of me, you'll find a friendly farmhouse where we can stay till help comes.'

Tom shrugged his shoulders and opened the car door.

'I might find a rabbit-hole, if I'm lucky,' he muttered.

'You'll need this,' said Mary, and handed him a torch.

Rannoch Moor is one of the most inhospitable places this side of Greenland, especially on a dark, filthy winter's evening. Tom shivered and switched on the torch, which emitted a feeble beam that hardly cut through the horizontal rain. He walked on. He fell over a couple of boulders and was soon soaked to the skin. About five minutes later, his torch picked out a building.

'Never,' he said. 'What a stroke of luck.'

Tom went back and fetched Mary. She clung on to his arm as they stumbled towards the building.

'A farm cottage,' he said as they approached the front door. 'Goodness knows what they farm round here – heather and red grouse, most likely.'

'Never mind that,' said Mary, 'knock on the door.'

Tom did. There was no answer.

'There's no-one in,' he said.

'Knock louder.'

Tom did so. There was still no answer.

'Maybe they're away somewhere. Try and find an open window,' said Mary.

'Mary, my knuckles are red raw with knocking on the door. If you think I'm....'

'Just do it.'

Tom shrugged and moved to the side of the cottage. One of the windows was slightly ajar, and he was able to insert his fingers and yank it open. He clambered through the aperture and fell heavily onto the floor.

'Bloody hell. I've broken my leg.'

Mary, at the window, said:

'Tom, don't be silly. You've only fallen three feet. Go and open the front door.'

Tom had to brush gossamer-thin cobwebs from his face. It was as if he was walking through Miss Havisham's sitting-room. He opened the door and admitted his wife.

'Switch on the light,' said Mary.

Tom flicked a switch.

'No electricity.'

'They mustn't have paid their bill,' said Mary.

'Mary, look around you. No-one lives here.' He shone the torch. Thick dust lay everywhere, untouched for years. A trail of tiny feet in the dust showed that there were some residents - mice. Mary wasn't too fond of mice. They jumped up your skirt when you weren't watching and nibbled at your thighs.

'Light a fire,' said Mary.

'What with?'

'There's some old newspapers over there. You've got some matches. There's the fireplace. Now go to it.'

Tom rolled the newspapers into sticks, grumbling that they never taught this at dental school, laid them in the sooty fireplace and set them alight. There were some lumps of coke scattered round the hearth and as soon as the paper caught properly, Tom laid a few pieces on the fire.

'Tom, I'm tired.'

'There's a horsehair sofa in the corner, so you can bed down on that.'

'Tom, it's filthy.'

'Well, there's a clothes-line in the kitchen. I ran into it when I entered. You can always drape yourself over that.'

'Very funny.' Mary grabbed one of the old newspapers and spread it out over the sofa. She pulled her coat tightly over her slender frame and lay down.

'Where am I supposed to sleep?' asked Tom.

'The floor.'

Tom kicked away the worst of the dust, spread a newspaper out and lay on his back with his hands across his chest. He was drifting into sleep when he heard a voice.

'Help me, please help me.'

'Mary. Is that you?' No answer.

I'm dreaming, he thought to himself, and lay back down.

'Help me, please help me.' It wasn't Mary's voice, for it had a definite Scots accent and Mary came from Saffron Walden.

Tom jerked awake and looked around. Nothing.

It must be this place. It would give anyone the creeps.

He drifted off again, but, minutes later, he felt a cold hand brush his face and he was instantly wide awake.

In the dim light of the dying embers of the fire, he thought he saw a diaphanous figure silhouetted against the fireplace wall. A mirror that lay gathering dust on the mantle-shelf suddenly flew up and dashed itself to pieces.

'Kind sir, I'm sorry I startled you. I needed to attract your attention.'

'Bejesus, a burglar. I don't have any cash on me,' said Tom.

'Pardon me, sir, but I am no burglar.'

'Where in heaven's name are you?'

'You cannot see me. I can only appear for a few seconds. After that, it takes all of my energy to speak to you.'

'If you're not a burglar, then you must be a ghost, and you can forget it. You don't exist. I'm overwrought and freezing. I'm imagining things.'

'Sir, you are not imagining things. What you perceive is all too real. I am the poor unfortunate Bryony MacTighe. I was murdered in this cottage and bricked up behind the fireplace. My spirit is locked in this place and I cannot leave until someone smashes down the wall and releases me.'

'Murdered?' asked Tom. 'Here?'

'Right here, in Honeyman Cottage. I was married to a very bad man, sir. Do you blame me for loving another? Dear sweet Eorghan, with the smiling eyes and tinkling laugh. My brute of a husband found out, and struck me down one dark November night with a flat iron. Oh, he was a wicked, evil, man.'

'What happened to him?'

'He confessed to my murder to a baillie when he was deep in drink. He never revealed my tomb. He was ashamed, sir, of where he'd buried my body. If people knew, they would have torn him limb from limb. He said he'd taken me in a cart to Loch Rannoch, weighed me down with rocks and cast me into the waters. Of course, no-one checked. Why should they?'

'His sentence?'

'He was hanged, sir. He was found guilty of uxoricide by a jury of his peers at the assizes.'

'Uxoricide?'

'The killing of a wife by her husband.'

'I'm dreaming,' said Tom. 'It's a nightmare.'

'All I ask, sir, is for you to release me from my burden. Let me go and join my dear Eorghan, who lies lonely in his grave in St Blane's Chapel churchyard.

'I cannot just smash down a wall for the fun of it,' said Tom, 'Besides, I haven't any tools.'

'There are tools in the outhouse behind the cottage,' said Bryony. 'There is a sledgehammer in there. That ought to suit your needs.'

'Just a minute. When did all this happen?'

'Queen Victoria had just ascended the throne,' said Bryony, 'and it was the time of the Highland destitution.'

'What was that?'

'Crop failure, sir. Many people here were starving.'

'I'm sorry to hear that,' said Tom. 'In all that time, why has no-one else released you?'

'I do not know, sir. I think it is because you are a sensitive and kindly man. I can reach you. Most of the other occupants of Honeyman Cottage have been illiterate and ungodly farm labourers.'

'I see.'

'And you, sir, what profession do you follow? I can see you are a man of refinement.'

'My wife wouldn't agree with you. I'm an orthodontist.'

'Pray, what is an orthodontist? I am unfamiliar with the term.'

'I mend people's teeth. Not very well, I admit.'

'You are a dentist?'

'Yes, for my sins.'

'A noble profession, sir. I had need of dentistry myself. I was in the hands of Ewan MacTavish, the blacksmith, for he was the only man with the necessary equipment.'

'Barbarians,' said Tom.

'What is your name, sir?' asked Bryony.

'Tom. Tom Eastman.'

'Well, Mr Eastman. I am very pleased to make your acquaintance. Will you help me?'

'It's a pity I cannot see you,' said Tom.

'I will make a final effort to manifest myself, but my spirit energy is almost gone.'

For a brief second, Tom saw her when he shone his torch on the fireplace wall. She was a pretty young woman with a full head of red hair, freckles, a smiling face and pellucid green eyes.

'Goodbye, sir, and God bless you,' Bryony said, as she faded from view.

The next morning dawned frosty and bright. Mary awoke, shook herself and rose to her feet.

'Tom, I'm hungry.'

'Well, I can't suggest anything except mouse droppings.'

'Don't be facetious.'

'Mary, don't bother me now. I have something very important to do.'

Tom made his way to the outhouse at the back, put his shoulder against the rotten door and felt it cave in under his weight. As Bryony pointed out, a sledgehammer stood in one corner. He checked to make sure the boxwood shaft wasn't rotten and when he satisfied himself that it was sound, he walked back into the cottage.

Mary shrieked.

'Tom, what are you doing with that?'

'Stand back, woman,' he said, and swung the hammer. The fireplace wall was made of plaster and laths of wood and it gave in immediately to his repeated blows.

Tom stood back and looked at the hole he had made.

Mary screamed..

'Oh, my God, Tom, it's a skeleton. It's murder, unless it's suicide. Fetch the Police. Dial 999.'

'How could it be suicide?' Tom said. 'Unless you've discovered the secret of entombing yourself from the inside.'

'No wonder the place is empty. They must have scarpered after they'd done the evil deed. Tom, maybe it was just last week.'

'Mary, have a look at the skeleton closely, would you?'

'No fear.'

'It's ash grey. It's old as the hills. Besides, if the deed was done last week, it wouldn't be a skeleton at all, would it? It takes about ten years for a corpse to decompose completely, especially in a freezing hell-hole like this.'

'Tom, you're so macabre, knowing stuff like that. It must be all that peering into people's mouths that's turned you into...Burke and Hare.'

'Mary, don't be absurd.'

Tom felt a current of cold air rush from the fireplace and sweep across his face.

'Job done,' he said.

A motorhome driver gave them a tow to a garage in Corrour, where a mechanic replaced the car's alternator and the battery.

'Something I have to do,' said Tom to Mary.

He asked the mechanic for directions to St Blane's Chapel and drove there.

'What's this all about?' asked an exasperated Mary.

'Just checking on something,' said Tom.

He took a walk round the small graveyard. He came upon the only ancient grave upon which the grass had been removed and the soil disturbed. He bent down to read the inscription, almost worn away, on the modest headstone.

'Here lie the mortal remains of Eorghan Fraser, died April 20th, 1880. May God protect his soul.'

'So you're with him at long last,' said Tom. 'Well done.'

THE GHOSTS OF FAIRFIELD
by Jane Langan

I grew up in a house (called Fairfield) that was built in 1894. It was big, cold and very Victorian. My mum favoured dark red carpets and embossed wallpaper. In the hallway there was a large antlered stag's head that was sagging from the neck. At the top of the first-floor stairs there was an oil painting of an old hook-nosed woman who my brother and I called The Witch. The electrics were ancient and erratic (there were issues in the 1970's in the UK with power), there was no central heating or double glazing and the only heat came from an open fire in the living room and the Rayburn (like a small Aga) in the kitchen. My brother and I had the two top rooms on the second floor. We had beautiful uninterrupted views of the Stretton Hills and it was a great area to grow up in. We were very lucky.

The house's garden backed on to a piece of common land and across from it was the small village church.

The house itself was on a road called Burgs Lane and the Burg it referred to was just down the road from us where there had been a small Roman settlement. Naturally, I grew up hearing about the ghost soldiers marching along the road. Allegedly, you could only see them from the thigh up as the road had been built upon and built upon. I never saw a Roman soldier.

When I hit my adolescent years, I struggled to sleep in the house, there were creaks, bangs and mysterious shadows aplenty. My mum and dad put it down to my overactive imagination. Still, I kept my bedroom door open and a landing light on until the day I moved out to go to university at eighteen. As soon as I left home, I could sleep in complete darkness. The house gave me the creeps.

Several things happened in those adolescent years that underlined the creepiness of the place. The first was the nightmares. Nowadays, they would call it night terrors. I would wake up screaming as I believed I was a sailor on a ship during the war with the Spanish in the sixteenth century. I knew I had to jump into the sea as the ship was on fire, but I

couldn't get my armour off. If I stayed on the ship, I would burn, but in the sea drowning was inevitable. This dream was on repeat for several years and may have been based on a poem I'd read, unfortunately, I can't remember which one.

The second thing was the black hook-nosed shadow. Yeah, I know all shadows are black, but there was a particularly scary shadow who used to appear at my door. I suspected it was The Witch come to get me.

The third thing was the visiting of dead relatives, both, an uncle and my gran came and sat at the end of my bed. I swear to this day I had a full-blown conversation with both.

Years later my mum told me that the girl who lived just down the road from us, when she was the same age as me, had some psychological issues. This girl's mum brought in a psychic as the girl was convinced she was seeing ghosts.

The psychic told them that the ghosts from the graveyard at the *church across The Common were very active and would walk through our houses looking for their families.

I am glad I didn't know that at the time.

As an adult I have visited and stayed overnight in my parent's house, but it continued to give me the heebie-jeebies'. When my young daughters stayed there, they both ended up in our bed in the middle of the night having been spooked by something.

When my mum passed away and my dad had gone into a home, we had to sell the house to pay for my dad's care.I spent quite some time alone clearing it, so it was ready for sale. I never stayed after dark but one evening as the light was changing, I saw my hook-nosed dark shadowed friend appearing in the doorway of my bedroom like she used to. Or maybe it was just my over-active imagination?

*Nowadays the church across the common is a house. I am not sure whether they relocated the residents of the graveyard or if they are still there.

CRUMBS TRIPTYCH
by Laura Theis

I.

You were so young the first time your parents tried to
murder you.
Putting your trust in breadcrumbs
when you should have put your trust
in the birds.

And the crazy old lady with her edible house -
wasn't she justifiably upset when you started
munching her walls?
She was always worried about that place.

Especially her sugar spun roof
when it inevitably rained in that forest.
But she still took you in.
She still fed you.

She was still as good a mother as she could be to her
foundlings.
However you had been raised in the language of cruelty.
You burnt and ate her
without a grain of remorse.

And afterwards, you burnt it all down, the entire forest.
The flames spread as far as the woodcutters hut.
They say you laughed at the ashes.
You swore you'd never go hungry again.

II.

I try to explain to you
why I should not be a mother

in the end I bring out
the book: look I say

this is me
who I would be in that story

the kind of woman who
lets her children go hungry

who hopes they get lost in the forest
and never darken the door again with their

endless demands for things I cannot give them
becauseI just do not have them myself -

sustenance or love or
the skills you need to get either

raised by a woodcutter's wife
like myself and as such knowing only survival (my own)

I would refuse to be someone else's daily bread
I would speak only to the birds

who will be happy with crumbs
the way no human child ever is

III.

once upon a time
I was all of these:

the desperate father and also
the children he leads away from the safety of home
into the deep forest dark
so a story can happen

and also the witch that waits
with the treats
on the other end
grinning

I was also those crumbs that happen
to get consumed
before they can fulfill
their intended purpose

I was the oblivious birds that don't give
two shits about the other storyline
assuming the unexpected feast was always
meant for no one else to find

I was the hut that's
too small for four hungry people
and the big house that would willingly

I LOVE THIS HOUSE
by D.H.L Hewa

I love this house, and never want to leave.

It's all thanks to my beloved Albert that we're here. In an architect designed house. Just for us. A house by a lake—all paid for by the money Albert's making—mining the coalfields of South Lancashire. After years of being a concert pianist, it's an idyll of rest and recuperation for me, whilst for Albert it's a place of respite, away from the daily hooting and clanging of his mine.

Today, we do what we've been doing most evenings since we moved in. Stretching out on the oak bench at the edge of the lake, I rest my head on Albert's lap as his fingers run gently through my hair. Silent, we listen as two buzzards call, gliding and soaring high above us. I'm told buzzards mate for life. I pray it's the same for us. A duck family quacks and waddles, secure in their small unit, ignoring our trespassing into their home. Giggling, we watch the antics of the ducklings. So like human children. What fun Albert and I will have here, with our own little ones.

'Shall we have a house warming on Halloween?' Albert's voice breaks into my thoughts.

'But...thought you wanted to be a recluse Bert,' I tease.

'Call it a last hurrah. Celebrate. Plenty of time after...' Albert laughs, making the bench wobble.

'So who's gonna organise this?' I nudge, looking up at him.

'Weeeelll…'

Giving him a slight shove, I stand up.

'Let's make it a good one then. Fancy dress and all the trimmings,' I smile.

'Great, thanks,' Albert says, squeezing my waist.

The fading light makes a final glisten on the rippling water, then gasps out, letting the darkness descend. We amble back home, arm in arm, guided by beacons of light from the house.

****

Standing at the bay window in the lounge, I wave, as Henry, our driver takes a smiling Albert off to work. The silver Rolls winds its way along the tarmacked drive slowly, vanishing into the distance. Albert's promised to be back early today. Help decorate our house for its warming—set out the twenty cut pumpkins—install outdoor flame lamps along the long drive to welcome our guests—hang dangly skeletons—spiders webs—giant spiders—witch's hats—candles—indoors.

A gossamer mist, which Albert calls 'dragon's breath,' hovers, as it often does, over the large stretch of water at the bottom of our landscaped gardens. The rising sun will soon burn that off, revealing the mountains beyond. The trees in their myriad colours of yellow, red, orange, purple, green and brown, will reflect on the water, blurring the line between the lake edge and grey pebble shore.

Dragging myself away from the view, I walk to the shiny black Steinway which occupies half the room. Gently raising the lid, I sit on the stool. The smell of fresh leather, mingles with the aromas floating in from the kitchen.

Mmmmm.

Parkin, toffee, cooking apples, brownies, treacle tarts, fudge, melting chocolate.

It's ten hours to the start of the party. May have to venture into the kitchen to do a taste test before then. Albert will be back in five hours. He's kept his grim reaper costume secret. Says he wants to surprise me, so I haven't told him what I've decided to wear. A dust sheet with two holes for eyes. I've been preparing to be the scariest ghost ever by holding my arms up shouting, 'whooooo, whoooo, whooo,' into our bedroom mirror whenever Albert hasn't been around. Can't wait to see his face.

I suppose I'd better have a last practice of my piano piece before tonight. Make Albert proud. Taking a long, long breath, I close my eyes, caressing the ivory keys into Liszt's 'Totentanz', a special request from the Master of the house. Swaying to the crescendo, my heart bangs hard into my ribs as I feel a tug at my shoulder.

'I am really sorry Madam, I knocked…'

'What is it Ruby?' I snap, staring into the maid's frantic eyes.

'It's just, just…'

'Yes?'

'Henry's on the telephone, says it's urgent…' Ruby stammers.

'Don't tell me Albert's going to be late,' I say, jumping up.

Dashing past Ruby into the hall, I grab the receiver.

'Hello. Hello. Henry? Is everything OK?' I pant into the phone.

'Oh Madam, madam…' Henry's voice is brittle.

'What is it Henry?' I ask, feeling goosebumps rising on my arms.

'There's been an explosion at the mine.'

'Oh my God. Is anyone injured?' I gasp.

'Yes, yes, and the Master...the Master…' Henry sobs.

'Is he helping the injured? OK. OK. Tell him not to worry. I'll cancel everything here. Come back when you're able…' I say.

'No Madam, the Master…'

'Oh God. Is he injured? Gone to hospital?' I yelp.

Henry's voice on the other end of the phone, fades, comes back.

'He's...he's dea…'

Oh God. Oh God. Oh God. So that's why Henry, not Albert is on the phone. Because, because Albert, beloved Albert is dea..

An iron hand wraps around my chest, squeezing, squeezing, squeezing, as the room swirls, swirls, swirls, disappearing into darkness.

****

Our house is now where I spend my days, wandering the rooms. Each day, I open the wardrobe in our bedroom, taking deep, deep breaths of the now empty space, once so full of Albert's precious suits.

Ahhhhh. Old Spice. Albert's favourite. The familiar smell of spicy vanilla helps me prepare for each day. Leaving the bedroom, I trudge along the landing, and start down, down, down the grand mahogany staircase. A staircase fit for a princess. It's what Albert asked for. What Albert got. Now I am left with a princess staircase for a princess without her prince. Shaking my head, I shrug against the silence bouncing off the walls, and enter the lounge.

Walking up to the piano, I lift the lid, and let my hands travel along the keys, fast, slow, slow, fast. Liszt's 'Totentanz' shatters the stillness. Glancing across to Albert's chair my body warms. He's there, stretched out as always, eyes closed, lips curling up in a smile. Heart fluttering like a caged bird, I play, play, play, until finally, my fingers stop, just stop.

Pushing myself off the piano stool, plodding to Albert's now vacant chair, I sit down. The cold seeps through my navy slacks. Ugh. Shivering, I pull the collar of my black turtle-neck sweater up to my ears, and wait.

Wait.

Wait.

Wait until the sky starts turning to a slate grey. Until the shadows descend.

Standing up, I walk to the bay window. The water still glistens in the far, far distance, at the bottom of the garden in the last light of day. I never go down there these days.

I have no need.

No need to look at two mating buzzards.

No need to watch a family of ducks.

No need to sit on that oak bench. Just let it sit there, forlorn, fading, with its inscribed brass plaque. I don't need to read it. I know what it says.

'Albert. Always in my heart. Forever missed.'

Forever missed. How silly that sounds. So trite. So distant. Something a stranger would say. What I really want to say is, my darling, my whole world ended the day an explosion ended your life. My life, your life, they were, they are, intertwined. Living, breathing, when you're unable to do either, makes me feel I'm cheating in some way. I look forward to joining you some day.

I wish I could still stretch out on that bench by the lake shore, with my head in your lap. I wish I could feel your fingers brushing through my hair, while we wait for the light to fade, to watch the twinkling stars light up an inky jet sky.

But who'd want to hear all that?

I wonder what you're doing now?

Who you're with?

When the shadows start to lengthen, I move away from the window.

So dark.

So very very dark.

So quiet.

So very very quiet.

We had everything.

We have nothing.

There's no longer even an us anymore.

Leaving the lounge, I tread up the wide, winding staircase. Up, up, up, in the pitch dark. I know each step like the back of my hand. Up, up, up.

'I can't get the door to open darling, can you give it a shove?'

Someone's pushing against the front door.

Standing stock still, part way along the landing, I hold my breath. Thieves. Breaking in. They must know I'm on my own these days. That even the servants have left. I've forgotten how long everyone's been gone.

'Hold on, hold on, I'll carry you over the threshold,' a young man with a girl in his arms struggles through the door, dropping her unceremoniously on the wooden floor.

'Cheers,' she says, dusting herself down.

'Sorry darling. Just wanted to do it properly for our first home together,' the young man replies.

'Smells very musty. Look at all the cobwebs and dust. Gross,' the girl retorts.

Wrinkling her nose, she runs her index finger along the banister of my beautiful stairs, then holds it up like a trophy.

'It's 'cos it's part of an estate darling. We'll soon make it our own,' the young man says wearily.

'Switch the lights on will you? Feels weird in the dark,' the girl sighs.

Taking a small torch out of his pocket, the young man waves it around, searching the hallway. Moving towards the switches by the front door, he flicks them up, then down.

'Hell. Forgot to tell the electric company to switch us on,' he shouts.

'Shhh. Shhh. No need to shout. There'll be candles or a lamp. There's a fireplace isn't there? Have you got your matches?' the girl murmurs.

Using the light from the torch, they walk into the lounge, and busy themselves lighting the fire with the coal that Albert and I had so plenty of. Finding the brass candlesticks on the mantelpiece, they light the remnants of candle in them. The lit coals in the fireplace blaze, making dancing shadows in the room.

'Better?' the young man asks, placing one arm around the girl, drawing her to him in front of the hearth.

'Better now we've got rid of the draught. Feels strange though. Like someone else is here,' the girl says, pulling her cable-knit cardigan tight around her.

'There's definitely no one else darling. This place has been empty for years,' the young man says reassuringly.

Neither of them see me lurking in the darkness of the stair landing.

I *love* this house, and I will *never, ever*, leave.

GEORGIE
by Daniel David

Georgie is vermillion.

More than this.

Georgie is frankincense. Georgie is nightingales. Georgie is hashish.

When Georgie walks around, forgotten words and exotic intonations crackle out of him like old Spanish folk songs from a wind up record player.

The kids in the village don't like it.

"Fucking hippie!" They yell out.

"Jew boy!"

"Queer!"

It's "Jew boy" that Georgie hates the most.

Sure, he always wears the same baggy, faded jeans. He prefers hoodies and long jackets to sparkly dresses or bra tops, even on the hottest day of the year. But Georgie isn't a boy. They aren't a girl either.

Georgie is all possibilities. A rain storm. An oboe concerto. Christmas cake.

Georgie keeps a piece of old rope in their bedroom. They find it one day walking through the marshes, knotted around a snapped branch and snagged on an old hip bone. They use it to count the abuse the kids in the town throw at them. One ridge for one slur. Georgie doesn't measure in metric or imperial. They measure in twists of wounding. Ninety eight twists is about three and a half meters or however many feet that is.

They keep caterpillars from Uncle Walter's garden in an old tobacco tin next to the wounding rope. Big, fat, red and hairy caterpillars that might be dangerous but never bite or sting or explode their hairs at Georgie. They all look after each other. Georgie gives them water and green cabbage leaves whilst they give Georgie information. You might think caterpillars can't speak, and you'd be right, but they die deliberately. Each one dies on a particular day and that day, every day, is a letter on a wildlife calendar that Georgie has adapted. Death spells out a word. Then words.

"Hey" is the first word, then "Please".

Georgie thinks they might be spelling out a whole sentence, but the next word is "Canal" and Georgie thinks that doesn't make any sense at all, so they just jot them down as single, miracle caterpillar words instead. Important words that will mean something to someone else one day if someone just keeps a note of them.

Georgie wets the rope sometimes with rainwater from the blocked gutter underneath their window. It makes their room smell like the sea and old bones. Broken grass from underneath a tent. Dad.

Dad takes them camping by the sea in an old bell tent that's almost white and has little patches of mildew around the peg holes. They collect fish bones and crab shells from the tide line and tie them together to make aeroplanes and star maps. At night they take the maps and aircraft up to the cliff edge and read the messages in the stars, before throwing the aeroplanes hard into the wind and watching them float up towards Capricorn.

Georgie misses Dad. One day he just isn't there anymore and nobody talks about him ever again. When Georgie asks Uncle Walter, he says he doesn't know what they mean. Georgie is Dad, always has been as far as they know and they must be dreaming. When Georgie gets cross they give them pills that make them feel sick and sleep for a week. When they wake up, the kids from the city have stolen their bike and they have to do the washing up every night with a person they've never met.

When everyone is asleep, Georgie creeps back downstairs and opens the cupboards and drawers all around the house looking for clues about Dad. They find a letter addressed to someone called Ash that just says "not yet", an old bus ticket to Glastonbury and a single dark hair on the back of an armchair that looks a lot like Dad's when he was younger.

In one room there's a baby standing up in its cot. It smiles at Georgie when they come in and offers them a soft fabric bunny. They take it and stroke down its ears, but it makes Georgie feel a little sad so they give it back with a half smile. The room smells of old milk and stale nappies. It makes Georgie want to get out.

There's a short piece of rope in the cot. Georgie almost doesn't see it, what with the pillows and knotted up blankets. But it's there in the top corner. It has three twists. Georgie smiles at the baby and runs a sympathetic hand through their fine straw hair. They whisper an apology and pick a sippy cup up from the floor, sprinkling a little apple juice on the rope to make the room smell nice.

When Georgie disappears, everybody goes looking for them. The police, the neighbours, the kids from the nation, but they can't find them anywhere. Dad is back, talking quietly and crying on TV as if he knows who they're looking for, but he doesn't. He only talks about purple t-shirts and punk rock and lop eared rabbits and nobody knows what that means. He says Georgie has brown eyes, is six foot two and has three parallel scars on their left arm, but Georgie doesn't have any of those things. They wonder how anyone will find them looking for all the wrong stuff.

The police hunt all over the house, in the small backyard with the rusty basketball hoop, in the alley ways that criss cross the estate and in the wasteland behind the garages behind the off license. At one point somebody calls out that they've found something and everybody rushes over. There's a body there, but it's not Georgie's body. It's the body of someone no one even knows is lost.

An old person. A writer apparently, who everyone thought was writing away in their caravan but wasn't. They've been here for so long that their hair is spread out through the soil like mushroom mycelium and their phone won't turn on anymore. The forensics team who dig them out say that their hair reaches all the way across the wasteland, under the paddock where the gypsies keep their horses and down to the canal. It tumbles out bank side in delicate grey ribbons that intertwine with the branchlets of a willow tree.

In a few months they stop looking for Georgie altogether. The laminated signs fall off the lampposts. The media go to Tokyo. Nobody wears their t-shirts anymore. Detective Hunt is still looking though. He has a picture of Georgie on his wall and lots of red string that knits together faces and places like a fisherman's map. He shuffles notebooks about and calls youth hostels in-between checking his Twitter feed and drinking green tea.

But Georgie isn't on Twitter, or TikTok, or CB radio. They don't have a handle, a hashtag or a page. They don't follow anyone, share stuff or like things and they aren't disappeared either. They're right here wondering why everyone is ignoring them.

They drop things in Detective Hunt's tea and rustle the pictures on his wall. They call out into Dad's face so many times their voice goes hoarse. They sing sea shanties into Uncle Walter's ears with their new found folk voice and tug at his huge leathery hands.

The baby is in Georgie's room now, so they kill four caterpillars over seven weeks to spell out "Help", but the baby isn't writing it down. They slap it across the face to make it cry, but no one who comes seems to understand that it's their hand pinking its cheek. They just wipe the baby with cream and give it juice and chocolate.

Georgie even finds the kids from the world and begs them for abuse, whatever they have they'll take it. They give nothing, so Georgie curls up at their feet, amongst the cigarette ends, drinks cans and little splats of greasy spit. They twine around their ankles, snuggling into the folds of their track pants and drifting in and out of sleep as they mouth the words of their banter absentmindedly.

Georgie is a galaxy. Georgie is the sound of wind in young chestnut leaves. Georgie is dark inside when it's still light out.

PUMPKIN
by Louise Wilford

The temperature drops as we make our way home over the moors.

It was a lovely anniversary - we'd walked round Nelly Moss lakes at Cragside (where Mark proposed to me ten years ago), crunching through leaves and pine cones, greeting other walkers and stroking their dogs, breathing in lungfuls of cool Autumn air with a hint of woodsmoke from the small fires the gardeners had lit to burn the bracken they were clearing. Mark was, of course, a serious hiker – he'd done the Three Peaks in Snowdonia and walked the whole of the Transpennine Trail. I was more of a casual rambler, but it was nice to walk together for once, even though for Mark this was only a gentle stroll.

I'd even gathered a few handfuls of late bilberries from a patch growing beside a small waterfall, as we walked through the woods back to our car. Mark loved bilberries, and I could use them to develop a new recipe.

In the afternoon, we'd stopped for lunch at a pub in Rothbury, the stone wall at the front guarded by a row of pumpkin jack-o-lanterns which flickered oddly as we passed them. The man behind the bar told us they'd had a pumpkin-carving competition for the local children. I smiled at him, remembering the pumpkins that we'd seen that weekend Mark proposed, adorning doorways and shopfronts, simultaneously jolly and freakish.

The barman recognised me from my cookery show and said I could take one of the pumpkins if I liked. 'Maybe you could do a pumpkin recipe and mention us in your next book,' he suggested. We set off home as the evening drifted in, our new carved pumpkin, now unlit of course, sitting on the rear shelf of the Audi like some weird Halloween satnav.

The moors had been glowing with orange light on our way west, but now the evening sky is darkening a little. White streamers of mist are gathering in the valleys, drifting into the roadside undergrowth. And on the hilltops, the moorland spreads out on every side like a gnarly duvet thrown over midnight sleepers.

'It's still gorgeous, isn't it?' I say, glancing sideways at him from the driver's seat. He's looking out over the moors and doesn't respond. He's always been a quiet man; it's what I first loved about him. He looks out over a landscape as if he's breathing it all in, making it a part of himself. The moors, of course, have a special place in his heart. He was brought up in Alnmouth and he walked here often as a young man.He knows these moors like he knows his own skin.

There are no other cars on the road.In front of us, I can see it stretching ahead, a pale ribbon dipping and rising, and through the rear-view mirror it stretches backwards, vanishing into the darkness.I can also see the carved pumpkin grinning toothily at me, and for a second it gives me a peculiar cold feeling that I wasn't expecting. I turn up the car's heater a little.

'We'll be back in Alnwick in twenty minutes,' I say, half sad, half relieved. I'm tired, if truth be known I've probably done more exercise today than I've done all year. I can't seem to get myself motivated. I seem to spend my days sitting round the house, waiting for Mark to return so we can curl up together on the settee and watch our favourite box sets. Even the cookery book I'm supposed to be writing is taking much longer than usual. My publisher has been quite irritated by me missing deadlines, says I'll be lucky to have it published by the Christmas after next when people might have forgotten I exist. You have to strike while the iron's hot in this business, she says. Well, at least I've got those bilberries now – I'll make Mark's favourite bilberry and almond cake when we get home. I try to include his favourite recipes in the book when I can. Maybe I should do a pumpkin recipe? I glance back at the ghoulish face on the parcel shelf and grimace.

I wasn't even sure about this anniversary trip north, if I'm honest.I did wonder whether it would be too much for me. But I'm glad we did it.It's been a real pleasure. I haven't been to Cragside since he proposed, all those years ago, and it was great to visit it again. He's been up here lots of times since, of course, hiking with his friends and sometimes alone, while I've been busy filming my new TV series or working on my latest book. London is so far from Northumberland and I know he's missed the countryside – Greenwich Park is nice but it isn't really a substitute for the moors! But he never complains. He knows my work means I have to be in London, and he's always been happy to support me as long as he can go on his hikes now and then. 'Recharging' is what he calls it.

Looking at his profile now I can see how these hills have shaped him. His skin is browner, more weather-beaten than mine, his hair just beginning to turn grey – I think it makes him look interesting, along with his pale blue eyes and the lines round them from squinting in all weathers. He's always been an attractive man. Seeing him beside me in the car provokes a sudden need to kiss him, tell him how I feel about him. But he seems so self-possessed, so wrapped in his own thoughts, that I don't feel I can disturb him.

We are at the brow of a hill when it happens. Suddenly, I see a flicker of yellowish light in the mirror, like a distant flame, and the murky interior of the car suddenly becomes brighter. For a moment, I think that a car has come up behind us, headlights on full beam, but where could it have come from? A moment earlier there were no cars behind or in front.

I glance over my shoulder and the car swerves into the edge of the road as I slam on the brakes in shock. The pumpkin face is now lit up by a candle flame that has suddenly, inexplicably, re-ignited.

'Christ almighty!'

The car judders to a halt, the anti-lock brakes kicking in, one wheel on the mossy, muddy verge. We both turn round to look at the pumpkin. It must be a prank, of course, a joke pumpkin – some sort of mechanism inside to make it light up at random moments. The barman must have let us have it as some sort of Trick or Treat nonsense. Very funny, I think, though I'm not amused. He might have caused a car accident, or a fire.

The pumpkin continues to glow eerily, light spilling from a jagged mouth and frowning eye-holes that seem now somehow more devilish, less charming, than they seemed earlier.

I realise Mark's no longer in the passenger seat. He has somehow got out of the car, though I didn't hear the door opening, and he's standing on the edge of the moorland staring out, away from me. The bag of bilberries has spilled across the seat.

Suddenly I am angry. What's he doing, leaving me to deal with this while he arses about staring dreamily across the landscape like some sort of cut-price Heathcliff? I open the driver's door, clamber out of the car, my legs stiff, and open the rear door, sticking in my head so I can blow out the flame in the pumpkin before it sets my bloody car on fire. It's giving off more heat than I expected and I can't get close enough to see whether it's a conventional candle or not, but I blow at it anyway, with little effect. The flame simply flickers and then grows bigger. The grinning face laughs silently at me.

I back out of the car and run round to Mark. He is still standing there, his hands in his trouser pockets in that familiar stance. Why is he doing this to me?

He turns and smiles that sweet old smile he always gave me before he left on one of his hikes. He'd hoist up his backpack, then smile down at me, wistful and kind, as if he wished I could go with him but knew I wasn't ready yet. I can see the ghostly outline of a backpack on his shoulders now.

Then he steps forward onto the brown heather, pulling a bilberry from his pocket and popping it in his mouth as he always used to do, and strides onto the moor towards the place where he died, last year, alone, of a heart attack.

Behind me in the car, the pumpkin's flame winks out. I lean against the passenger door, defeated, watching my husband stride away across the moors.

THE MIRROR AT MIDNIGHT
by Beck Collett

I catch myself pondering a great deal these days; how can it be that I am studied so very much by them, and yet never truly seen? A cruel joke from the creator, I am the very definition of irony. It's a cold existence. Between you and I, I feel used, though I know that is my role. I'm not foolish enough to expect any more out of it. Still, I dream of being looked at, seen for the very first time; virgin eyes on my sleek form. It will never happen, though, it is not allowed. I see them, the flesh mother and father, and the little fleshy girl. The girl gets closest to fulfilling me; sometimes I think she is looking at me, seeing me, and I gasp – silently, of course, but then she pulls a face and laughs, so perhaps not. One day maybe, I shall surprise her, and pull a different face back; see how she likes that. I keep them all inside me, all the ones who looked my way. Maybe today will be the day. At midnight, little fleshy girl stares, baring teeth, looking off to one side, not seeing herself, but, maybe, looking for me. Does she know I am here? I am feeling (can I feel?) devilish, so I shiver (a trick I have learnt, designed to thrill), let all the other distorted faces I remember show themselves. She screams, runs off to tell her parents of the demons.

I feel…nothing.

AFTERNOON TEA
by Diana Hayden

I took my tray to a table tucked away beside the pond
next to a hideous two foot tall gnome.
Ping. Sue's text. "Just parking."
"Look for me near pond," I replied.
My right eye caught something. Was it a wink?
"You're in the lucky chair," the gnome said.
Before I had time to think I'd morphed into a gnome.
Any moment Sue would arrive.
The gnome put his hand over my face.
"Why did you do that?" I growled.
"So, she doesn't recognise you," he sneered.
Sue texted frantically. "Where are you?"
I screamed but nothing came out.

A SPECIAL OCCASION
by John Bukowski

I'm a salesman from a long line of salesmen. My grandfather sold Studebaker's before he moved up to Cadillacs. At various times, my father sold jewelry, cosmetics, and eventually printing supplies. I sell menswear. Not as lucrative as in decades past, when suits and ties were a fact of day-to-day life, but still a living. My salesman's smile is always ready, needing only a door chime to bring it forth. Today that patented smile widened into a look of surprise.

I'd worked at the Fashionable Male for twenty years, ten as owner. I thought I knew all the types; had learned how to handle them. The young guys looking for prom attire usually arrived in groups amidst horseplay and crude language. A firm hand and exclamations of "That looks hot" worked well with them. The nervous, slightly older fellows sought wedding apparel, typically accompanied by a bride-to-be. In those cases, defer to the decision maker not the living male mannequin. Older businessmen had a well-fed look; they bought quickly and in volume: Fratello ties, Brooks Brother suits, Daniel and Ellissa shirts. Service and kiss ass. Cha-ching! But men near the century mark were a rarity. Rarer still was one coming in under his own power–alone.

"May I help you, sir?"

"I don't know, young fella. But I'd appreciate it if you tried."

There was sadness in his smile, weariness as well. Perhaps he recently lost a friend or relative. Or maybe this was just how you looked after a lifetime of fatigue and pain, woes and worries, loss and grief. A frayed sport jacket draped loosely over slumped shoulders and bent spine. A yellowed-white shirt rising and falling rapidly under an old bow tie; the breath barely able to find its way in before it needed to escape. Sweat beading on a broad forehead with a feverish look, as if the skin tags and wisps of white hair might smolder at any moment. Maybe this was how I'd look if I lived long enough.

"I'll certainly do my best. What are we looking for today?"

"Well, son, we are looking for a chair and some clothes, in that order."

"I think I can help with both. Please, have a seat."

I ushered him to a straight-backed chair, holding one frail arm as his shiny pants lit lightly on the cushion. Then I shook the withered claw protruding from a ragged tweed cuff. "Welcome to The Fashionable Male. I'm Robert Crown, but please call me Bob."

"Thank you kindly, Bob. Jack Mayhew." He mopped his head with a balled up red hankie. "Whew. That's a long walk."

I looked outside for a companion parking the car. "Will someone be joining us today? Your son or daughter perhaps?"

"My son died nine, no make that ten years ago. Just two years after his mama. Heart attack. Never had a daughter. Would have been nice, though."

"I'm sorry to hear that, Jack."

As the old man waved off my condolences, my eyes scanned the lot for a senior's shuttle or maybe a caregiver parking a Buick or shiny black Lincoln. But nothing moved outside. The three handicapped spaces remained empty.

"May I ask, ah, how you got here today?"

"Bus," Jack said. "Got my senior's card." He patted his breast pocket, eliciting a cough. "That and six bits gets me where I need to go."

"You walked all the way from the bus stop?"

He nodded, again mopping his brow before repocketing the balled hankie. "Long way."

"Can I get you some water? Coffee?"

His smile lit up a bit. "Water'd be nice."

I reached into the mini fridge hidden under the haberdashery shelves. Unscrewing the cap from a cold bottle, I said, "Cup?"

He shook his head and winked. "Not so old yet I can't drink from the bottle."

"Of course not." I smiled. "What can I show you today, Jack? Sport jacket? Slacks? We have some nice Joseph Abboud sweaters on sale."

"I'm in the market for a dark suit, Bob. Nothing fancy. Nice black suit. Maybe gray."

"Is this for a funeral?"

My grandmother once told me that the saddest thing about growing old was watching your friends and family die off, one by one. I figured Jack must be near the end of the line in that regard.

He nodded. "You could say that."

"Close friend?"

His sad smile returned. "Yeah. Most of the time, anyway."

"Well, I'm sorry for your loss. You just rest a moment and I'll bring out some selections."

I eyeballed him as a size thirty-four-short but brought out thirty-sixes. A bit of a bag hides a multitude of stoops, crooks, and sags. I shied away from names like Brioni and Armani; they looked to be out of his price range, judging by appearances. And I didn't think he was looking for a continental flair. I kept it moderately priced. And I kept it American.

For the next hour and fifteen minutes, Jack Mayhew and I danced the clothier's tango. He took his time, touching material, slowly and carefully rising to try on jackets before slowly and carefully sitting again to recover and sip water. I didn't mind. I had nothing better to do at ten on a Wednesday morning. Maybe sell a pair of sox here or there. Besides, how often do you get to hear the life story of someone who voted for Thomas Dewey – more than once. And something more. I think we both found it therapeutic, at least I did.

My dad passed away just one year ago this month. For the two years previous, I spent every Wednesday (my day off) and Sunday afternoon with him. At first it was a chore, a duty I'd promised my mother when she passed. Then it became a habit. Finally, it was a familiar ritual that brought pleasure to us both. My dad enjoyed the company, although he never said so. I came to enjoy getting to know the man who'd sired me but with whom I'd never really connected. Not until those last two years. Now that it was over, I missed it. Or maybe I just missed him.

"You were actually a door-to-door salesman during the depression?"

Bob's grey wisps bobbed. "Hammond's Illustrated Bibles."

"Bibles? Door to door?"

He sipped water and smiled. "Yep. Gilt edged. Hand-painted flyleaf and book headings."

"And you were able to make a living doing … What I mean is, I can't imagine that expensive bibles went with twenty-percent unemployment."

He winked. "You'd be surprised. But you had to know how to sell. Whose doors to knock on."

I draped a dark Brooks Brothers over his sunken chest, shook my head and exchanged it for a Kenneth Cole. "And how did you know that?"

"Did my homework. Got to know the neighborhoods." He coughed, a hollow rattle that shook his skinny frame. "I was just a pup myself, barely sixteen. But I learned fast. Found out where the rich Presbyterians lived; Catholics were likely to slam the door in your face." He chuckled at an old memory. "Sometimes it paid to grease the wheels a bit, too."

I nodded at the Kenneth Cole, then helped him put it on over the new white shirt I'd selected for him. "Grease the wheels?"

Jack rubbed thumb and fore finger together. "Payola. Lettuce. Moola. Buck slipped to a doorman could get you into a posh apartment house. Get you the names of a few likely prospects too."

The jacket was a bit loose, but as I say, covered a multitude of sins. "Where was that Jack? What city, I mean."

"Chicago," he replied. "Before the war." His eyes took on a far-away cast. "Just a year before I met Evelynn."

"Was that your wife?"

He nodded; gaze focused on visions from eighty years ago.

"You must have been married a long time."

He kept nodding. "Yep. Long time."

I gave him a few moments then cleared my throat. "How about we try on these trousers?" I helped him up and stumble-stepped him to the dressing room. "You going to need help in there, Jack?"

"Guess I can still change my own pants," he said. "As long as there's a place to sit."

"There's a bench in there, at the back," I said. "Take your time." I stood at the door, listening for sounds of trouble. "Were you in World War II, Jack?"

"Yep." The reply sounded strained with effort. "Eighth Air Force. Ball turret gunner."

I whistled. "I understand that was quite a dangerous job."

"So they tell. But I guess they all dangerous. Tail gunner was probably worse...dratted zipper."

"Need a hand?"

"No, I got it."

The fitting-room door clicked open and Jack shuffled out, his stockinged feet gliding over dark material.

"Hold on," I said. "Let me turn up those cuffs before you trip. We'll hem them later." I folded material around one bony ankle, then started on the second. "So, the tail gunner was most dangerous. Why was that?"

"You see, if they could take him out, that left the whole back of the plane open. Just sit in the six o'clock and lob cannon shells into us. Lost my best friend to a Kraut twenty millimeter. Tommy Wheelan. Hell of a guy." He swayed on his feet.

"Here, let me help you." I sat him back down. "Would you like more water? Or maybe coffee? I was just going to pour myself a cup."

His smile brightened. "Mighty kind of you. I like coffee. Black. Yes, mighty kind. Thank you."

"Don't mention it. Thank you for your service."

I returned from the back room with two cups. "Why don't I put this down to cool?"

He nodded.

"I guess you probably lost a lot of friends in the war."

His eyes lost focus again, as if staring through me to the past. "Yep. Yes indeed. War. Heart attacks. Cancer. Car accidents. Even a boat accident." His voice took on the huskiness of strained emotion. "I lost a lot of friends. Lost em lots of ways. That's the hardest part of growing old."

"Yes," I said, not knowing what else to say. "So I understand." I smiled to change the mood. "But I guess it beats the alternative."

He looked directly at me without a trace of humor. "Not really."

"Well, um, … let me see." I appraised him sitting in his black suit. "That looks sharp. Would you like to look in the mirror?"

"I'll take your word, son." His voice sounded distant, as if it came from wherever his unfocused eyes were gazing. "Not really." I could barely hear him now. "Not this long. Too damn long." His eyes glistened.

"Ah, well, Jack. Um, can I show you some dress socks? Belts? We're having a special on Tommy John briefs."

"No," he whispered. "I guess I won't be needing socks or underwear. Why piss money on something that don't show."

"Well, ah, … how about a new tie? Perhaps something in grey?"

He nodded, still staring far away or within himself, a smile rising to the corners of his mouth. "That'd be fine. Pick me out a nice one." As I left, I heard him add, "Thank you for your kindness."

I selected a Saks printed silk, grey with a white stripe. "How about this," I said, returning from the tie rack. "It'll break up the solid colors without breaking your wallet." I held the tie next to his dark jacket. "What do you think?"

His eyes had closed. His right hand was clutching something.

"Jack?" I touched the hand, which had gone from feverish to cool. "Jack?" I tapped his arm. The hand opened, a money clip plopping to the carpet next to the stub of a number-two pencil.

I hesitantly picked up the clip. A business card sat beside a wad of hundred-dollar bills. Printed on one side of the card was Mangione Funeral Home. There was writing on the other side. I read the words that had been penned by a less than steady hand.

'All arrangements have been made. Keep the extra for your trouble.'

Below this, five words were scribbled in pencil.

'Don't bother hemming the cuffs.'

It was only then I noticed that Jack Mayhew had stopped breathing. The smile on his face looked peaceful.

THE INSIDE OUT GIRL
by Jane Langan

Once upon a time, the boy found an inside out girl who lived in the cave on the side of the mountain next to the forest and lived happily ever after.

But this isn't the beginning of the story. I have started at the end.

I'll try again.

Once upon a time, there was a boy called Billy. Billy was like most boys; he liked to play and jump and explore. He came from a large, happy family and had six older brothers and sisters.

His father was the local carpenter and spent all day in his workshop building things for people. His mother looked after the cottage and the children. It was all very traditional. But Billy didn't want to be traditional. He felt different; he didn't want to be like his brothers and sisters. Billy didn't want to learn woodwork with his father. Billy didn't want to learn to cook and clean with his mother. He wanted to be a travelling minstrel. He wanted to wear fancy clothes. Some days he felt like wearing his sister's clothes and some days he felt like wearing his own. He didn't understand why they had to be different. His mother and father tolerated his behaviour and believed that he would grow out of it. His brothers and sisters were less kind.

'Baby Billy wants to be a little girl. Baby Billy wants to cut off his little winkie and wee sitting down. Baby Billy is a silly Billy…'

You can imagine. Children are cruel.

Billy played less and less at home. He would get his chores done in the morning and disappear until dinner time in the evening; he was exploring and building his minstrel-ling
repertoire.

In fairness, Billy had only ever met a minstrel once; but it had made a big impression—the minstrel had sung, danced and told stories impersonating all the characters. So, Billy sung as he ran through the forest. Billy danced and did acrobatics in the pine covered clearings and Billy would shout and sing his stories to the birds and squirrels in the trees.

Billy was a gifted storyteller and had a fine voice. Even his acrobatics, with persistence, practice and quite a few bruises, had become an impressive tumbling show. Soon, Billy thought, I shall leave home and make my way in the world telling my stories. People will throw money and I shall live a wonderful minstrel life.

Billy wandered further and further from home every time he went out. Each time finding a new route, a new tree, a new stream. Until one day, he finally reached the other side of the forest and found the mountain he could see from his bedroom window.

For a moment, Billy couldn't quite believe he had made it that far. He stood with his hands on his hips and gazed up and up to see the snow-covered summit.

One day I will stand on the top of this mountain and see the entire world, he thought. Then he heard a noise. It wasn't a normal noise. It wasn't a squirrel in a tree. Or the heavy step of a bear on a branch. It wasn't a bird call he was familiar with. It was a very odd noise indeed. The noise was like a gulp and a yell all at once, a kind of swallowed scream. He couldn't describe it, but Billy was a fearless young man, so instead of running from the noise, he went towards it. First though, he looked at the forest floor and grabbed a sturdy stick, just in case.

The noise continued, almost like an ugly hum, continuous. Quietly, Billy crept. Until he came to the mouth of a dark cave. The noise was echoing out of there.

Now, between you and me. This is where I would have returned to the forest to continue with practising my minstrel-ling. Not Billy.

Billy was an industrious fellow. He looked about, got his knife from his pocket and pierced the pine tree, making a hole – resin seeped slowly out. As it did, Billy removed his undershirt and placed it at the bottom of the tree to catch the resin. While this was happening, Billy gathered several similar sized sticks and tied them together with a vine, then he got his resin covered undershirt and knotted it firmly to his sticks. He had his torch. Now he needed to light it. He looked to the forest floor again and found a flint. A spark. The torch was lit.

The noise continued throughout his efforts and seemed to become more desperate.

'Ugh gulp ahh. Ugh gulp ahh. Ahh. Ugh. Gulp.'

Billy stood in the mouth of the cave for a moment as his eyes adjusted to the darkness. He couldn't make out how far it went but he could see a smallish lump about fifty feet ahead of him. The smallish lump seemed to be where the noise was coming from.

'Hello. Hello,' shouted Billy, 'Is anybody there?'

'Ugh, gulp, ahh,' said the lump.

Billy edged closer, he thought he could make out arms and legs, but something wasn't quite right.

'Do you need help. Can I help you?' shouted Billy.

Still the same noise. The lump uncurled itself and stood up. Billy was only ten feet away now. He dropped the torch. He couldn't believe what he saw.

There in front of him stood a girl. But she was all the wrong way around. Her insides were on the outside and everything looked a bit like a bloody mess. She held her arms out as if for help.

Billy slowly leaned down, keeping his eyes fixed on the poor thing and picked up his torch. He took another step towards her.

'How can I help? There must be something I can do.'

Her hands beckoned him forward. She had stopped making the sound.

He took another step.

Close now, Billy found her quite terrifying to look at. Of course, he had seen his father butcher animals, but he had never seen anything like this. How was she still alive? Had someone done this to her? He had so many questions and he had no way of finding out. The sight of her made him feel very sad.

Still her fingers bent and beckoned. Billy took another step.

'Can you write, is there something you want to say? Although, I suppose you can't see. Can you hear even?' Billy was talking to her as she stood, arms akimbo, fingers moving.

He took another step. She was almost in touching distance.

'Was it an evil witch that did this to you?' That was the last thing Billy said before suddenly, the girl had peeled herself around him, covering him, from head to foot so her right side was on the outside and her insides were all over Billy; his face, his body, his limbs, he felt her attach herself, he felt the stalks of her eyes, push into his eyes. He screamed and then fell to the floor, the girl with him.

Hours later they woke up. Billy wasn't just Billy he was she, they were they, together and one. They looked down and didn't recognise themselves. They walked to the stream and looked at their face, their eyes had merged. Billy had brown eyes; the girl had green. They had Hazel. They smiled and realised how attractive they were. They were perfect. They felt whole. They tried singing and suddenly their range was twice as good, they tumbled higher than they ever had before. And when they tried their stories, they were better than anything Billy could have come up with alone.

They shared every thought and memory but how the girl became inside out in the cave was a mystery, and to be honest they didn't care. Meanwhile, Billy's family thought he had run off to become a minstrel and never heard from him again.

The first thing they did was climb to the summit of the mountain and see the entire world. Then they founded a hugely successful travelling theatre company.

They lived happily ever after.

BRIDGE ECHOES
by Lily Lawson

The girl appeared, dripping wet, on the path in front of me. It was unusual for me to see a girl in a dress, my kids lived in shorts or trousers. I stepped back. 'Where did she come from?' I shivered despite the sunshine.

"Sir, don't go there, it's not safe." she pointed behind her.

I looked and saw the bridge was out.

"Right, I see. What happened to you?"

"Fell in, didn't I."

"Are you hurt?"

"No Sir, don't you worry about me, my Momma will take care of me."

"Ok, go and get warmed up, you'll catch your death hanging around like that."

"Will do, Sir"

"Where's your Momma?"

"Back there, Sir."

"Right, thanks for the warning."

"Thank you, Sir."

The warmth returned to my bones. I looked to see where she went but she'd disappeared. I turned my bike round and went along the path in the other direction.

My encounter kept nagging at me. 'Who was she? Where was her Momma? What happened?'

Later, reading the local paper which had been pushed through the letterbox that evening, I came across this:

One Hundred Years Ago

2nd September 1921

Bridge collapse fatalities

An unfortunate incident occurred at Longdale yesterday resulting in the death of Mrs L Watson, wife of Mr G Watson of Willow Green, together with their daughter Miss G Watson 10 years of age.

Mr A Jackson lost control of his barge, which he was using to ferry goods to Storley. The vehicle collided with the Albertine bridge causing its collapse. Mrs Watson and her daughter were traveling into town on foot via the structure. They were cast into the Jubilee and caught up in its current. Onlookers reported screaming before silence informed them of the victims' untimely demise. The bodies were recovered this morning.

We extend our deepest condolences to Mr Watson, a well-respected gentleman of his parish.

Jackson has been called to answer to the court Monday next to account for his actions.

Jackson was later cleared of any wrongdoing; the barge was found to be faulty.

PITCH FORK
by Sharon Rockman

Steaming cargo trains of food
Call them bain maries if you like
Manned by serious conductors
Call them chefs if you prefer
Leaning in to stoke the fires
Leaning out towards the roving plates
Of diners who respond to service
As hunter gatherers of a new age
Gliding smoothly between stations
Balancing their helpings whilst
Traversing polished tracks

I was attending to my appetite
An orderly abatement-
Until the old woman by the toasters
Raised her gleaming pitchfork
Most murderously aloft
0m/s at the top of its trajectory
Before its deadly downward stab
I might have sounded the whistle
From between squared teeth
As Lady Macbeth filled the frame
Invoking fears of the underworld
And the quake of destination -
The old lady was Maleficent
Transmogrified to dragon
Sparking the internal wiring
Of hidden tubes and tunnels

Rolling her fireball through
Those schematic networks
Multi-coloured fare zones –

It became possible to imagine
Her meal and subsequent mortality

I snatched madly at her fork and folly
She hissed at me and sputtered to a stop
She did not want her toast to burn

(after Charles Simic and a random diner)

Makarelle – Anthology ONE

THE WORST CYBER BULLY
by Helen Rana

Veena, one of the forensic computer analysts, peered hesitantly around the door. 'Sorry to disturb you sir, but I've found out who sent those messages to Daniel Smith.' She hovered in front of the desk, holding the deceased teenager's computer.

'Show me.'

She placed the laptop on the desk and turned it to face her senior officer, pointing at a name on the screen.

DS Colin Blackwell bent down to look into the screen. 'What, all of them?'

'Most of them, yeah. Eighty-seven percent of the messages come from different accounts all belonging to the same person.'

'Good god!' He ran his fingers through his hair and stared at her in bewilderment. 'How can we explain this to his family?'

In the short time Daniel had been dead, his family had set up a 'Justice 4 Dan' anti-online bullying crusade, using the strength of their anger and loss to marshal people, crowdsource funds and resources. They wore t-shirts bearing his face, had set up social media campaigns, spoken to local and national media, and organised a candlelight vigil for that evening. Almost everyone in the local community had joined in, and those who hadn't were viewed with intense suspicion – had they contributed to the sixteen-year old's untimely death?

The youngster had drunk a bottle of vodka and swallowed two packets of his mother's strong codeine painkillers. He lay dying on his bedroom floor for hours, discovered when his twelve-year old sister came home from school. The last messages he had received were still on his computer and phone screens, surrounded by vivid emojis:

Have you done it yet?
You gays make me sick
Go on, are you too scared to do it??!!
Kill yourself, you fat poof!

They were all visible to other people online, some of whom had interjected in his defence:

People who are homophobic are usually gay themselves but too scared to admit it
Stop picking on him!!!

The police had acted with speed and force, interviewing Daniel's family and friends, confiscating the devices of several likely suspects to find who was behind the intimidation and incitement to suicide.

Meanwhile, Veena had been scrutinising Daniel's own online footprint.

'I don't understand,' Colin said.

'It actually happens quite a lot,' she explained.

'But why? What would anyone hope to achieve by doing this?'

'Attention, I suppose. You make up online personas that attack you as a way to try to gain sympathy or support. To make people rally round. For validation.'

Colin was bewildered. 'What a world we live in,' he sighed.

Veena nodded. 'They call it sadfishing. It's self-harming, digitally.'

'Right. Well, shall we wait until tomorrow to tell the family?' Colin suggested. 'Let them have their vigil tonight, it might give them some solace in the meantime. They're going to be very upset when they find out what's really happened.'

He would let the Smiths fight against perceived injustice until tomorrow morning. Then they would have to be told the identity of Daniel's cyber bullies.

Daniel Smith himself.

HARD BARGAIN
by Leila Martin

Today, she must catch all the leaves. She sprints for the treeline, her boots lifting woodchips. I trail in her wake, past shifting branches and the steel glint of a tossed crisp packet. She doesn't look back. The wind dashes my smile away.

She's pouncing now. Her scarf is a flame, ferocious against the drab flanks of bark. Wait, I call. I fold onto an iron bench. Its chill seeps through my jeans.

She's lost her hat. Her hair lashes her ears. She's only playing. It's what kids are supposed to do, though she ignores the chirping gaggle at the swings.

Her lips are moving. I shiver, pull up my collar. The wind grips me with the sudden, strange urge to leap from this bench and run to her and claim her; to peel across the grass behind us, slam myself into my car and roar away. I'm clenching metal, my knuckles white teeth. A senior in tweed clicks past with a beagle in tow. His eyes graze mine and narrow.

I rub warmth into my hands and try to convince myself I just need sleep. No-one knows those yawning years in the beginning; she could never remember being captive in glass. She could never remember herself tiny, luminous and raw.

But her face skewers with such determination as she springs to snatch the last stray leaf. I can't deny any longer what I could never have guessed back then, rocking desperate bargains over a hot clod of tissue: keen ears can always hear you.

Branches creak their empty fingers. The sky's dimmed to stone, and the only colour left is the licking flame of her scarf, now advancing. She struts, puffed with pride, her hands hooked over two damp bunches. Here.

It's getting late, I say. Let's go home. The leaves are clammy in my grasp. Too late, I try to resist the impulse to release them. They swarm, frantic; pinwheel away.

Her eyes are lamps.

BANSHEE
by Louise Wilford

Your lost voice, slithering over the hilltop scree,
wailing over the wood's moonshading fingers,
breathing its scared-to-stone soprano sigh

against my rattling door. That lonely cry, surfing
on the air's curling wave, skimmed across my roof-tiles,
funnelled down my chimney, fills the rooms of my life

with the wild outside. Cat-yowl, owl-shriek, whine
of a rising tornado, complaint of metal against metal,
lunatic's moan, the keening of a doodlebug before

the menacing silence, before true night begins.
Give it your best shot, omen-screecher, warner,
worrier. See if I wake in the grey hours, stiff

with terror at your drunk-on-shadows scream.
See if I cringe and shiver as your stinking
wings flap against my bedroom windows

and your yellow eyes search the nightmare corners
of my mind.

HERCULANEUM
by Edward Alport

I read those twisted signs,
The tortured casts of dogs and men
Frozen in fire.
Some perfect monument to pass
Word of when the end could come:
So sweet and soft and hardly a whiff
Of Hell on its breath.
Huddling on the beach,
Striding down the street,
All of life on display on a shelf:
Frozen in fire.

I read those twisted signs
Of life frozen on its way to somewhere else
And sometime else.
Waiting for the word that never comes
Waiting for a key to turn, a spark to jump
Permission to unwrap myself
From suffocating breath
From tangling shrouds
From caltrops, scattered on the road.
Waiting for life to start again, one day,
Sometime else.

WHEN SHE COMES HOME
by Cheryl Powell

He always watches for her. Knowing she would come in darkness. He feels her, a vibration in his blood, as she moves swiftly across the dark water of the Fen. She is almost home now, and he and Maeve are anxious, waiting.

This time she leaves it till the last moment, when dawn is about to break, the first blade of light cutting sky from earth. Her skin will soon seethe with heat and he thinks how much she had once loved the sun. 'Tell me about the sunshine flower, Daddy,' she would plead, a small child, climbing into his lap with a storybook. And he would smell the fruit-bread sweetness of her as she pressed her cheek to his, feel the flutter of her childish heart. He would want to hold her then, forever, not like later when she was older, becoming a woman. Then, he was tortured by the way she looked at him, her touch, what she took from him.

He and Maeve have grown old. They have lived too long, willed themselves on for her sake. For who will love her when they are gone? And how will she survive eternity without love?

She is on the threshold now and his voice falters. 'So many years,' he tells her. 'So many years.'

'Has it been so long, Daddy?' Her voice is girlish still, unchanged by decades of wandering, her lips red and moist. She is always seventeen, the same as the day she was taken, yet he knows her corruption.

'Jack?' Maeve is calling him. She is weak, failing.

'It's the girl.' He can never bring himself to say her name, call her daughter, for that would make him a monster. His daughter, his Evie, had died that terrible night, out there on the causeway, though it was he who had gone looking for her and had carried her home. It was he who had dressed the wounds on her neck, held her tight through her night-long convulsions, waited as her blood cooled and her heart fell silent. It was he who had given her what she craved, what was forbidden, and for that he was being punished. They both were.

Maeve had known at once what Evie had become, and dare not draw back the curtain or let daylight in.

But Maeve's life-force is beaten thin now. 'Oh, Evie,' she murmurs. 'My girl. My girl,' and puts out her hands to her.

Evie draws back, but he knows she is taking in every detail, recalibrating her assessment of her once-parents, realizing she has almost left it too late.

'Are you in trouble, Evie?' he says to her. He thinks again about journeys to the grim marshes, the uninhabited place beyond the outer islands of Black Fen, the sluggish rivers choked with sourgrass and vast bogs that would swallow a body in minutes. Yet he knows he no longer has the strength to punt the distance or lift a corpse, however shrunken and depleted she has left it.

'No,' she smiles. 'Can I come in?' Even now, she will not step over the threshold uninvited, though dawn is breaking and her peril great.

'This is your home, Evie,' says Maeve, and takes her hand, and leads her into the dark closet of the kitchen, and doesn't flinch at the rankness of her; the stench of brackish earth and foul breath. Barefoot walks Evie, still wearing the dark green dress Maeve made for her years before, though it is mildewed and threadbare now and stained with silt. Evie has no need of clothes except to help her hunt, to move more easily among humans.

The cottage is disintegrating, walls fretted with ivy, the orange glow of day burning through the cracks. He must lead the girl to her resting place, the rotten chamber beneath the cottage, lest she perish.

'Do you need me?' he asks

He does not look at her but feels her starving eyes upon him.

'I've missed you, Daddy.' She turns to him, and he feels his blood sing as she examines his face, probing, and he knows she has detected the self-loathing in him, and the disgust for her; the never-diminishing guilt. But he will give in to her, like he always has, because he can do no other.

'Come by the fire,' Maeve entreats. 'You look so cold.'

It is night again and Evie has risen, her hair clotted with earth, the stink of her foul. But she complies, allowing her skin to grow rosy from the warmth of the fire, as if radiant with youth, the way she was when alive, that last night striding out in her summer dress, hair loose and copper-bright and he in anguish as she had kissed him, forcefully, and he still reeling from her earlier violence. There was no life in her now, no humanity, her yearning for him was a sinful hunger only. And yet, despite it all, he felt that something of her was still his daughter.

Her eyes glitter in the firelight and he can see the hauntedness there. He knows how difficult it is for her to be with them, to smell their blood, control her addiction. That's why he must let her use him. For the sake of Maeve. That's what he tells himself. For Maeve could never shut out the girl, even after she took Michael from his crib, and drained him and left him bleached, a soft bag of flesh they had to bury. The girl had shown no remorse, felt none, for such, he knew, was the pull of her hunger.

In time, Maeve forgave her. He had never understood that. He had wanted to destroy the girl, thought he hated her enough to do it, and was young and strong then. They could have been free of her. He could easily have driven a stake into her heart when she slept. She was a depraved thing, after all, an abomination, and so was he for giving himself to her but, in the end, Maeve stayed his hand.

'I can't lose Evie too, Jack.' she had said. She always blamed herself for Michael, believing garlic and holy water would protect him, thought the crucifix would hold the girl at bay. She knew nothing then of a vampire's voracious appetite, the blood lust they were at the mercy of, and the iron strength of them. Even now, he remembers the look of the girl after the kill, satiated and jubilant, for to her kind there is nothing sweeter than the blood of a sleeping infant.

After that she lusted for him, her father. His blood. And he allowed it, desired it even, though each violation left him guilty and roiling with self-disgust.

But even now Evie looks beautiful to him. And she still wears the locket they bought years ago, fixing their portraits in the oval frames. 'We thought you might wear it, Evie,' Maeve told her. 'To remind yourself you are never alone. Our love goes with you. Always.'

He had seen no reaction, no expression on the girl's face, though she had sat perfectly still and allowed Maeve's trembling fingers to fastened the chain. The girl didn't look at the locket or touch it. He wonders whether she ever had.

It is deepest night and Maeve turns and strokes Evie's hair. She whispers the words he has always dreaded would come.

'I'll not last the night, Evie. Take me with you.' Her plea is like the soft hush of the sea.

'No, Maeve.' He does not raise his voice, or move towards her. 'No, my darling. This is not the way.'

'She will have nobody,' she beseeches him. 'For all eternity. Nobody. Oh, Evie, sweetheart. Take me with you.'

Evie stirs. 'I will be nothing to you, mama,' she says and her voice is hollow, like an echo in an empty room. 'You will not love me. You will not love anyone. You will feel nothing but hunger.'

He knew this was true. But Maeve would not believe it. 'You no longer know the human heart, Evie. What it is capable of. How it endures. Take me with you.'

Evie sits still and says nothing, and he watches Maeve take a comb and untangle the girl's clotted hair and wash her face, dabbing at her skin with great tenderness, though he knows the girl feels nothing. And so they remain, all three, silent and waiting, until the fire burns low and the room grows dark. Night wears on towards dawn and Maeve's breathing shallows.

'It is time, Mama,' says Evie, rising at last. She takes Maeve in her arms. 'Come. It is time.'

....

He is at the window now, watching the sky, a blue-black skin holding back a world unknown. Two dark figures move on the land, one carrying the other, lost on a great sea of emptiness. Maeve, he knows, will soon be gone and he will follow. He looks on. The figures are still. And he too is still, excluded, waiting for first light, for the trickle of day, the blood-light on the horizon. He knows he will not turn away even as his daughter's skin begins to ignite, as the flames break her open and the fire catches at Maeve's hair and consumes them both. But he will hold on to that moment earlier, when Evie came to him and took his face in her cold hands and pulled him close so their cheeks touched. She held him there as if to warm herself, a tenderness he had almost forgotten. 'Sorry Daddy.' And for a second something juddered in her chest, he had felt it against him, a spark that flared momentarily and then.knew that spark; knew it right away. For it was the memory of her heartbeat.

THE LADY
by Dave Sinclair

One summer day, my lover and I
walked hand in hand, around Hampton Court.
We came to the maze and entered within
following no plan, just steps without thought.

Our path was ushered by cool laurel walls,
our voices were silent, but our minds were entwined.
At each branch in the path, with arm around waist,
we chose as if one and walked as if blind.

We came to a clearing and sat on a bench.
My head on his shoulder, we dozed in the heat.
Did we dream that we heard a murmured exchange,
as a couple appeared and stood by our seat?

The lady wore pearls on fine gold brocade
while the man had a doublet with rapier at his waist.
'My sweetest Jane, you must no longer delay'
and with the palest of cheeks, she accepted his embrace.

The breeze chilled my skin as the couple turned away
and faded from sight into corridors of green.
I looked to my love, and asked him to say
if he shared my dismay at all that we had seen.

As he kissed away the tears that ran down my cheek
my heart ran wild like a young girl betrayed.
Then his lips softly touched the nape of my neck
with the loving caress of the executioner's blade.

Often, I think of the events of that day,
and I hold my love tight in a desperate embrace.
And though we returned many times to the maze
our steps never found the path to that place.

THE VISITOR
by Sue Davnall

Ron was a fine craftsman. He'd honed his skills over many years until no one could match him in the whole of South London. But times change and Ron was feeling his age. Keeping up with every new wheeze that came along was more trouble than it was worth.

Propping up the bar in his local one evening, he grumbled into his beer: 'It's not like when I started out, Stan. Single-glazed sash windows, no mortices on the doors: I could be in and out in a jiffy. Now it's all fancy alarms and video doorbells and the like; you'd think they had the Crown Jewels locked away. I'm fed up with it.'

His old mate nodded. He'd met similar problems in his own line of work. Fobless car keys: what a nonsense.

'Perhaps you should retire, Ron, put your feet up. You could stay with Pauline for a bit. Get a breath of sea air.'

'Are you having a laugh? You know what she thinks of me, her and Frankie both. They don't care that I put food on the table for them when they were kids, they've hardly spoken to me since their mum died. A social worker and a bloody accountant, I ask you.'

He snorted and swigged moodily at his beer. Stan pondered a few moments before having another go.

'What about trying a different patch? Somewhere out of London? Folk are more trusting in the sticks.'

'Don't know about that, you know what they say about teaching old dogs new tricks.'

'That's my point; it'd be more old-school, right up your street.'

'I'd have to do a few recces first, check out the lie of the land. Wouldn't I stand out like a sore thumb, a London geezer like me?'

'At your age they'd likely think you were just some old codger out on a jaunt.'

'Maybe. Fancy keeping me company? It'd look less obvious if there were two of us.'

'Yeah, could be a laugh. Find a decent pub or something for lunch.'

'Sorted.'

With that settled, they ordered another pint. Lovely stuff, London Pride.

It was a beautiful summer and the two mates enjoyed their sorties. They were chuffed to find that beer was much cheaper in the wilds of Kent and Essex, Hertfordshire and Surrey. Ron hired a different car each time, something small that would go unremarked as they pottered through the villages and along the country lanes. The most promising area, they concluded, was in and around the Ashdown Forest: they identified several likely properties for Ron's personal attention at a later date.

In mid-September, once the kids were back at school but the weather still pleasant enough to lend credibility to Ron's 'OAP on an outing' facade, he decided to put his new venture to the test. He chose a house on the edge of a small village, a hamlet really. This was commuter country and most places in the area could be guaranteed to be empty for several hours. Ron knew that the safest time to strike was mid-morning when everyone was out and about their business.

Leaving the car a little way down the road, Ron slipped in through the side gate and round the back. French windows, poorly secured – he was inside within two minutes. He was always selective about his haul: there was no point in lifting electronic goods, his fence wouldn't give him the time of day for them. Jewellery was better, small ornaments, collectable items. There wasn't a lot of that here but it was a useful dry run. Once he'd got enough to make it worth his while he strolled back to the car and headed for London.

Over the next few weeks he paid a couple more visits to the area. These trips were more rewarding and he began to enjoy his new venture. He even stood Stan a round of drinks to say thanks for giving him the idea.

But on his fourth trip he came a cropper. He'd switched from hiring cars to buying a different old banger for each outing, picking them up at dealers who were happy to accept cash in hand and 'disappear' the vehicle afterwards. Ron took it on trust that the car was roadworthy: on this occasion, it wasn't. After a succession of inexplicable squeaks and bangs and some alarming grinding noises, steam began to pour from under the bonnet. Ron stuttered to a stop at the side of the road and considered his options. He plumped for abandoning the useless heap of metal (with a good kick to the tyres for luck) and walking to the nearest pub. Like many country inns, it had rooms and Ron opted to stay over.

He had a terrible night: the mattress was lumpy, the room draughty and the landlord clattered and clanked around downstairs until the early hours of the morning. As soon as it was daylight Ron was up, dressed and away. When he got back to the car it seemed better for a night's rest and sputtered into action.

Ron was too tired to stick to his original plan and didn't trust the car not to let him down again so he set off to find the most direct route back to London. That took him into an area of Ashdown Forest that he had not seen before. Passing through a denser stretch of trees, he spotted a neat white gate and picket fence. Beyond was a track that ran straight for a short distance before disappearing around a bend. Black lettering on the uppermost bar of the gate declared the property to be The Spinney. Ron was intrigued; whatever was at the end of the track could yield enough to make up for his hitherto disappointing outing.

He pulled the car onto the grass verge and began to walk carefully along the track. It seemed that no vehicles had driven up here for a long time. Thick tussocks of grass had crept into the middle of the track and drifts of fallen leaves blurred the line between the roadway and the trees on either side.

After a quarter of a mile the track turned a corner before entering a clearing. Ron saw before him a stone cottage one storey high with a thatched roof and dormer windows. It looked well maintained but modest and he almost turned back, guessing that the pickings would be thin.

'Still,' he thought, 'Now that I'm here I might as well have a closer look.'

Ron surveyed the clearing for signs of life. Nothing stirred. As he approached the cottage he could see that the door was solid but warped; there were deep indentations in the wood around the handle. He lifted the latch and was surprised to find that the door opened readily.

'Hello? Hello there. Anyone at home?'

Silence. He stepped inside. The ground floor was a single large room with a steep flight of stairs leading to the attic with the dormer windows. It was much smarter than Ron expected. The walls were painted a fashionable shade of grey, the window frames picked out in olive green. To the left was a kitchen area: an Aga was set into a wide hearth and nearby stood a rustic table and three dining chairs. At the other end of the room Ron saw a coffee table, two padded armchairs and a three-legged stool. On the range was a saucepan, steaming appetisingly. Soup, by the smell of it.

Ron turned to leave: the inhabitants couldn't have gone far if they'd left a pan on the stove. But the alluring odour reminded him forcefully that he hadn't had any breakfast. It was a long drive back to London and he was feeling woozy from lack of sleep. He checked the view from the cottage door again: no movement in the surrounding forest, not a sound to be heard. So, taking a ladle from a nearby hook, he dipped it into the soup and sipped cautiously. Lovely! Before he knew what he was doing, he'd scoffed half the pan.

He thought he'd better get on his way sharpish and stepped out of the front door. But the forest was as silent as before. It seemed a shame to come all this way without any reward. Maybe just a quick look in the attic?

As he crossed the room towards the stairs he caught his foot under a thick rug that he'd not noticed before. Pitching forward, he landed flat on top of the stool. There was an almighty crack as one of the legs snapped and Ron sprawled onto the floor. Hell! That had torn it. Ron scrambled to his feet and stood rigid, straining to hear approaching footsteps. Still nothing. He waited for a few moments then scurried up the stairs as fast as his advancing years allowed.

The room contained little apart from a king-sized bed with a cabinet either side and a smaller bed at the far end. The window shutters were painted in the same olive green as the woodwork downstairs. Ron sat on the edge of the king-size to look inside the nearest cabinet. More disappointment: the cabinet held only a bowl of nuts. Night-time nibblers, eh? No wonder they needed a huge bed. Ron yawned. His disturbed night was catching up with him. He decided to sit there for a little while until the floor stopped moving. A minute later, he was gently snoring.

Ron jerked awake, confused. He couldn't remember where he was. Someone was moving about downstairs; Ron heard a low murmuring followed by an indignant roar of indignation. They'd found the broken stool, then. Or was it the missing soup?

Ron knew that he was in serious trouble. The dormer window was too small for him to climb through, there was no way out except down the stairs. The treads creaked as whoever was below came up to the attic. There was only one thing for it: Ron rolled off the bed and scrambled underneath, pulling down the edge of the coverlet to hide him.

Now they were in the room. There were heavy footsteps, laboured breathing, and a peculiar smell. Ron, his eyes squeezed tight shut, sensed the coverlet being lifted then felt the touch of a very hairy hand on his cheek as whoever it was reached under the bed and prodded. Peering up, he saw a pair of big brown eyes looking down at him. Registering the identity of his unwitting host, Ron screamed, scrabbled out from under the bed and ran for his life.

'Hey, Stan, where's Ron got to? Haven't seen him in ages.'

Stan picked up his pint from the bar and gulped down a third of it before answering.

'Really sad, actually; he went a bit funny in the head. He's living with his daughter in Bexhill. Nowhere round here would take him, said they weren't equipped to deal with whatever's wrong with him. So much for the NHS, I ask you.'

Stan turned back to his pint with a sigh. He really missed the old Ron. He'd go down and see him later in the week. He wouldn't stay too long though: it was tough having to sit there listening to his old mate raving about trees and cottages and bears.

Printed in Great Britain
by Amazon